I0733678

Fierce MONARCH

MJ CROUCH

FIERCE MONARCH: GILDED EMPIRE

Chapter 1
Mari

For the first time since Cash poked his head out of the ground, I let myself get drunk. It was a safety measure for everyone, really. I was angry enough to burn down more than a few more buildings.

Nate was a Beckstrom. Cash's brother. An Ace.

He'd betrayed me.

And now he was gone.

Cash dropped his bomb and ran before the dust settled, shepherding Nate out the door while I tried to figure out if the other leaders were going to kill me on the spot. In the end, they walked out first with the silent, seething disrespect that started coups, and I knew we were poised on the brink of an all-out war. I didn't know how to process any of it, so I packed it away like I could shove it into a corner of my mind and forget. A problem for another day.

Today, all I could think about was my broken heart.

All this time, the traitor was closer than I ever thought possible.

I'd let him into my family, my home, *my body*. I'd given him all the insight he wanted into me. I'd practically *begged* for it. Then there were the things we talked about at night in the dark, wrapped in nothing but the soft sheets and each other's warmth. The dreams I'd had while I was desperate for love and commitment. The words he whispered into my hair when no one was looking.

All of it—lies.

Every time I remembered, I took a drink to dull the rage, grimacing the entire time. I hated vodka. Having to drink it to numb myself made me even angrier, so I drank more until I was stuck in a vicious cycle.

Drink, rage, drink, rage.

In no time, I was through the first bottle and reaching for the second.

Which was how Greyson found me, smashed out of my mind and throwing punches at a heavy bag in my gym. I normally left the door open, but the thought of seeing someone when I was so far from okay made my skin tight. I couldn't do it. So the door stayed closed.

I should've fucking locked it.

"Mari."

His voice was careful. So careful. I hated it.

"Don't treat me with kid gloves, Greyson," I snarled. My knuckles were aching, swollen, and split already, but I didn't care. I needed an outlet.

Grey stepped behind the bag, holding it for me. "Even if you need them?"

His gaze was a brand on my shocked skin, warm and so full of love I could feel it. I didn't want to feel anything, so I avoided his eyes like it was my goddamn job. If I looked, I'd break, and I couldn't afford to break.

"I don't."

I did. I absolutely did. Because I was dying inside.

Nate lied to me. He betrayed my trust. He put my people in jeopardy. He'd put *me* in jeopardy.

Traitor.

Was he still a traitor if he was never actually mine to begin with?

"He lied." My voice was smooth, but my insides roiled. Grief, still fresh and bruising, pummeled me, threatening to bring me to my knees. I'd become accustomed to it early in life, the idea that no one was permanent, but the first bite was still the worst. This was no different.

"I know," he said with a sigh.

I didn't respond, nor did I stop punching, but Grey never stopped talking, even when I tuned him out. For the first time in so long, his voice wasn't the soothing balm it usually was. It didn't heal me; it made me ache. It was a reminder of what we'd lost. A future I hadn't realized I'd been looking toward. It hurt so fucking bad to see it all blown to smithereens.

"You're going to hurt yourself." The words pulled me back, and I stepped away from the bag. Grabbing my water bottle, I swished my mouth out and spat into the nearest trash can. Red caught my eye, and I realized half my knuckles were cracked and bleeding. The sight, the physical manifestation of my pain, made me laugh, though it was borderline hysterical. "Pretty sure I'm already there."

"Mari, I'm—"

"Don't," I snapped. "This is on me. *I* brought him here. *I* inducted him. *I* fucked him. This is *my* fault. Everything is *my* fault."

Greyson looked like he wanted to argue, but at my glare, he

backed down. I knew he'd beat himself up too, but there was only enough guilt in this room for one, and I was determined to carry it until I died. A permanent reminder of how foolish trusting someone made me.

"How deep did he get?" I asked, stepping over to the first-aid cabinet. I wanted to let my knuckles fester, but who knew when the others would come after me. I couldn't afford a handicap when it could mean the difference between life and death.

Grey leaned against the wall, swiping through his tablet as I cleaned the cuts, layered on some salve, and wrapped them. The stuff was a family recipe from Tennessee's mee-maw and the shit worked miracles, so I'd probably be healed up in a day or so.

"I'm not sure. His credentials didn't give him access to much, but he could have found out any of ours by being observant, though that would've only given him access to the archives. He didn't have biometric access to anything but the house unless he hacked the system." He paused, writing himself a note in his phone before continuing. "Regardless, I already changed everything. Passwords, biometric scans, et cetera. I've moved the location of the safe houses, swapped warehouses, and even gotten the three of us new phones and numbers, but honestly, there's really no telling what he could have found out. He was here for a long time."

Just long enough to make me love a lie.

Nate knew everything. All our plans, my goals, everything—and now, so did Cash. Nate had said he believed in me, that he believed I was doing the right thing against his brother, all so he could gather all the ammo he needed to shoot me in the back.

I'll never stop loving you, he'd whispered last night while he'd held me in his arms. While we'd made love.

What a fucking joke.

"He knew." Knew he was *coming home* and fucked me anyway. Held me anyway. Told me he loved me anyway.

I thought the look in his eyes was devotion when it was really goodbye. He'd wanted one last orgasm before he broke me. The fact that he'd been so cruel, so disgusting, made me want to scrub my skin until I got rid of the cells that touched him.

Greyson's sigh was sad. "We have to keep moving, Mari."

"How?" I turned to him with burning eyes courtesy of the booze, desperate for an answer I wasn't sure he could give.

How do we fix this?

How do we move on?

Where do we go from here?

My chest ached because we both knew what I really wanted to know. *How could he do this to me?*

"I don't know, *reina*." His voice broke for me. For us. For the family that we thought we'd made, and just like I knew I would, I broke too.

Tears ran in tracks down my face, though I caught the sob before it could leave my throat. Nate could have my tears—could fucking drown in them if he wanted—but he didn't get my voice. My body curled in on itself, desperate to protect my soft spots as I let myself fall. Grey wrapped himself around me, following me down to kneel at my back on the floor. He held me tight, whispering nonsensical words in my ear and running his hand down my hair as I tried so fucking hard to rein it in again.

I would not break. Not for Nate. Not for Cash. Not for fucking anyone.

When I felt stable enough to stand on my own, I did. My legs wobbled like a newborn foal, but they held. They would always hold. I had to be strong enough for that.

Greyson's scent lingered on my skin, a reminder of the home I'd always had, and it gave me the courage to ask, "What would you do?"

"If it were anyone else, I'd suggest normal protocol for spies."

Assassinate him, he meant.

Grey cleared his throat quietly, like the noise would set me off. "I can find someone to do it discreetly if you'd prefer, but I didn't want to assume."

I debated it. Truly, I did. But I couldn't imagine a world without Nate Black in it, even if Nate Black wasn't real.

He'd hurt me, broken my trust, and still, I couldn't sic my people on Nate like a pack of dogs. I couldn't hurt him. Pain or not, my heart beat for him just like it did for Greyson and Dominic. Until I cut his part out and cauterized the wound, I couldn't sign his death sentence.

"Leave it for now. If anything, it'll lull them into complacency until we've decided the correct course of action." I sighed and moved over to the weight bench. My legs were too unstable for running, so I'd lift until my arms fell off. Although, they were already feeling wobbly. "Where's Dominic?"

"Destroying his room. It'll need a complete overhaul."

Couldn't blame him. If I could destroy the house itself, I would. The walls were too ingrained with memories for me to ever feel happy between them again. They were already closing in, and I dreaded the reminders I'd find upstairs.

So, don't go up there.

Sometimes I forgot that I was rich.

"Start looking for a new house. We'll need to move." I slid under the weight rack, fine to keep the base weight as a warm-up, but I didn't reach for it yet. I was too caught up in my own head. The idea of a fresh start appealed more the longer I considered it.

Greyson tapped something else and flipped the tablet to show me two homes. From the pictures alone, I liked them. "Already done. These look good."

"We'll buy them both, retrofit, and then move to whichever one suits best at the time. We can always use the other as a decoy."

He made a note on his phone then slipped both it and the

tablet into his jacket. "For now, I've got the penthouse at the Celestine ready for the three of us."

I was always grateful for Greyson, but in the middle of a personal crisis, I was in awe of how well he knew me. He could take care of me in ways I couldn't fathom.

"The Celestine's perfect. Thanks, Grey."

It was a luxury condo building not far from Shara's place, deep in the heart of my territory. With building security some of the best outside our compound, we always kept the penthouse ready in case of emergencies. Plus, we owned the whole building, so we could keep the family close while we worked through Nate's treachery. Considering how dangerous life had just become, it was the best solution we had.

Cash had placed a target on our backs, and Nate helped him.

I sat up on the bench without lifting a thing. My head was too messy to be holding anything above my body. I'd be just as likely to slip and hurt myself. "I'm going for a shower."

As I moved past him, Greyson stopped me with a soft hand around my bicep. "I'm sorry, Mari."

Staring at him, I saw the agony I was carrying reflected in his eyes. When I hurt, he hurt, and I was fucking decimated.

"Me too." I looked away, swallowing tears and anguish in one shard-filled gulp. He was right; we had to keep going. "I want us moved in to the penthouse by the end of the night. The others can follow tomorrow."

"I love you, *reina*."

I couldn't say it back. All I could think about was last night in Nate's arms.

I'll never stop loving you.

Smiling tightly at Grey, I went upstairs, locked myself in my bathroom, and cried into the shower like someone had died.

Chapter 2
Nate

My first memory was my brother trying to kill me.

I was just a normal five-year-old at day care, playing with cars and laughing with the other kids, when this man showed up, saying he was my brother. I'd never met him before, but we had the same hair, the same eyes. He took me from the day care before I had a chance to say goodbye, telling me we were going on an adventure, just the two of us.

I was a fatherless kid, desperate to belong to someone. Who was I to say no?

According to my mother, Cash had suspected his father had sired another son, but for years, he had no proof.

Until he did.

Our father sent money to my mother, not enough to survive on, but enough to "help." Apparently, Cash tracked it. He'd been in his twenties at the time and well into the underworld, so checking a few bank statements wasn't out of his capabilities. Neither was hiding his tracks.

We drove around in circles for an hour before he took me to this little pond just outside of town, only stopping to pick up burgers for lunch, which we ate on the shoreline. As we munched on the fast-food fries, he told me all about being raised by our father. The good times, the bad times, the anger, the joy. All of it.

Then he told me to take off my shoes because we were going swimming. I didn't know how to swim, but he was my big brother, and all the books said brothers could be trusted, right?

Wrong.

For a while, he taught me to swim. To hold my breath. He held me up and let me float along the surface, smiling and laughing at his silly face. I had no warning when everything changed. I had no clue what flipped the switch, but he went from holding me above the water to holding me under it. I remembered clawing at his arm, desperately trying to get up, to find air. Crying under water for my mom. The terror when I swallowed. The absolute certainty that I was going to die.

Then he stopped.

Decades later, I still didn't know why he'd come for me or why he'd let me live. Only that he did.

That was the day my debt began.

Walking back into his compound after months away was eye-opening. It was no Marcosa mansion, that was for sure. The walls were solid, but the floor was scratched up, the couches old and destroyed. There was an air of desperation to the space that the mansion never had. Not to mention, there was booze in every hand, drugs on every flat surface, and women on every lap.

So many women.

A hand clamped down on my shoulder, squeezing just tight enough to hurt. That alone told me who it was. "Welcome back, little brother."

I grunted my hello and jerked my head toward the room. "What's with the party?"

Cash snatched my bag off my shoulder and tossed it at an Ace with a gruff command to take it to my room. I latched on to it, hauling it over my shoulder, and waved him away. "Don't want anyone in my room."

"Right, forgot about your little need for privacy." My brother sneered, like the idea of a locked door was disgusting. Maybe for him, it was.

I held the bag firmly against my side, and he wrapped an arm around my shoulder, forcing me into the room as if he knew that if I had a choice, I'd run. "It's a celebration. A welcome home for the prodigal brother. See anything you like?"

This was part and parcel for Cash. Throw women in my lap as if he didn't know I hated his guts, hoping it would make me more amenable, when we both knew I was only here because I had nowhere else to go. Luckily for him, I'd learned early that going with the flow made him more tolerable, and I wasn't looking to make my situation worse.

Rolling my eyes, I looked over the crowd, realizing something interesting. All the women looked the same. Blonde hair, blue eyes, thin and wispy enough for their clothes to fall off their bodies. All lightness when I wanted dark hair and dark eyes to suck me in and never let me go.

Had he intentionally picked someone the opposite of Mari as a kindness or because he wanted to make me suffer? Since I was fairly confident he didn't believe love was real, I was pretty sure it was his version of the former.

I was about to make a joke about Cash having a type, as he expected, when I saw him. The man sat on the back couch like a king, surrounded by women—though he didn't touch any of them —with a beer in his hand, which he tipped my way.

The Marcosa spy.

I didn't respond. I didn't nod or wink or grin. I just glared. Because Mari deserved better than him. His lips ticked up, thoroughly entertained by my irritation.

My brother saw where I was looking and grinned. "I didn't realize he was here already. Come on, let's get a drink."

Another hold on my shoulder, another reminder that no matter what happened, I wasn't free. I would never be free. I'd signed my life over to the devil at five, and I owed him until I was ready to shut my eyes for good.

Cash shoved a bottle in my hand, snatched a girl around the waist, and dragged the three of us through the crowd, which parted like he was fucking Moses. *Because he needed that ego boost.*

"Nate, Cash. Good to see you again." Marcosa gave us that good ol' boy smile that set my teeth on edge. "I see you've returned home and caused quite a stir in the process."

I barely swallowed the urge to tell him home was not here, covering my silence with a pull of beer. How could a place I couldn't rest my head safely ever be a home? No, my home was with soft sheets, soft skin, and brown hair on my pillow. My home was something I would never see again.

The urge to ask about her soured the beer in my stomach.

Cash's arm squeezed tight around my neck, and as always, I wondered if he was wishing he'd finished the job he started so many years ago. "Of course he did. Nate is excellent at his job. No one compares to my brother."

He said it like he cared about my feelings, like he would do anything to have my back. Like I was special. I had never been special. I was a tool, something to torment my mother and a weapon to make his army fear him. That was all I was and all I would ever be.

Marcosa's lips tipped again, still hiding that self-indulgent smile. "You must be excited to have your pick of women tonight. No more sharing for you."

He and Cash laughed loudly as I recited "fuck you" in every language I'd ever heard in my head.

I wanted to tell them how much I wanted to share, how beautiful Mari looked falling apart between the three of us and that I would rather be celibate for the rest of my life than touch another woman who wasn't her. But I couldn't do that, just like I couldn't do anything else. Doing so would make her wish she were dead, because Cash didn't like me. If he found something I enjoyed, he broke it, and Mari was not going to be another of his broken little dolls. I wouldn't allow it.

The reminder of what was at stake pushed me to act, and I pasted on a grin so similar to Dominic's playboy act we could have been twins, making a big show of looking around. "It has been a minute. I think I'll go do that now, if you don't need me for anything."

I looked at my brother, who tipped his beer, clinking our bottles together. "Nah, you're good. Enjoy tonight, little bro. We've got work to do tomorrow. The little queen may have fallen, but we need to make sure she stays down."

My nod was on autopilot, a movement completely detached from my mind. It unsettled me that I was already falling into *good soldier* habits, but what else could you do in deadly situations where fighting back got you dead? I had to hold it together for a little while longer.

Make a plan. Get to Mari. Kill Cash. "You got it."

Stepping through the crowd, I let the bodies swallow me up. I checked out the women, unseeing eyes skating over each body before moving on. It made my stomach roll. I didn't even want to pretend to check them out. It felt like cheating.

Hard to cheat when you blew your relationship to smithereens.

One of the women walked around with sealed bottles on a

tray, and I traded in my empty for a fresh one. Getting Mari back was my second priority. Surviving was my first.

I was almost to the other side of the room when she stepped into my path, and I had to resist the urge to curl my lip.

The woman was small, tiny in stature and body, but it wasn't healthy. She looked sickly, yet I knew from my time in the compound that she was one of the women who prided herself on having everyone in the gang at least once. I was just another notch on her bedpost.

"You looking for company?" she rasped, and I winced at how painful it sounded.

No was on the tip of my tongue, and then I looked back to see my brother and his guest watching.

Son of a bitch.

Filing through my options, I closed my eyes against a groan. I didn't have a fucking choice, and I hated it.

"Yeah." Snatching her arm, I pulled her behind me down the hallway and into my suite. Despite the fact that I'd lived here for years, the room was no-frills at best. It was nothing important, just a place to rest my head. A transitional space with three rooms, two bedrooms connected by a main living area and kitchen. I learned early on that Cash liked taking my things away. It didn't matter if I made him happy or sad—or even if he wanted the damn thing. If I had it, he wanted it. The good thing was, it taught me to care less about my possessions. I had nothing I would be upset to lose.

Except he'd done it yet again, this time taking away the only thing that had ever been mine, and I'd let him.

Pulling the girl into the spare room, I shut the door behind us and motioned to the bed. She went eagerly, then reached for my belt. I slapped her hands away before they could get close. "Don't touch me."

She looked around as if she could see a camera. "I don't understand."

Sighing, I looked up at the ceiling for patience, cursing Cash every way I could. "What's your name?"

"Ava."

"Okay, Ava. How much would it take for your silence?"

"Silence?" Her brows furrowed like she'd never heard the word, and I groaned. Christ, was she on drugs? I couldn't negotiate if she was high; she'd be too much of a liability. People with vices liked to open their fucking mouths whenever possible, and this had to stay between us.

"Are you high?"

"No."

"Drunk?"

"No," she growled.

"Would you pass a drug test?"

"Sober as a church mouse."

I stared at her, and she rolled her eyes. "Fine, two beers, but I'm not a lightweight. I can still consent."

"Do the men in this gang really stop to ask that?"

"No." That one word killed me. For a moment, Ava sounded as small as she looked, and I ached to tell her to run, to leave and never look back. This wasn't a life for anyone, and she was in her early twenties. Still plenty young enough to start over and be happy. Then her eyes sharpened, and I knew she wouldn't go, even if I promised her a way out. She was ready to die on this hill, and I had no doubt she would. They always did.

"You got an old man?"

"No."

"Boyfriend?"

"Christ. No boyfriend, fuck buddy, or husband waiting for me. No one I give a shit about. Why, you looking for a new girl?"

"Absolutely not."

The sharpness of my words made her flinch, and I decided that honesty was the best policy here. If she opened her mouth to anyone, she'd be dead before dawn anyway. Even if Cash wanted me to control, he needed my reputation intact more, and that meant he'd do anything to ensure I was as big an alpha male douche as possible. "I don't want to touch you and I really don't want you touching me, but I need them to think that we screwed."

"But you don't want to?"

Not in a million years, but that felt unkind to say, so I shook my head.

"I'm supposed to—what? Sit in here?" She sounded incredulous, but I saw the way her hand ran across the soft sheets. I didn't let women into my room, even when I did fuck them, so the guest room had the best sheets I could buy. Soft and supple and so good against naked skin.

"Yes." She looked like she'd interrupt, but I kept talking. "I won't fuck you. Not now, not ever, but I need you to make it seem like we did. That means messy hair, messy makeup, walk of shame tomorrow—the whole enchilada. In return, you can stay here in this room. Alone. There's a massive shower with unlimited hot water and all the streaming channels. I'll even order you whatever food you want. I don't give a fuck, as long as you stay until morning."

We had a pretty good kitchen staff in-house, so room service was an option, but even if she wanted the most expensive meal in the city, I'd have it delivered. I just needed to buy myself some time.

Ava toyed with the bedspread as she looked at the floor. "How do I know that you're not just going to change your mind and come in here when I'm asleep and vulnerable?"

"Because I'm not an asshole or a predator." She just stared and I sighed, my patience beyond worn. "There's a lock on the door, and I don't have a key. Other than the window, it's the only exit. You can put whatever you want in front of the door to keep me out. I just need you to keep your mouth shut unless it's saying that I fucked you into that mattress. Can you do that?"

"They're not going to believe it."

Oh, for fuck's sake.

I didn't know how to tell her that her reputation would protect us both, but I didn't need to. She took one look at my face and laughed. "Look, I know I get around—I'm not ashamed of that—but it means most of the men out there know what I sound like. News flash, I am not quiet."

Discomfort settled under my skin, and I had the urge to flee the room. "I don't want to have this conversation with you."

Or any other woman. The only person whose screams I wanted was Mari, and I doubted I'd be that lucky again.

Ava's face softened. "I get it. I'm just saying, we need to make it believable."

"I am *not* touching you," I said through gritted teeth.

"I didn't ask you to." She pulled her purse over onto her lap and dug through, pulling out a suspiciously large silk pouch.

Oh my fucking god. "Is that a vibrator?"

"Obviously. Wanna see?"

"No!" She dropped the bag to her lap and set her purse on the floor. "Do you just carry that thing around all the time?"

Ava raised her eyebrow like I was dumber than a box of rocks. "You just pointed out that I sleep with a bunch of criminals. Do you think most of them know where the clit is?"

I wasn't touching that comment with a ten-foot pole.

Ava clapped her hands and grinned. "Here's the plan. I'm going to stream some audio porn onto the TV and use my vibrator to make myself come. If anybody passes the room, they'll hear what they expect. I get an orgasm, you get the street cred. They'll expect an all-nighter from the conquering hero, so I'll stay in here tonight and repeat a few times. In an hour, you can order room service and leave it and my fee outside the door."

"What's your fee?"

"Two hundred."

I would've paid triple to keep her away from me. It sounded like too good of a deal, and I learned a long time ago that anything that good typically meant I was getting fucked.

Crossing my arms over my chest, I narrowed my eyes. "What's in this for you?"

"I already told you, a few orgasms, food, and a quiet place to rest." I lifted an eyebrow, and she huffed. "Fine, it's because you're paying me."

The sass was strong, but it was a lie. I could see it. There was something else, some other reason she agreed. When I continued to stare at her, she sighed.

"Before you left, you were surviving—and barely that—but you weren't here. Not really. Now you're back, and even though I can see you slipping back into that survival mentality, you look sad. Actually, you look wrecked. I just want to help."

Destroyed was a better word, but she wasn't wrong.

"Besides, you've always been nice to me and the other girls. Don't think that just because we haven't been in your bed that we haven't noticed." My ears burned, and I tried to ignore the earnest stare.

My brother was a sadist and an asshole. I couldn't count the number of women I'd poured into taxis and sent away because I was scared he'd go too far and kill them. Or the ones I took to the clinic to get tested or birth control or morning-after pills. The ones I'd subtly warned away from the worst members of the Aces in an effort to keep them safe. I thought I'd been invisible, unnoticeable. My mistake.

"So, do we have a deal?" Ava held out her hand to shake.

"We have a deal, but I'm not going to touch you."

She shrugged and lifted the bag again. My lip curled at the reminder that I was in the same room as a sex toy and another woman. *Mari is going to have my balls.*

Except, no. She wasn't. Because she wasn't mine anymore.

Fuck, I missed her. The ache hit swiftly, almost taking me out at the knees, and I knew I had to get out of there. I quickly got Ava's order and headed for the door. "I'll send your food in an hour."

"Don't worry, baby. I'll make it memorable." She smirked, tossing the bag onto the bed before standing to follow me out.

"Don't call me baby," I said clearly. I had no room for miscommunication.

Ava smiled, winked, then shoved me out the door, the loud click of the lock falling into place behind me. Running a hand over my face, I wondered just what I'd gotten into, then decided it didn't matter. I was all in if it would get Cash off my back, even for a little while.

I'd unwillingly heard rumors about Ava's prowess more than once and figured I could get away with not picking anyone up for at least a week if she made it convincing enough. The woman was a hellcat on a good day.

"This is fucking ridiculous," I mumbled, walking into my room and locking the door behind me. It was just as bare as the rest of the apartment and twice as heartless.

I missed Mari throwing her clothes on the floor, only for Greyson to pick them up and fold them. I missed Dominic slouching everywhere, putting his fucking feet on the couches. The low hum of the radio that one or all of them always seemed to have on. I didn't even think they realized it most of the time. They just couldn't stand the silence.

And my suite was all silence.

As I sat on the edge of the bed, it hit me that I was alone for the first time in months, and the weight of that was crushing.

I'd been avoiding thinking of Mari as much as possible since we left the meeting because I knew the second I did, I would have to come to terms with how badly I'd fucked up. I'd have to relive her beautiful face twisted in agony. The fire of betrayal not just from her, but the men I had started considering brothers. Real brothers, not like whatever toxic relationship Cash and I had.

Dominic and Greyson were supportive and kind. They were warm and welcoming once I'd proven myself. They invited me into the fold and made me feel like an equal, even though I had far less history with Mari. They never once made me feel bad about who I was, and I found myself standing taller in their presence. As if just having them and Mari nearby made me stronger, better.

And then I'd gone and screwed it up.

I need to talk to her.

My phone was in my hand before I even finished the thought, and every ring screamed that it was a mistake. But I couldn't stop myself. I had to hear her voice. I had to explain, even if she wouldn't believe me—and she wouldn't. I wasn't stupid; I knew the truth like I knew her, but I couldn't let the last time we interacted be with my brother in the room. I couldn't live with her thinking I didn't love her. If I could only tell her one thing, I'd tell her that.

The call connected, but there was nothing but silence for a minute.

"Angel—"

"What do you want?" I'd seen Grey in pain. I'd seen him terrified and worried and desperate for news. I'd seen him so angry he was ready to rip someone's head off, but I'd never heard his voice so fucking cold. This was worse than frostbite. It was hypothermia in a voice.

"Can I—"

"No."

Of course he was playing guard dog. "Greyson. I know you have no reason to trust me, but I need—"

"How dare you call and ask for anything. Do you have any idea what you've done?"

Betrayed the love of my life and ruined any trust she ever had in me or anyone else. I could see it right there in front of me, as I'd stood behind Cash, watching every painful second of her closing herself off to people.

But Grey already knew that.

"I just want to explain."

"She doesn't need your explanations. She needs you to leave her alone. Stay the hell away from her, Nathaniel Beckstrom. If you step within a hundred feet of her, I will wipe out your entire fucking bloodline. You hear me?"

That would probably be a mercy, I thought. But I couldn't say that either. The consequences for spilling our fucked-up secrets meant death. And not mine.

My throat was tight and sharp as I swallowed. "Yeah, I hear you."

I barely had the words out before the beep of my phone told me he'd hung up. I wanted to throw it at a window, but the device was my only access to Mari. Then again, if Greyson was answering her phone, that avenue was likely closed. Still, I didn't want to let it go. Couldn't, really. Not yet.

Tossing it and myself onto the bed, I stared at the ceiling. I'd known the moment the text came in that I'd have to burn any possibility of a life with Mari, but living it was far worse than I'd imagined. I felt an emptiness behind my breastbone that I wasn't sure I could survive.

You have to, I told myself. *You did this. You could have told her. She would have listened. She could have helped you.*

But I didn't because it wasn't just myself I was trying to

protect, and now she was gone. Nothing but a memory of a time I'd never enjoy again.

The weight of my actions had been pressing on me for hours, but alone in my room, it hit hard and fast.

There would be no hand-holding in the car on the way to meetings, no standing at Mari's back and watching her over-achieve when others thought she'd fail. No climbing into bed with her fresh-faced and soft from the shower. No snuggling up to her with the others close by.

That life was over, and I would never get it back.

Still, I couldn't let her go. Not really. She was the heart in my chest, the breath in my lungs. I couldn't exist without loving her, so I wouldn't try to. I'd let the love sustain me, even when it faded for her.

The more I thought about it, the better I felt.

Just because I couldn't have her didn't mean I couldn't keep our history safe, and it didn't mean I couldn't keep *her* safe. If Mari was gone from me forever, an option I could never return to, then the least I could do was make sure she was alive and happy. Even if it killed me to watch someone else take my place.

Chapter 3
Dominic

It was strange waking up in a place that wasn't the Marcosa mansion. The penthouse suite at the Celestine was comfortable and cozy, but it lacked the warmth the historic mansion had. Or maybe it was just because the suite lacked Mari.

Since we'd gotten home, she'd been quiet and reserved, pulling away from everyone, including Grey and me. Could we blame her? She'd fallen in love with the enemy. The burn in my stomach rose again, and I wondered if I'd need to start carrying antacids soon. Did rage cause ulcers? I wasn't sure. Just like I wasn't sure rage was an appropriate term for the cataclysmic-level anger I felt on Mari's behalf.

Nate lied. He tricked her—he tricked us. Greyson and I gave him the most precious thing in our world, and he destroyed her. Mari might be harboring some sentimentality toward him, but I didn't, and neither did Grey. He'd earned his death fair and square. Especially knowing this was a hurt that Mari would never heal from.

Pulling on some clothes, I went straight to her door, knocking even though I knew she wouldn't answer, just like she hadn't any of the other times I'd tried before I attempted to crash. She'd asked for space, but it went against my nature to leave her alone to lick her wounds. I was her partner. I wanted to hold her through the worst of it, and she wouldn't let me. Couldn't, Grey corrected when I asked.

She has to process on her own before she can let us in again.

I was worried she was shutting us out, but Greyson assured me when she came to terms with what happened, she would come for us. I just had to be patient and hope that he was right.

For now, all I got was silence.

I pressed my forehead against the door, sagging a little, desperate to let her know that I was waiting for her with open arms. "I love you, *mariposa*."

Come back to me.

After another minute, I stood back, and the frantic energy under my skin pushed me into movement. Knowing sleep wasn't coming again, I decided to burn it off. Maybe if I exhausted myself, I'd forget why my bed was empty.

Grabbing my keys and my phone, I left the suite, nodding to Moore and Tennessee standing guard outside our door. None of us were comfortable leaving Mari alone, even for a second. Cash had put a target on her back, not just in the city, but within the family, and if we weren't careful, we were going to end up with a dead queen.

Taking the stairs at a quick clip, I let the descent warm up my muscles. By the time I made it to the tenth floor, I was ready to go. With a beep of the card against the lock, I whipped open the gym door, only to walk straight into Joaquin.

It took less than a heartbeat to realize he knew.

One of the only things Mari had said before she'd shut down on us in the car was that she wanted to keep things quiet, just for a few hours. Just until she wasn't so fucking raw. We'd kept our mouths shut, but it hadn't been enough.

I wasn't sure how, but the glint in Joaquin's eyes told me he understood what had happened and was using it to his advantage. Honestly, it made sense. If he was going to overthrow Mari, he would do so when she was at her most unstable, which was now.

The thought made me nauseous.

Careful to keep an eye on him, I casually grabbed a mat, laying it out near the mirror so I could stretch. With Mari in danger, I couldn't afford even a pulled muscle. As I moved my body, falling into the routine of it, I realized Joaquin wasn't alone. The other capos were there as well. Hmm, all of Mari's uncles in the same place at the same time on a day that was monumental in its danger...that was totally innocent.

I may have been born at night—but not last night. I knew what they were doing.

No one spoke while I stretched or when I moved to the bench, adjusting the weight so that I could do some presses. It wasn't until I was occupied with my warm-up that Joaquin walked over, eyes at the ready like he was spotting me.

"I'm good," I said casually, not wanting him hovering over me. If he wanted to get to Mari, Greyson and I were a good place to start, and a well-placed drop could take me out. Death by barbell.

Fuck that.

Keeping my focus on my form and my muscles, I let the silence fester, but Joaquin stayed where he was. "What would our queen say if she found us letting you work out without a spotter in such *troubling* times? No. I think I'll keep an eye on you."

As if he hadn't already been doing that. Feeling other eyes on me, I decided I wasn't in the mood for subtlety. "You don't give a fuck about what she thinks."

For a split second, there was a tidal wave of shock, then Joaquin threw his head back and laughed. "My niece is an incredible woman. She's smart and savvy and stronger than most people think, but she's also weak."

Thinking of everything Mari had endured, everything she had done and overcome to create the safety in the city that we were profiting from at this very moment inside a building *she* had prepared to keep her people safe, I wasn't sure how they could ever consider her weak.

As if he could hear my arguments, Joaquin continued. "She let that boy into her home when she knew nothing about him, and now look at us. We're steps away from war."

"That wasn't her fault." It was Nate's for lying. It was Moore's for getting a false background check. It was Rafael's for getting a doctored file on Cash, one that conveniently erased his little brother.

None of it was Mari's.

"She's still a liability." Gabriele gave me a significant look, but I didn't need him to finish. Liabilities didn't survive our world. "You, on the other hand, have been nothing but helpful since you returned."

I snorted, reracking the barbell and sitting up to add more weight, but Joaquin was already doing it. I watched carefully and tried not to point out the hypocrisy of Gabriele's statement, considering he was conveniently forgetting the fact that I had disappeared for twenty years and been out of contact with Mari for the better part of ten. "You're looking for a scapegoat."

I saw Joaquin's grin in the mirror as he leaned on the bar behind me, all malice and misinterpretation. "Am I, though? We both know you're meant for something more."

I narrowed my eyes at the not-so-subtle threat, then lay back, taking the bar again to continue my reps. The last thing I wanted was to be vulnerable, but when swimming with sharks, you had to pretend they were beneath your notice. You had to be the predator. "I'm not interested."

"We didn't make you an offer yet."

Yet. Fuck, I'm going to have to tell Greyson. We knew they'd make moves, but we thought we had more time. "Is there an offer to be made, Joaquin?"

He smirked. "You know there is."

"With everything I know about the Marcosas—and I know a lot now—taking over involves killing off the old regime. I'm not interested in killing the woman I love." It was probably a mistake to admit that I had a weakness for Mari, but they weren't blind. If they didn't know it already, they were being intentionally obtuse.

Joaquin scoffed. "Of course not. Your generation is soft."

"And yet you're asking me for a favor."

"Not a favor. Consider it a job offer."

Another press. My arms were starting to burn now, but it helped me focus on the land mines we were crossing. "Not interested. I like the job I already have."

Joaquin's laugh was just short of a bark. "Of course you do. The job you already have lets you get your dick wet when you want."

"Watch yourself," I snapped. Part of me wanted to keep going until I knew exactly what he wanted from me and for Mari, all of his plans, but he didn't get to talk about her like that. No one got to talk about her like that.

"That was disrespectful," he said, bowing his head as if that was enough of an apology. Yet he didn't say it was wrong.

"What's your point, Joaquin?" The longer he talked, the less patience I had, and I was already running low on it.

"What if we come up with a plan that gets us all what we want?" Joaquin rolled his eyes like the words were hippie bullshit as he helped me rerack and add more weight. "We want you as our new leader, and you want Mari alive."

"And do you think you can make both those things happen?"

Joaquin's smile was all vain confidence.

"How do I know this isn't a trick? That you won't just kill her as soon as I agree."

"You don't," he said simply. "You also don't have a choice. It's either take the offer, or become part of the problem. Which would you prefer?"

It'd been a while since I'd had a full-blown threat lobbed at me, but that was an almost elementary one to figure out. "How would you get Mari to agree to abdicate her throne?"

It was unheard of in the Marcosas, and I knew for a fact that my *mariposa* wouldn't willingly hand over her crown. Especially not now.

"We wouldn't, but in this family, the husband rules the roost." Joaquin moved to grab his things, not looking for me to answer. Which was good because I didn't know what to say to that bullshit.

A forced marriage, even to Mari, was not on my agenda, and I knew it would kill her just the same as a bullet. She deserved to choose her husband after everything. In spite of it. Even though I knew she loved me, I also knew that letting this happen would be the death of us.

"Don't give us an answer yet. Just think about it. We'll be in touch." Joaquin watched carefully as I racked the bar for the last time before disappearing with his minions, leaving me alone in the gym and more confused than ever. I hadn't had nearly enough of a workout, but I couldn't avoid going upstairs any longer. Mari had to know what just happened.

As soon as I was sure the uncles weren't waiting, I sprinted to the stairwell and up until I shoved onto the penthouse floor with a heave. Tennessee's hand rested on his gun, and he sagged against the wall seeing it was me. "Christ, Dominic. Was that necessary?"

"Sorry," I said absently, pulling out the keycard to get into the suite. "I just—sorry."

What else could I say when I needed to tell Mari and Greyson first?

Tennessee's eyes, which were normally happy and laughing, were sad for the first time since I'd known him. It hit me then that Nate's treachery wasn't just a surprise to us. There had been far more casualties than I expected. "I'm sorry about—"

He immediately waved me off. "Don't worry about it. Just take care of the boss."

"I'll try." I slipped inside, not quite sure I could promise that.

I beelined for Mari's door, knocking again and again and again when she didn't answer. "Look, I know you want to be alone, but it's important. It's about Joaquin."

I heard the click of the lock and ignored how much it hurt that she was physically locking us out of her life. Then the door opened, and there she was.

Mari in the hospital bed had been heartbreaking. She'd looked so small and vulnerable that when I'd seen her, it had been like being transported back to our teen years again when she was fragile and needed protection.

This Mari, though fragile, was not the same. There was no warmth, no laughter, no love or joy. Everything about her was just full ice queen, and when she spoke, it gave me chills and not in a good way. "What do you need, Dominic?"

Her tone didn't give a single indication that she had any feelings for me, and it made my pulse race. "I just ran into Joaquin at the gym. He's making moves against you."

Her face didn't show a hint of surprise, which was understandable, but the slight tick of resignation bothered me.

"We have to stop him," I said, trying to get her to understand, needing her to agree. The silence dragged on for one second, two, three.

Finally, she spoke. "He's the least of our problems right now."

Disbelief filled my whole being. "The man who lives two floors down and has access to the security of this building and you at all times is the least of our problems?"

Her flat look was enough of an answer, and I was baffled by how to proceed. Had the thing with Nate screwed up her brain so much that she wasn't seeing what was in front of her? Did I need to call in Grey to explain things to her or take shit off her plate so she could get her head on straight? Did kingpins have therapists? "Mar—"

"We'll deal with it later."

Then the door was closed, the lock clicked, and I was on the outside again.

What the fuck?

"Give her some time." I whirled around to find Grey leaning against the wall, frowning at the handle just like I was.

I stepped closer, lowering my voice so she couldn't hear through the door. "Obviously, she's struggling, but this is important."

He ran a hand through his hair, pushing it off his face, and I realized for the first time he wasn't fully dressed. The man was in holey sweats, for fuck's sake. He hadn't shaved, and the slightly unkempt tilt of his collar told me he'd been pulling at it. Staring at him, I had to wonder if this was his version of a breakdown.

Where Mari isolated herself, Grey fell apart. No doubt when she opened the door for good, he'd be back on his axis soon after. The two of them were too connected for it not to happen. But what did we do in the meantime while our biggest players were out of commission?

You step up. You're the underboss.

Fuck me running.

He jerked his eyes away eventually, turning back to me. "She needs time. We'll deal with this on our own."

"Is that a good idea?" I looked back at the door with more than a little reluctance. "I can't lie to her again."

I had already been on my last shot before Nate, but I knew if she found out I lied again—hell, if she thought I'd withheld something from her—that was it. She'd dump me faster than I could say her name, and she'd never look at me that way again. I'd have to watch her feelings wither on the vine right in front of my eyes. It sounded like torture.

"It won't come to that. Besides, it's not like you didn't tell her first." When he saw I still wasn't convinced, he sighed. "She can't handle anything else right now, Dominic. We'll take care of this for her, and when she's ready, we'll loop her in. No lying, no cheating, no secrets. All you have to do is play double agent."

"To what end?"

He looked at the door again before heading toward the kitchen, beckoning me to follow with a nod. "The only reason Joaquin's still alive is the fact that he's the next in line for the throne. If Mari killed him on our word alone, it would look worse for her."

Taking out the competition wasn't unheard of—again, that was what most Marcosas did to earn their throne—but in this case, it would look more like killing the opposition to prevent them from removing her than a protective move. "So we just let him think he's won?"

"For now, yes. We want him gone, we need proof. Find it, and we'll tell her together."

I wasn't so sure that would work, but Greyson knew Mari better than I did, and I had to trust that he knew best in this too.

"This better work," I said softly. "I don't want to lose her."

"I don't want that either," Grey agreed. "She's already lost too much."

Chapter 4
Greyson

The cheerful knock came the next morning when the sun wasn't even up.

"Come on, cousin. Let me in." Cameron's singsong voice barely reached through the door. "I brought you presents from our travels."

I wasn't sure presents were going to help, but I was pretty sure that Cameron would. Whatever we did, whatever went down, Mari found safety in her cousins, and Cameron was the last man standing. *God, I hope this works.*

I pulled open the door, nodding to the dining room, where she stared into her cup of coffee the same way she had for the last twenty minutes.

Instantly, all that peppy cheer was gone, replaced by nothing but worry. Pitching his voice low, he asked, "What the hell happened to her?"

"I'll let her explain." I took the bags out of his hand, putting them on the kitchen counter. Mari was keeping this as quiet as possible despite Joaquin's interference, and I didn't want to step on her toes. She'd give her cousin whatever he needed to know, and that was it. "Just be gentle. It's been a rough few days."

With a nod of pure resolution, he plopped down on a chair, snatched her coffee, and took a sip, grimacing at the no-doubt cold liquid. "You look like a zombie."

"Is that a compliment?" she asked, voice raspy with disuse.

"It wasn't supposed to be. Care to tell me why I'm not allowed to go home?" He asked it casually, but the way he glanced back at me said he was trying to be gentle. He just had no clue he'd slapped his hand onto a bomb.

Mari looked over at me, a fleeting wish that I could fix this crossing her face before she threw her shoulders back. I stayed silent as she explained the meeting, Cash and Nate. The pain I could feel floating through the room was a blade digging into my own side, and knowing Mari was hurting ate at me.

"Are you fucking kidding me?" Cameron's harsh voice broke the soft silence after Mari finished. To his credit, he'd stayed quiet while she spoke, but more than one napkin lay shredded in front of him. The man moved quickly. "He was an Ace the whole time?"

"Yes," Mari said through gritted teeth. "Which is why we're here. The mansion isn't safe anymore. If you need to get your things, do it, but we need you and Aislynn here."

"No."

The answer was immediate and without question.

Mari sighed and tried again. "Cameron, I know this is too close for you. I know you need your space from Joaquin and us, and I promised that you could have it after the wedding, but I need you to be safe more than I need you to be comfortable."

"I didn't say I won't be safe, but I can't live here. Besides, I told Ash I would take her home."

"Home?"

"To my place."

I wasn't aware that her cousin *had* a place that wasn't the mansion, but Mari nodded in understanding. "I'd prefer you to be here, but if that's not an option, your house is secluded enough."

Meaning, it was a decent option for now. But if anything else happened, she'd pull rank and yank him home before the sun set. Cameron grinned, relaxing in his seat. "Considering barely anyone knows about it, I would hope so. Either way, the missus will be pleased."

He said that with a little too much relish to be anything but sincere.

Mari rolled her eyes, continuing as if he hadn't spoken. "Keep your guard up. Make sure you have security members close by, if not for you, then for Aislynn. She is not allowed to go anywhere alone. If that's a problem, she can talk to me."

"Agreed," he said easily. "Not that she was going to anyway."

Mari smiled, the barest suggestion of laughter on her face, and it took my breath away—the faintest hint of who she'd been yesterday and a reminder of why I was desperate to help her heal. "Of course not."

They talked a little more about plans and Mari's expectations, but eventually, there was a lull.

"I'm sorry." Cameron reached out to lay his hand on hers. Immediately, she pulled it back, hiding it in her lap where she thought neither of us could see the trembling.

"It's fine." He looked up at me, brows furrowed as Mari stared unseeing out the window. That one look told me we were on the same page. Mari wasn't okay.

I wasn't sure she would ever be okay again.

But we would be there for her, nonetheless. We'd help her, guide her, tether her until she was grounded in her own body again.

Then we'd burn Cash's empire to the ground and hope Nate went with it.

Cameron cleared his throat, catching her attention, and pasted a smile on his face. "What's the plan for the empire, boss?"

"We redo everything," Mari said, falling back into the leadership role. "As of now, everything we know about Cash could be fake, so we pretend it is. If no one could figure out that he has a living brother, there's no way the rest of it is right."

I wasn't so sure since the best lies were rooted in the truth, but I also wasn't going to correct her. She needed this. We all did.

"We already moved some safe houses, but pull whatever favors you can. We need to figure out who we're up against, and we need to take action."

"And the uncles?" Her cousin wasn't stupid. This big of a stone in the pond would send ripples so far-reaching, everyone would feel them. The fact that Dominic was already feeling the effects was a very bad sign.

"They're tomorrow's problem," Mari said firmly, glancing at me before looking back at her cousin. Luckily, Cameron was a smart man who shut his mouth with a nod.

Obviously ready to be alone again, Mari stood. "If you need anything from the mansion, let me know. We're going to head over there soon to pick something up."

Cameron frowned, likely remembering we kept doubles of everything in the Celestine so we didn't have to go back to a compromised location. "Is that safe?"

"I won't be long. I'm only picking up a couple of journals."

"Journals." His voice made it clear that no journal was worth her life, and while I agreed, these were worth the risk.

"My father's journals," Mari explained. "And Antoni's, if I can find them."

"You want to read your dad's diary? Do you think that's a good idea, considering—"

Considering he had been a fan of the ladies and he'd had no problem writing that shit down. Cameron didn't know Mari, Antoni, and I had snuck into the library more than once as teens to read all about it. It had scarred us for life.

Mari snorted, her lips twitching as if she almost wanted to smile before smothering it. "I'm not looking for my father's sexcapades. We think there might be information on Cash in there."

Cameron tilted his head. "Are you sure? I thought you already looked through them."

"Apparently not far enough back."

Her cousin hummed then shook his head. "Well, be safe. I already had most of Aislynn's stuff packed up and shipped to the house while we were gone, so we should be good to go. I think I saw them in the library last time I was there."

"Perfect." There was a pause and an uncomfortable silence, and I saw Mari squirm for the first time in ages. "Cam—"

"I know about the bomb," he whispered, his hands clenching at his sides as he followed her to his feet. "Warner, too."

Even though the news should've come from her, Mari looked grateful she didn't have to say it. "I'm so sorry."

"Don't. It's part of the life. They all knew what they were getting into, and even if Warner had known he was going out that way, he still would have done it. He loved this job, he loved you, and he was loyal to this family. He wouldn't have changed a thing."

"I hope you're right," Mari said sadly.

"I know I am." Cameron pulled her into a tight hug, whispering in her ear. "Take care of yourself."

"Be back later. We have a meeting with the capos."

"You got it." He turned back with a wink and a pointed look. "Don't forget your presents."

Then he was gone, leaving us alone. I stepped closer, wrapping her up the second the door was closed. She sagged in my hold, her breathing choppy and unstable, but she didn't cry. She wouldn't.

"Not yet," she whispered. "I need a little more time."

I could see her pulling her walls back up, but when she looked at me, I saw a crack of something warmer. Something closer to my Mari, my *reina,* and it gave me hope.

"A little more time, love," I said, letting her go. Knowing that in doing so, I would get her back all the quicker.

While most of the Celestine had been remodeled into suites, three floors below the penthouse, we'd created an office in case we were compromised. The place was bare and beige, but it did the trick. The chairs were comfortable, the coffee serviceable, and the space big enough for what we needed. This was the first time we'd had to use it.

I stood behind Mari in the massive conference room, knowing that what she was about to say was potentially deadly.

"Why are we here, Mariana?" Joaquin asked. Even if Dominic hadn't told me what happened, I would've had no doubt Joaquin was in the know. He was just too fucking shifty not to be.

"We had a security breach," Mari said simply.

He hummed in his throat, tapping his pen against the table. *Tap, tap, tap.* "A security breach. Care to be more specific?"

Mari took a fortifying breath. "Nate is an Ace."

"Not just an Ace, but a Beckstrom," Joaquin corrected with a cheerful smile, like his niece's pain made him happy. Dominic and I both growled, and he rolled his eyes.

Cameron's voice was droll, but his gaze was soaked with rage. "If you knew what was happening, why ask?"

"I wanted to make sure everybody else was aware."

"How did *you* become aware?" I asked softly, pinning him to his seat with a glare.

"One only has to look outside to find out what Cash is doing."

It was only through years of practice reading her body language that I saw Mari tense. Just the slight hitch of her shoulders to betray her nerves. "What exactly does that mean?"

Joaquin pulled out his phone, scrolled, then slid it down the long table to land in front of her. Mari didn't touch it, but Dominic, who sat to her right, did. He scrolled through, cursing under his breath.

"Cash has been flaunting him around town." Dominic tilted the phone so Mari and I could see, and sure enough, there was Cash on his mystery tour, shaking hands. Although, instead of kissing babies, he was kissing up. The first picture was Kosas, then Ajilon, and finally O'Bannon.

"Has he been seen with everyone?" she asked quietly.

"Every single one," Joaquin said. "And you'll see it's not just the leaders either."

"I think I'll take your word for it." Mari nodded, and Dominic slid the phone back harder than necessary. Undeterred, Joaquin caught it and slipped the device back into his pocket with a satisfied smirk.

"What are we going to do about this?"

"Nothing."

Joaquin laughed, though it was as fake as ever. "You want to sit there and let him disrespect us—"

"Is your ego so fragile that it can't handle a little disrespect, Uncle?" She spoke with a chill cold enough to burn, but the passion gave me renewed hope that she was coming to terms with everything. That sometime soon, I'd have my partner back.

"It's the principle of the matter." Joaquin leaned forward on the table like he was ready to leap down and attack her. "He's disrespecting the Marcosa name, our power structure, the family itself—and you're letting him."

"I'm letting him do nothing. Cash's actions have no bearing on ours, and right now, I'd rather take our time and extinguish him permanently than poke holes big enough for him to escape. Nate is a nonstarter. He doesn't matter."

"If you really think that it doesn't matter, then you're a fool."

"Is that so?" The temperature dropped ten degrees with every word until I felt like we were all breathing frost. "If you think you can do so much better than me, maybe we should trade seats."

"Maybe we should," Joaquin snapped, only to wince and look away at Gabriele's scowl and the *very* subtle shift of the table.

Joaquin was silent, chewing on his own petulance until he bent his head to Mari once more. "Apologies, niece. Seeing how upset you are about this situation has me feeling some sort of way. I worry the boy will become a problem for you."

I held back my scoff, but Dominic's disbelief was audible across the table.

Mari smiled, sickly-sweet and poisonous. "Thank you for your concern, Uncle, but I assure you there is no problem for any of us. Nate was a mistake I don't intend to make again."

"So what do we do now?" Moore asked, guiding us back on track.

"We kill the Beckstrom boy," Gabriele suggested. It didn't escape my attention that only two of the capos were speaking.

"If we could kill Cash, he would be dead already," Dominic pointed out.

"Not Cash. The brother."

Again, I watched the hitch in Mari's shoulder, the single tap of her foot betraying her agitation. I stepped forward, giving her a moment to collect herself. "We need to be smart about our course of action. An assassination is one thing. A *failed* assassination is another entirely. The last thing we need is Cash getting another head of steam."

"I think we could figure out a way."

"Then do it," Mari snapped, and Joaquin's head jerked back to her. "If you believe that's true, then you plan things, Uncle. Bring me an assassination proposal that won't get this city burned down around our ears, and I'll consider it."

Joaquin's surprise was nothing more than a widening of his eyes, then a grim smile lit his face. "Agreed."

Mari turned to the rest of the table, dismissing him entirely. "We're operating under the assumption that everything has been compromised. Credentials will be reallocated, biometrics rescanned, profiles recreated. We're starting from the ground up. Moore will text you with your time slot to get it redone. Until then, assume whatever information we got on Cash and Nate was a lie and start from scratch. Get on the streets and pull info on both of them. Poll the dealers, check the DMV, find their fucking school records. I don't care what you do, but get me facts."

"What's going to happen when we get this information?" Joaquin asked.

Mari looked him dead in the eyes, no flinching. "Exactly what should happen. You find me the information that I need to take out Cash, and he goes down."

"How is this any different from before?" Gabriele asked, throwing another glare at Joaquin when he tried to poke at her again. Those two had always been oil and water.

I shifted enough to see Mari's face, sad to notice it was grim and determined. "Let's just say I'm motivated."

This was the deadly queen who took out gangs and protected her city in blood. This was the queen who armed her guards and took no mercy. This was the queen who lost a little bit of herself every time someone died.

Right now, this was the queen we needed, even if it sucked.

Mari handed out the orders, excusing people as she went, until all that remained were her closest allies.

"That won't hold them forever," Cameron said, eyes tracking his father on his way down the hall. There was no doubt that was the truth. Joaquin was leading the charge against Mari, and if we didn't end the war before it could actually start, we were going to lose everything we'd worked for.

Moore cleared his throat, tapping his knuckles against the tabletop as he thought. "I might have some options we can try to seal this up quickly."

"What kinds of options?" Mari asked.

"The nontraditional kinds. They'll cost us, though."

"Cost isn't an issue." Mari stared at him, unruffled, but Dominic and I both frowned. Moore was as straitlaced as they came, despite the fact that he protected a crime boss. What exactly was his version of a nontraditional intel source?

Moore cleared his throat again, looking every bit uncomfortable. "One of my friends from the service is a Fed."

Alarm bells rang, and I swallowed the urge to snap at him. "If finding an Ace in our home was enough to put Mari's head on the chopping block, what do you think using a Fed for intel is going to do? The other leaders will decimate the city if they find out."

"They don't have to find out," Moore countered.

"How do you expect to hide it from them?" Cameron asked. "The uncles are ruthless. They'll figure it out sooner than you think."

"They didn't last time." Moore shrugged.

Cameron froze in his seat, and I groaned. We hadn't told him where the original info on Cash had come from. Moore's friend had given us just enough to use to convince the leaders to help take him out, but it was outside his investigation and, honestly, barely anything to go on. That wouldn't be the same case here. We needed cold, hard evidence to get through this shit.

Trying to defuse the situation, I turned to Cameron. "It may not work anyway. We need more than they had."

If Rafael's information wasn't accurate, I doubted the federal government's would be. A glance at Mari and Dominic—hell, even Tennessee—told me I wasn't alone in that thought.

"It doesn't hurt to check," Mari mumbled, turning to Moore. "Do you think your source will give it to us?"

I wasn't sure if I wanted him to say yes. Getting in bed with the Feds could hurt as much as it helped.

Moore scrubbed his hand through his hair with a sigh. "Honestly, I don't know, but it couldn't hurt to ask."

"Actually, it could," Cameron said, earning a nod from Dominic.

"How much will it cost us if we don't try?" Mari's words sank into the silence, and I knew she'd made up her mind before she turned to the head of security. "Do it. Let Greyson know what you need."

Moore nodded, grabbed his phone, and headed outside. Immediately, Dominic turned to Mari, ready to launch an offensive argument, but she shut him down with a single look. When she spoke, her voice was quiet but powerful, even as it nearly shook with rage.

"I don't care how much money the Fed wants or that it puts us on unstable ground in front of the others. *I don't care, Dominic.* He was in my home. He was in my *bed*. I have to know who he is." She took a breath, holding it for so long my lungs hurt in sympathy. "I know you're just trying to protect me, but you can't protect me from this."

The suffering in her voice, the way she clenched the pen in

her hand so hard that it cracked, obliterated any hope of an argument he had. "Okay."

His agreement eased some of the tension in Mari's shoulders and between the two of them. From my spot, I could just see under the table where he grabbed her hand, running his thumb across her skin to soothe her. My breath stuttered out in grateful spurts when she didn't pull away.

Tennessee clapped, rubbing his hands together with a cheeky—although absolutely fake—grin. "Since we're in an agreeable mood, let's talk security."

Mari sat back in her chair but kept Dominic's hand. "What did you have in mind?"

"While the Celestine is protected to the heavens, you aren't."

Mari raised a single eyebrow. "Doubting your abilities?"

"Never, but this is unprecedented territory. Anyone who thinks *for sure* they could keep you safe is a fucking idiot." We all stared at him, and he shrugged. "Guarantees aren't a thing in this life, and I don't deal in absolutes."

"What are you suggesting, then?" Mari's shoulders were heavier, the weight of the world on them once again.

"We put you and the capos under twenty-four-seven guard."

"It shows we're weak," Dominic argued.

"It shows you're protected," Tennessee corrected absently, keeping his focus on Mari. "Everyone knows you can handle yourself. It's not a concern in this city. Despite whatever it is they think now, no one's going to come after you like that. Your family is another situation entirely. They were already a threat, and now they're sharpening knives. They need to know they aren't getting to you without a fight. You know I'll follow orders, even if I want to argue. If you really don't want more security, I won't put it on you, but I think it's best. Plus, it'll give us the availability to watch them too, see if we can figure out what they're doing before they make a real attempt on you."

"Is there anything in our world that isn't a double-edged sword?" Mari murmured.

Another shrug came from Tennessee. "It's the way things go."

There, in the silence of the conference room, Mari cracked just a little. Her shoulders slumped, her fingers rose to massage her brow. She let a little bit of the exhaustion she was feeling leak out until she stoppered it again in front of our eyes. Like all soldiers, we steadfastly ignored our leader's breakdown. If anyone was entitled to one, it was Mari.

Finally, she turned back to Tennessee. "If you think this is best..."

"I wouldn't suggest it otherwise, and you know it."

"Okay."

Tennessee smiled, looking more than a little relieved. "I promise it's only until this is over."

Mari stared at him with speculation, but it was gone before she voiced it, leaving the room heavy with the unspoken question of *how long will that be?*

Chapter 5
Mari

If the meeting with my inner circle was bad, I considered the phone call with Dr. Grant, though necessary, even worse. "Ms. Marcosa, I wasn't expecting to hear from you so soon. Is someone dying already?"

I kept my fingers tight to stop the shaking. "I need a house call immediately."

"For what exactly? I'm very busy running your ward."

I tried to recall if she was doing immunizations today or something else, but the knowledge was lost in the haze. "STI tests."

She scoffed, though she tried to hide it. "Can they wait?"

The thought of waiting even a single day made my stomach roll. "No. I need them done today."

"For all four of you?"

My heart ached at how easily she'd accepted my relationships. How easily Nate had fit.

He's a liar.

"No. Three."

My voice cracked, and silence filled the line until her voice came back softer and weighted with understanding. "I see. One moment, please."

The sound of paper shuffling and her muffled voice as she spoke to someone else kept me company until she returned. "I'll be right there."

"Thank you."

"Don't thank me yet, Ms. Marcosa. You haven't gotten the bill."

I didn't give a single fuck. I'd pay her entire yearly salary tonight if it meant I could get this done ASAP.

"It shouldn't take too long to get to your home. Expect me in twenty minutes."

The reminder that my home was compromised stung, and I struggled to keep my voice even. "We're on vacation at the Celestine downtown. I'll send you the address and a code so the front desk will let you up."

"Understood."

Somehow, I had no doubt she really did get it. *Grey picked the right doctor.* Doc was great, but he was an institution in the Marcosa family. Dr. Grant was new blood we desperately needed. A breath of fresh air that would benefit us greatly in the years to come if we survived the next few months.

I hung up the phone before rapid-firing texts to warn the front desk, as well as Dominic and Greyson, of her arrival. The boys replied back that they were in a meeting with the club managers explaining new protocols the security team came up with, but they'd meet up with her after. Fine by me.

Even though it was unfair to put everything on them, I wasn't quite ready to have them close when I still felt vulnerable. I needed a little more time to separate them from Nate and his mistakes. *If he even thought they were mistakes.*

I shut down that line of thinking before I fell down the proverbial rabbit hole.

With nothing to do but wait, I sat by the windows in the living room staring out at the city that I'd nearly lost every part of myself for and wondered. Would there ever be a moment when I would find peace in the view again? When I could look at each building without wondering if that was where Nate was or if he could see me? Would I ever look at the streets without wondering if he was close by? I'd bled into the ground and bound the city and myself together, but would he take that from me too?

The knock on the door startled me from the idea, and I got up before the concern could take root even more.

A look through the peephole showed Dr. Grant patiently sandwiched between Moore and Tennessee. Though it felt impossible, I schooled my face into a relaxed mask and whipped open the door. I didn't need more of her sympathy or I'd lose it. "That was quick."

She shrugged casually. "I was in the neighborhood." I hated that her gaze was gentler than it usually was, but I didn't feel the need to call her on it.

Knowing the boys had frisked her, I let her inside and waved a hand. "What do you need for this?"

"That table will work." She pulled out an alcohol wipe to sanitize the cozy four-top in the kitchen, then washed her hands and dug through her bag. "We should be able to get everything done with a blood test. We can do a pelvic exam if you'd like, but I'd prefer that at the office."

"Let's wait for the results." I sat when told to, grateful for the sleeveless top I'd chosen earlier. Dr. Grant was quick and efficient, barely looking at me as she went forward with the blood draw, handing me a stress ball, though she raised an eyebrow when I white-knuckled it.

"Who aren't we testing?" she asked softly, and I knew what she was asking.

"Nate." Christ. Just saying his name felt like razor blades in my throat.

"Is he dead or—"

"An Ace."

Her eyes widened with shock, but she quickly schooled her face into the disinterested mask she normally wore. "And the others?"

"Alive, but angry."

"I can imagine you all are."

When I said nothing, she hummed to herself, sliding the needle into my arm and clicking the vial in when it was time. I watched my blood fill it up, transfixed by the sight of it.

Something so innocuous, barely thicker than water, was the thing that kept our hearts beating, our brains functioning, and our bodies moving. It was so powerful. What would it be like to hold that much power?

What would it be like to hold that much potential?

The snap of the rubber strap falling off my arm pulled my attention back, only to find Dr. Grant's head tilted in question.

Shit. "Sorry, what did you say?"

She smiled again, and I had to grit my teeth to keep from screaming at her. "I asked if there was a chance of pregnancy."

God, no. "I have the implant." Showing her my arm took seconds, but a brief hesitation crossed her face, a moment of discomfort that stole my breath.

Dr. Grant steeled her shoulders and looked me straight in the eye. "With the reason I'm here, the likelihood of tampering is high. I suggest we do a pregnancy test as well."

I was a woman who ran an empire, the queen in a traditionally king's world. I'd seen and done some awful shit, but the idea of someone impregnating me against my will was apparently the final straw. Dr. Grant passed me the closest trash can as I threw up everything I'd ever eaten.

When I was done, numbness, blessed and quick, stole over me. At least until we found out if it was true, I wouldn't have a moment when I felt clean ever again.

Nate had initially told me that he'd had a vasectomy some years ago, but going forward with the assumption everything he'd ever told me was a lie, I needed to assume that was too.

I wanted to ask if she really thought Nate would do that to me, then stopped. None of us knew Nate. His capabilities were limitless, and asking would only hurt more if it turned out to be true.

Dr. Grant bandaged me up, then took my bicep in her hands, poking and prodding at the implant. She asked a few questions before pulling out what looked to be a scanner of some sort, lifting it with an excited grin. "A new toy, thanks to you. You'll be the first person I'll use it on."

I didn't watch the screen, knowing I wouldn't be able to tell a thing. Finally, Dr. Grant put me out of my misery. "It doesn't look to be tampered with."

Thank fuck.

She sat back, dropping the scanner back into her bag. "I think it's best to replace it, just in case. I can do it here if you need."

"Please."

She said nothing, turning away to label the blood draw before moving on to cleaning the area again. I watched her until a single hard pound came at the door.

"Guest?" Dr. Grant asked.

I didn't answer her, pulling my gun as I peered through the peephole again. Moore stood there, frowning down at a courier bag like it had personally offended him. I opened the door, keeping the gun out and ready. "What the hell is that?"

"It's for you."

As if I didn't already know that. "Did you scan it?"

"Yeah. Twice." I didn't know why he was still frowning at the bag, and I didn't have time to care. Propping the door open with my shoulder, I held out my empty hand, and the second he opened the bag to show the label on the box, I wished I hadn't. "I can get rid of it if you want."

I decided then and there that he was getting a raise. Instead of accepting the offer, I took the box and slammed the door behind me, the masochistic part of me rearing its ugly head.

Dr. Grant looked worried, but she didn't need to be. Nothing in the box could hurt her; it only had the power to hurt me.

I holstered the gun and carried the box to the counter. I used a kitchen knife to open the tape, and inside the pristine packaging was another box with a luxury logo on it. A custom artisan jeweler that Aislynn had turned me on to.

Don't do it, I told myself, staring at the thing that was my very own Pandora's box. *Don't open it.*

Even though I was positive there was no hope at the bottom, I had to see for myself. I needed closure.

My fingers shook as I unclasped the lock and lifted the lid.

Three rings sat on silk, each one polished to a high shine, matching but not quite identical. Like my soul knew which one would hurt the worst, I pulled out the center ring to see the words engraved on the band.

Forever.

Because I'd been about to offer him that. My life for his love. I thought it would be a simple trade for Nate, an easy one. I hadn't expected this. Pain crippled me for a single second before I put the ring back, carefully closing the lid.

"Don't move," I told Dr. Grant, heading out the door with my prize in hand. As if shoving it into the back of my sock drawer would work for something so emotionally damaging.

He'll never see it, part of me cried.

He didn't want it, the other part said.

Back in the kitchen, I dropped into the chair and flung my arm onto the table, desperate to forget every thought of Nathaniel Beckstrom. "Let's get this over with."

* * *

A few hours later, with a bandage on my arm, a dose of painkillers in my body, and some sleeping pills in the bathroom *just in case*, I called the girls over. I'd asked my cousin to keep quiet about Nate, knowing that I wanted to tell Aislynn and Shara myself. The rings were a reminder that time wasn't on my side.

Curling up on the couch felt like waiting for a death sentence. I didn't want to do it. I didn't want to tell them I'd fucked up so bad. I didn't want to rehash things with Nate.

I didn't want it to be true.

Dominic and Greyson hovered in the kitchen, banging pots, though not actually cooking. They just existed in the same space. I thought my trust issues with Nate would become theirs, yet as I watched them from the corner of my eye, knowing they were doing the same to me, I felt no worry. No fear, just gratitude.

I was grateful that they stayed, that they were honest, that they were here. Just so fucking grateful.

The knock came, and Dominic was halfway across the room before I could slip my hand under the pillow for my gun.

"Who is it?" He must've got the answer he wanted because the door swung open, and Ash walked in.

For a moment, Ash and I just looked at each other. In all the years I had known her, I wasn't sure I'd ever seen her so happy.

She looked like she was gliding on air, and a petty part of me was grateful I'd get to pop her bubble, even as I knew she'd never had this before. Misery loved company, after all.

And I got it.

While Ash hustled over to the couch, landing next to me and sweeping me into a major hug, Shara barreled through the room with a backpack that clinked suspiciously. Her eyes tightened as she looked me over, and I could only imagine what I looked like to them.

Could they see the heartbreak on my face? The slump of my shoulders and the tightness of my jaw? Could they feel the ache behind my breastbone like it was their own? Did they know?

The sympathy in Shara's eyes said that she did.

I glanced at Greyson, and he grabbed Dominic by the shoulder, steering him out of the room with nothing more than a nod to me, and again, I was grateful. So fucking grateful for them.

When we were finally alone, I turned to Shara. "Who told you?"

"It's not hard to figure it out. You're missing a Musketeer." She grimaced, despite the softness in her eyes. "That, and the rumors around town."

Aislynn, who was resting her chin on my head, angled back, glancing between the two of us. "Rumors...missing a Musketeer, what the hell are you talking about? Did something happen while we were gone?"

Everything.

"Considering you've been very busy with your husband, I'm not surprised you don't know." The faint blush on Aislynn's face told me just how busy she'd been, and I was happy for her. So fucking happy. I also wanted to die inside too.

There was only so much I could handle in a day, and I was rapidly hitting the point of no return, so I pulled the bandage off quick. "Nate is a Beckstrom."

At my side, Ash pushed me away until she could see my face. "Are you shitting me?"

"Nope," I said sadly, though part of me wished I were. That it was all just a cosmic joke.

"Nate is a Beckstrom," Ash said quietly. I could practically see her mind whirling as she cursed. "My intel was wrong."

"Yeah." Her intel hadn't mentioned Nate. No one's had. He was a ghost, exactly what Cash needed him to be. Exactly what he'd trained to be.

Was the military a lie too?

Knowing I couldn't go down that road, I focused on my friends. I could see Ash falling into her mafia princess role, thinking about the consequences of letting an Ace into my home. "I'll reach out to my sources again. Somebody has to know something."

"I'd appreciate it." I filled them in on the rest, and when it was done, I leaned out of their hold, needing a little space. I felt hollowed out, but somehow better. There was something different about being held up by your girlfriends than being held up by your partners. Although I trusted Grey and Dominic, they just weren't who I needed.

I looked up to see Ash frowning at Shara. "What's your problem?"

I turned, and the look of pure heartbreak and regret hit me straight in the solar plexus. Then she grabbed my hands and squeezed.

"It's my fault," Shara said quietly. "I'm the one who pushed you toward him. I told you he was a good guy."

"I made my own decisions," I said, though the reminder hurt as much as it confused me. "He walked away from me, and I couldn't let it go. I threw myself at him, while he refused all of my advances."

That was the part that still didn't make sense. Was it part of his game, prodding the part of my brain that wanted to chase? Had he needed to wait until he gained my trust or access to my home before he moved to the next phase? I didn't want to believe that was true, but I didn't want to believe any of it was true.

"The only person in charge of Nate's actions was Nate," I said firmly, cutting off Shara before she could speak. Aislynn's eyes burned into me, and I realized I had a choice.

I could sit there and let the pain control me, or I could move on, push forward, and hope I could fix the mistake I'd made before it was too late.

"We are not taking on the guilt for what he did."

"Amen." Ash pulled out her phone. "I think this deserves wine."

"I think it needs something harder," Shara muttered, stomping over to the kitchen to grab three shot glasses before pulling an entire bottle of booze out of her bag.

I glanced at the label, noting it was top-shelf. "Did you take that from Gilded?"

She turned her most innocent look on me like I didn't know she practiced it in the mirror. "The boss was in trouble."

"Of course."

Ash laughed and Shara winked, pouring the shots and handing them to each of us. "To men who ain't shit!"

"And the women who survived them," Ash added.

"Hear, hear." We clinked our glasses and took the shots, slamming them onto the table with a shared laugh.

No more wallowing. I had given myself a day, but I had to move forward and move on. My people needed me to be strong, put this behind us, and end Cash. So I would drink myself stupid, talk shit about my ex, and when morning came, I would put on my big-girl pants and reenter the world for good.

Come hell or high water, the queen was back.

Chapter 6
Nate

The call came in the middle of the night as I stared up at the ceiling. Ava had long since gone to bed, giving not one, not two, but three rounds of earsplitting orgasms loud enough for the entire fucking city to hear. Even after I turned on my noise-canceling headphones as high as they could go, her audio porn leaked through. I was desperately in need of brain bleach.

Every part of the charade made my fucking skin crawl, but she'd been right. No one would've believed the silent night I'd planned. The fact that she was in my suite *again* was even more annoying, but Cash's digs over text made it apparent that Ava's first performance wasn't enough. We needed a steady stream of simulated sex to prove I wasn't "whipped by that Marcosa pussy."

It had taken every ounce of self-preservation not to kill him for that, but I knew it was another loyalty test, one I couldn't afford to fail. Not when so much rode on my surviving and more than my life was at stake.

Thankfully, Ava was more than fine with a little break from her usual nightly activities, especially when the cash was good, the food was free, and I gave her all the space she wanted. If I never had to be in a room with her again, I'd feel like I'd won the lottery.

It wasn't her fault, truly. I just didn't want a woman in my space. Or, a woman who wasn't Mari.

I hadn't even been gone for a day, and my chest ached at being away from her.

Get over it, I told myself. *She's never going to let you come back.*

That was the fucking truth. Had Cash done his reveal in private, I might've had a chance, but he publicly humiliated her. More than that, he revealed her mistake, her weakness, to a group of wolves slavering at the chance to destroy her.

Even if she still loved me, she'd never admit it again. The ringing continued as I rolled over and grabbed my phone from the bedside charger, only to frown at the dark screen. No call, but there was definitely ringing happening.

If it's not this phone, then it's...

My heart jumped into my throat, and I threw off the blankets, leaping for my backpack. I never let the thing out of my sight, so not even a second passed before I was yanking open the hidden pocket at the bottom. I had a few burners scattered around so I could make calls without Cash tracking me, but the one in this backpack was the only one I wanted to keep safe. Had to, really. I'd even lied to Cash about breaking it just so he wouldn't get his hands on it.

Filled with pictures and videos I'd taken of Mari, even some of Dominic and Greyson, the phone was the most precious thing I owned. It was everything to me. There was nothing scandalous, just moments of us together, Mari's softness when she slept, the look of love Dominic and Grey gave her when she wasn't looking.

My family.

I had to walk away from them in the present, but I'd do whatever it took to keep the memories with me.

Knowing I couldn't keep the phone out for Cash to find, I'd bought a battery pack, using that to charge it whenever I was alone. Since it was the only number Mari had for me, I refused to turn it off, but I'd meant to at least put it on silent so it didn't go off at the wrong time.

Too late now.

I flipped over the flashing screen, and my heart thumped harder. It was her.

I clicked accept before I could consider the consequences. "Mari."

"I fucking hate you." Her voice was slurred, but I heard the words loud and clear behind all that ice. "I hate you so—*hiccup*—much."

"Are you drunk, angel? How much have you had to drink?" Mari trashed would've been cute any other time in our lives, but Cash was regrouping, and I knew firsthand that the other leaders were out for blood. If she was caught unaware...fuck.

Please let Dominic and Greyson be close by.

"Don't call me that," she snarled, or tried to. Her voice was as unsteady as I imagined her legs were. "You don't get to call me that anymore. You don't get to call me anything. You're nothing to me."

God, I hated that she was right. I hated that I'd had to walk away from one woman I loved, just to save another.

I'd chosen the family I was born with over the one I made, and all it had cost me was everything I'd ever wanted.

"Mari—" I swallowed thickly, trying to force something out of my mouth. Her pain burned in my chest, and I needed her to know *anything. Everything.* But I couldn't do it.

Yesterday, I'd been desperate to tell her everything, but nothing I said was a guaranteed fix, and I didn't want to hurt her worse. Not when I could hear the agony she tried to hide in her voice.

It killed me knowing that I put it there, that I had given her one more chance to distrust men. To distrust me.

"I should have known that first day." Her voice trailed off into a mutter, like she was mostly talking to herself. "It made no sense for you to stop for me, and even when you did, you should've run the second those assholes showed up, but you didn't. Of course you didn't. And there I was, ignoring the red flags like it was my life's mission to see what I wanted. I mean, *Christ.* I wanted to believe you were who you said you were. Normal. Kind. Real. I needed that so bad that I forgot everything else."

She paused, and I had to strain to hear the muffled sound of what I desperately hoped wasn't a sob. *Please don't cry, baby.*

"You were supposed to be my one good thing. My one *safe* thing. But you were always his."

Mari ripping out my beating heart with her bare hands would've hurt less.

"Baby." My voice broke at the agony she was in. That I'd caused.

"Don't."

For a moment, there was nothing but heavy, aching silence. We were two souls thrown together in the worst possible circumstances, kept together by subterfuge and lies, bound together by nothing but the bond we'd forged. One that I wasn't sure could ever really be broken.

But it didn't mean we'd get our happy ending.

I knew Mari. Even if she forgave me—which I sincerely doubted would happen—she'd rather starve our relationship than nurture it. More pain for the both of us and a scar to remind her of her troubles.

To remind her of the stakes of falling in love.

Honestly, the only reason she was even speaking to me now was because no one would believe me if I told them. Mari was drunk, her inhibitions down, but she knew her reputation preceded her. She knew not a single soul would believe she'd called the man who jilted her in front of everyone, and that alone would protect her. At least for this call.

"I hate you." It was so quiet I almost couldn't hear her. I wished I hadn't. Mari had never sounded so bleak.

You did this. You deserve everything she says.

"I know." I sighed, rubbing my chest absently like it would do anything to relieve the ache of knowing just how far out of reach she would always be. "I hate me too."

"I wish I'd never met you. I wish you'd never stopped that day. I wish I'd died."

The thought of her not existing brought me physical pain. A twisting, gnarling ache in my stomach.

"I don't." She scoffed, but I pushed on. "No matter how much you hate me, no matter what else happens, I'll never regret you, Marianna Marcosa."

"Of course you wouldn't. You weren't the one who was played, who was kissed and loved and fucked by a lie. You got to walk around knowing you were dipping your dick in *prime Marcosa pussy* while I looked like a fucking idiot." She said it like she was quoting something, and I swore then and there that if it was Cash, he was a dead man. I could suffer through a lot for the people I loved, but not that. Anything but making Mari feel like she was nothing but a hole to me.

I tried to center myself, to let her hear the honesty in my words. "I know you don't believe me, but it wasn't like that. I swear to god."

"You're right, I don't believe you. If we were anything other than a lie, you would've told me because we both know I would've listened. But you didn't. Don't worry, though. You don't have to regret me. I'll do it enough for the both of us."

Had I thought I'd hurt her? What an understatement. This was Mari shattered. Decimated. Living in a world without enough stitches to put her back together because I'd chosen to keep my silence and hide my secrets. I'd held my cards to my chest, hoping I could have it all—safety for my family and the people I loved—and instead, I'd walked away with nothing.

"I didn't want this to happen," I confessed. A small sliver of the truth she was owed.

It did nothing to thaw the ice in Mari's voice. "Even if that were true, it *did* happen, and now we both have to live with the consequences. Mark my words, Nathaniel Beckstrom, I'm moving on, and the day I forget you exist will be the happiest day of my life."

The beep startled me, and I pulled away to find the screen black again. She'd hung up on me, and I couldn't even blame her.

* * *

The day after I returned, two Aces and I made our way to a dilapidated warehouse downtown to shake down some of Cash's middlemen. The reason my brother was so successful in Seattle could be narrowed down to one thing: blow.

While he'd been waiting for Mario Marcosa to die, cocaine had become Cash's drug of choice, both as a buyer and a seller. His addiction got worse when Antoni took over, until Cash was a full-blown cokehead by the time Mari was sworn in.

She'd outlawed most of the harder drugs like fentanyl, meth, coke, and heroin before her throne was even warm, but her strategy wasn't perfect. She hit the dealers and the suppliers she knew about, but she didn't realize there was already an underground market, established long before she took over, one fed by secret cartel connections.

She didn't know about Cash.

When she started her war on drugs, he gained a platform. He kept his network low-key, not wanting to reveal himself too early, and the business thrived to the point that he could've bought the city outright if he wanted to. But that wasn't fun for Cash. He wanted to take it for himself and destroy the Marcosas in the process.

In trying to clean up the city, Mari gave Cash more control than she'd ever know, but I doubted she would've stopped even if she had. Some things mattered more than money or power.

One of Cash's drug dens was underground in a warehouse so derelict, it was practically falling down around my ears. It was also dead center in Marcosa territory, but the condition kept it from looking like a possible hiding spot, exactly why Cash liked it.

The three of us headed in through a hidden entrance, walking straight into what felt like a shitty movie. Women clad in nothing but ratty underwear with more holes than substance counted money and sealed the weighed drugs into small baggies. Unlike what most people assumed, every one of them was clean. You couldn't have addicts moving your product if you wanted to get paid.

A quick glance showed everything exactly how it was supposed to be, but I jerked my head for Cash's dogs to sniff around. I had other things to occupy my time.

It took seconds to find two men playing cards in the corner in their ill-fitting suits and big egos. They looked like kids trying to play king.

I said nothing as I invaded their space. I didn't have to. Everyone knew why I was there.

Cash was a psychopath, but he preferred to let his favorite enforcer mete out warnings...and punishments.

Cooper looked up first, concern flickering through his face before he schooled himself. Renaldi didn't acknowledge my existence at all beyond a single, lazy question. "Is there a reason you're here, Beckstrom?"

"Here about your last shipment. You were missing product."

Renaldi contemplated his cards before dropping two on the table. I'd never been one for poker beyond the few times Jorey and Stowe forced me to play, but it must have been the right move. Cooper cursed, despite his discomfort at having me close. I moved even closer out of spite.

The more off-balance he was, the better things would go for me.

"One kilo won't kill the bottom line."

I rolled my eyes, leaning casually against the wall at Cooper's back. "But ten could. Especially given that's the low end of the scale for how much you two have taken, am I right?"

Everyone froze, staring at me while I stared right back. I didn't move while I took in everything. Every guard in the room had a gun, but three of them had additional knives. One was strapped with a veritable arsenal, and that was just what I could see. The four of them stood close enough to Renaldi to defend him if necessary. Playing king, indeed. *An internal war will help Mari,* a voice in the back of my mind said. It sounded suspiciously like Grey. I wasn't sure how to fix what I'd fucked up with her, but this was an easy, untraceable start. The guards didn't have to be my problem.

If Cash wanted to play drug lord, he could do it himself. I wasn't interested in following in our father's footsteps, and he knew it.

Cooper was fidgeting under my silent gaze, sweat beading at his temples, but he didn't speak. He didn't admit shit. I expected it from Renaldi, but Cooper was the weak link. Stronger than I'd assumed, though. Stealing drugs from a psychopath who snorted as much of his product as he sold was just fucking stupid, and to keep their silence was something close to brave. I knew all about silence, though, didn't I?

The part of me that remembered Mari's drunken phone call last night winced. I'd had her right there and still couldn't tell her the only truth that mattered right now.

That I was sorry.

That I loved her.

That we weren't a lie.

I couldn't tell her shit, so why was I expecting Cooper to cop to anything?

"How much to make this go away?" Renaldi asked, facing me expectantly.

"You think you can pay me off?"

Renaldi tilted his head, smirking a little as he regarded me. "I think you've been gone too long, little brother. Too comfortable in the Marcosa mansion—and that Marcosa pussy—that you've forgotten where your loyalties lie. Maybe *she* was sweeter than anything your brother could give you."

It was so close to the truth that I was almost impressed. Not that I showed it. I was a fucking professional.

Renaldi's eyes narrowed, though he was still pretending to be relaxed. "Why are you really here, Nate? Because our shipment was missing a couple thousand bucks?"

His scoff was echoed with laughter around the room, and I joined in.

"A hundred thousand on the low side," I corrected.

Renaldi's eyes narrowed, and we held eye contact.

Staring contests were juvenile as fuck, but men like Renaldi stroked their dicks to images of themselves on top of the world.

They were also weak fuckers with even weaker backbones because they didn't have the training to take shit for themselves. They stole because they couldn't build, and that showed in everything they did.

Renaldi ground his teeth loud enough to hear when he finally looked away, eyes shadowed with his bruised ego. "I wasn't aware of anything being taken."

"Why don't we cut the bullshit since we all know I've got more important things to do than deal with you two. You want this to go away? Either replace the product, or pay back what you owe. Retail price, of course."

"And if we don't?"

He tipped his head, and those four guards straightened up like they'd been called to attention. I slipped my hand to one of my own guns, hoping Renaldi wasn't suicidal. If he killed me, Cash would burn his life down and make him watch.

"Do it, or I'll come back and put a bullet in your head." It was that simple.

Cooper spoke up, shaky voice and all. "What if we're not here when you come back?"

It was my turn to smirk as I waved a lazy hand at the Aces I'd brought. "That's what Tweedledee and Tweedledum are here for. Word of advice, don't try to cut them down and run. It won't work. Big Brother is watching."

I gave a pointed glance at the ceiling where the cameras—which they'd adjusted little by little over the time I was gone—had been refastened at the correct angles and caged so they couldn't be fucked with again. How Cash had gotten in without their notice, I had no fucking clue, but it was one more mark against Renaldi being an amateur.

Renaldi waved off the guards, and they stood down. I grinned at him, though I didn't care one way or another. "You have twenty-four hours. If you don't have the money my brother's owed when time runs out, you're dead, and we'll find someone else to run this shithole."

Both men swallowed heavily, and I motioned Cash's men to follow me out. We paused just out of hearing range as I gave them their orders. "No one takes a piss by themselves until Cash gives the okay. Check in every thirty minutes and again when your relief team shows up. Any fuckups, and it'll be your heads, not mine."

The Aces, both newer but still seasoned, nodded, and I headed for the door, ready to wash the gasoline scent from the coke off my body, even if it meant burning my clothes. I hadn't made it more than two steps when I heard the idiots whispering to each other.

"Do you think he knows about the Marcosas?" one asked. Pretty sure it was Ryan. He was only chatty when he was nervous.

"I'm sure he does, considering he just spent months in their house," Parker replied.

"I thought my family was fucked up, but I kind of pity her."

Parker snorted. "She's richer than sin and hot as fuck. She could have everything and anything she wants, but she's fighting for power she'll never keep. She's been spoiled her whole life, and now the uncles are going to put her in her place. Serves her right."

I didn't hear Ryan's reply. Rage rose swiftly through me, and before I knew what I was doing, I was pulling my car away from the warehouse. A quick turn had me driving toward Mari's house before I realized I had no clue where she was anymore.

Which meant I had to call in a favor.

Chapter 7
Nate

"You have a lot of nerve," Rafael Osorio said when he finally picked up the phone. It only took him four fucking calls. "Do you know the shitstorm you've put me in?"

Nope. Didn't care either. "Do tell."

Rafael ignored my sarcasm, as usual. "I wasn't aware Mari didn't know who you were, you little prick. Do you have any idea the damage this could do?"

Considering my relationship's implosion recently, yeah. I did.

"We can talk all about the ways that you're going to castrate me for this later. Where is she?"

"What makes you think I would tell you where she is?"

"Are you aware that her *other* uncles are planning to take her out? Soon, from what I've heard." The last part was a guess, but one I was pretty sure about.

"If Mari's uncles wanted her to bend the knee, forcing her

during a time of upheaval—like, say, when her boyfriend turns out to be an enemy spy—would be their best bet. She's unstable, and people are watching. She's hemorrhaging power daily, and it'll only get worse the longer my brother runs amok in her city."

Silence was Rafael's only answer, and my fingers *tap, tap, tapped* the steering wheel in impatience. I was desperate to move but unwilling to take action until I knew where to go. I couldn't run in circles when I wasn't sure Mari had time to waste.

"I see," he said flatly, and I wasn't even surprised that he already knew. I just needed to know if Mari did.

"Where is she, Rafael?"

Rafael's huff was grating to my already frayed nerves, and I sighed. "I'm not going to hurt her."

"I don't believe you."

He had no reason to, but it didn't change the fact that he was going to tell me one way or another. "Does she know?"

Does she know her family's out to get her?

Rafael's pause was as good as a *yes*, and I cursed again. Everything in Mari's life was going wrong and I wished so desperately that I could help, but I knew better. There was no helping. Not like this. Not when I was the cause of all this turmoil.

"Please just tell me where she is. I promise not to hurt her. Hell, you can follow me there if you want. I just need to make sure she's okay."

Another long pause. So long, I felt like I'd ground my teeth to dust until, finally, Rafael said, "She won't see you."

"Then what's the harm in giving me the information?"

"If she figures out it was me—"

"She won't," I said quickly, knowing he was going to give me what I wanted. He had to.

"I won't tell you exactly where she is, but I'll give you a general area."

"Fine." I could work with that. Nothing that a little stalking couldn't fix, even if it felt weird to think about following the love of my life.

Then again, if she never forgave me, I had no doubt that was going to be my future. Provided we all survived Cash.

Rafael rattled off the cross streets, more irritated than I'd ever heard him. I was about to hang up the phone when he snapped my name. "If she gets hurt because of this, I'll make you wish your brother had actually killed you."

"Wouldn't be the first time," I said, starting the car before I'd even hung up the phone. I had to warn my girl.

Finding Mari was easier than I expected after making my way uptown, per Rafael's instructions.

Hard to have true stealth when you ran a city.

I was barely out of my car before someone was pointing me in the right direction. Every other turn, I heard reverent whispers of the Marcosa queen, leading me to her like a trail.

My first glimpse of Mari since the damned meeting was a brutal one.

She looked put together. Makeup on, hair slicked back in a ponytail and straightened to a single sheet of silky brown, perfect suit, and heels to kill. She looked incredible, and I had to palm my cock where it was trying to tent my jeans.

Not the time.

Especially because I could see beneath the mask. Her lips were pressed together so tightly that twin lines bracketed them. Her steps were a little heavier.

The only thing I couldn't see were her eyes, and I knew she'd hidden them on purpose. Easier to fool the people she interacted with that she was fine when they didn't have a direct view to her soul.

She moved as a unit with Dominic and Moore, though she didn't touch either of them. She barely even looked their way.

Dominic was dressed casually, as usual, but even he seemed subdued. Angry.

When Mari stumbled and flinched away from his touch, his anger grew until more people were veering away from him. I wasn't even sure they realized it either. It was instinctual. A primal response to a predator losing his shit nearby and a desperate need to get out of the line of fire.

Fuck. I'd expected her to hate me, but I hadn't thought her trust issues would seep over to the others. The distance between them proved she'd lost even more because of me. Dominic and Greyson were her home, her shelter. She was supposed to lean on them and let them guide her through this bullshit. Instead, she was secluding herself and hurting all of them in the process.

You're a waste of space, Cash's voice lingered in my head. *Look what you do. You break people, hurt them. That's what you were always meant for.*

I didn't believe it, but it said something that the old words still had a place in my mind.

The small group stopped near the four-story monstrosity of a mall. Mountview Mall *screamed* privilege and luxury, but Mari didn't go inside. Dominic did, with Moore following close behind.

Meanwhile, Mari slipped into the flow of foot traffic and disappeared.

What the fuck?

I rocked onto my tiptoes, trying to peer over the bustling crowd moving around the entrance, but I couldn't see her.

Not until I spotted a flash of chocolate down the block.

Mari was walking around the city alone.

A distant part of me recognized that it wasn't normal, but anger and panic didn't give a shit. My girl had a target on her back and enemies coming from every direction, and she was wandering around *alone.*

Absolutely not.

I was halfway down the sidewalk, moving through bodies with slow, careful movements.

Don't be suspicious. Don't look like you're chasing her. Just a nice guy out for a leisurely stroll.

Mari took the next corner, and I sped up, desperate not to lose her. She took me through the city, keeping to her territory lines. I had no clue where the fuck she was going and no clue if she saw me, but some part of my brain wondered if she was playing with me.

Does she want to be chased?

I rounded another corner to find her gone. Vanished.

That anxiety pushing my heart into my throat got worse, making the vein in my forehead throb and ache. I was going to lose my shit if I didn't find her because, Marcosa or not, she needed protection.

My protection.

Careful to walk on silent feet, I checked every alley in sight until I found her. She was at the far end, talking quietly on her phone. I still had no clue why she was there, though I had a good idea where we were. The warehouse district wasn't too far off, where people worked around the clock and there was no shortage of witnesses. But in this unincorporated part of the city, it was probably just us.

With one eye on the ground so I didn't kick something and startle her too soon, I followed Mari down the alley, hugging the wall until I was right behind her. The second she hung up the phone, I pushed her against the wall, my hips pressing hers to the brick, and knocked her phone out of her hand.

As expected, Mari went feral. Kicking and scratching. Biting and clawing. All she knew was a man was holding her in an abandoned part of town. Of course she was losing it. I didn't want to scare her, but maybe she needed it, because who the fuck walked around alone in the middle of a war?

That thought brought the rage, the near-blindness-inducing panic at the thought of her being caught unawares or worse. What if someone grabbed her for Cash when she wasn't paying attention? Prisoners weren't treated kindly in his camp. I didn't want that for Mari.

"It's me."

She stilled, a dangerous tension coiling through her.

"You normally follow people who don't want you around?" she asked.

"When I have to protect them from themselves, yes. What the fuck do you think you're doing?" I snarled into her ear, despite the fact that I absolutely had no right to.

"I don't need your protection," she growled, kicking her head back. I narrowly avoided the skull to the nose and buried my face into her neck to protect it. Fine—and to smell her too. "What the fuck are you doing following me? Aren't you connected at the hip to big brother?"

"No, and I'm not the one under fire everywhere she goes."

"No, you're just the one who lit the match."

I sighed, hating the way the conversation was going already. "Where are Dominic and Moore?"

"Shopping," she deadpanned.

I flipped her around, shoving her right back to where she was. I didn't like trapping her, but what else could I do? She needed to hear me. She had to understand the dangers of running around like this. And I needed to see her eyes.

Those sad, broken, very angry eyes. My dick jerked in my pants at the thought of those eyes glaring at me while she was on her knees, and I gave it the metaphorical middle finger. *She's more likely to slice you off than she is to suck you.*

"You got a problem with my face?"

"No." She was beautiful, always. "You can't do this right now, Mari. It's not safe."

"What do you care about my safety, Beckstrom? Your life would be so much easier without me."

The words hurt to hear. A world without Mari wasn't a world at all. I just hadn't realized it soon enough.

Tell her that.

I wanted to. I wanted to talk about the phone call and everything that happened before, but when I looked at her, I saw no vulnerability, no recognition. I wasn't sure if she remembered our call at all or if it had disappeared in the haze of booze.

"Mari—" The press of a gun to my sternum stole my breath, but not as much as the ice on her face did. Also, how had I forgotten to hold her fucking arms? Was I really that blind when it came to her?

If so, I wasn't sure I'd be much help on the protection front.

"Why are you really following me?" she asked, peering around without ever taking her eyes off me. "Where's your brother?"

"I don't know. I came because I wanted to warn you."

Her bark of laughter hurt my ears, it was so angry. "I don't believe you."

"People are talking. Your uncles—"

"I'm aware."

She wasn't, not really. She didn't know what I did about them. About everyone. "Let me help."

She scoffed. "I've already made that mistake. I won't be doing it again."

"We weren't a mistake," I growled, tightening my fingers on her hips, as if a few bruises would prove my point.

"Yes, we were."

I wanted to argue, but Mari was a remote tundra with

nothing but miles between her and civilization. I missed the warmth she used to bring more than ever.

"I didn't mean for this to happen," I whispered again, loosening my grip on her. What good had coming after her done, beyond showing anyone watching that Mari really was a priority for me?

Fuck, if Cash caught wind of this, it was going to be bad. Very, very bad.

Especially since I hadn't helped her, hadn't warned her of anything she didn't already know, hadn't fixed things. I'd just made everything worse.

"Fuck your intentions," Mari spat, trying to weasel her way out of my grip. If she moved left, I countered it. If she dodged, ducked, and weaved, I mirrored her.

If she wanted out of my grasp, she'd need to pull the trigger.

"I never should've touched you." Her words stung, but all I could see was buried hurt. There was no way through it. Not now. Not until I earned back her trust.

Maybe not ever.

"Shoot me." My mouth moved on instinct, refusing me even a second to think things through, but I couldn't deny I'd have made the same choice over again.

Her eyes widened, her strong stance faltering just a touch. Mari wasn't as unaffected by me as she'd hoped I believed, but would that matter in the end?

Finally, she shook her head, restabilizing the gun pointing at my chest because she needed the control. I got it. I'd be upset too, given the circumstances. "What did you say?"

"If you think I'm a danger to you, pull the trigger."

I didn't tell her that I didn't want to live in a world where she hated me, or that it would be a mercy to take me out before my brother did. Because it was only a matter of time before Cash realized my loyalty had shifted that day on the side of the road, and if he got his hands on me after he did, I'd wish for an easy death.

I stayed silent and watched as Mari thought about it. She didn't dismiss me or pull the trigger immediately; she looked at the situation from every angle, like she always tried to.

I watched the moment her finger twitched *so damn close* to pulling the trigger, and I didn't flinch.

Didn't blink. Refused to look away. If I was going to die, I'd do it with her face as the last thing I saw. It was a mercy I wasn't sure I deserved, but one I was taking anyway.

Finally, the gun eased off, and so did she. "I'm not going to make more trouble for myself by killing you now. I'll wait until I can do it without risking the people I care about."

The heavy implication that I was no longer one of those people bruised, but I didn't dwell, because for the first time since I'd caught up to her, Mari let me *see* her.

And I liked what she was hiding.

"You can't do it at all."

She rolled her eyes, but I pushed forward, putting myself in her space and waiting to see what happened. When she neither retreated nor shot me, I smiled, knowing I was right. "You can't do it. You can't shoot me."

"I can—"

"You can't because you still love me like I love you." I brushed a hand over her ponytail, enjoying the silkiness against my skin and wondering what it would feel like hiding our bodies as we writhed—

Don't get ahead of yourself.

For her part, Mari looked completely unfazed. And pissed. Very, very pissed. "Love isn't real when it's built on a lie."

"Then what is this?" I pulled up her empty hand and placed it on my chest, right over my thundering heart. It'd been pounding since I'd gotten her alone, and it was getting bad enough that I worried I was having a stroke.

But what a way to die, right?

Mari flinched, ripping her hand away with a snarl. "It's adrenaline and bullshit."

Bullshit was definitely right, but I didn't call her on it. I wrapped my hands around her hips, pulling her against my body, and for the first time in days, I felt whole. My thumbs slipped beneath her suit jacket until I found the sliver of skin I wanted, and fuck me, if just touching her didn't make me hard as stone.

"Let me rebuild it," I whispered.

"Rebuild what?" She knew. We both knew she did, but if Mari needed me to say it, then I would.

"Us."

I thought she'd soften—hoped, really—but she stiffened instead, pulling away without moving an inch. "Did Cash ask you to do this? Get close and try to soften me up for round two?"

"No," I growled, because fuck my brother. "I'm not here for anyone but you, Mari. I know you don't trust me, but let me prove myself again. We can go slow. No sex, no kissing until you trust me. I'll even give you your space if that's what you want. Whatever you need. We'll take this at your pace, angel. Just let me try."

She didn't call me on the nickname again, though her eyes narrowed dangerously. "Does giving me space include following me around town?"

Ah, so she did know I was following her. "Probably."

Mari's huff was soft and annoyed. "Don't bother. I'm not interested in rekindling anything because there is no us."

My mouth was on hers before she could finish. I was already so tired of hearing her say that, even if it felt like the truth in her mind. But I pushed away the irritation because Mari tasted like home and heartbreak, and I was desperate for more. Threading my hand through her ponytail, I tightened my grip, forcing her head exactly where I wanted it. The bite that followed tore a groan from both of us.

Mari opened her lips, and I took it as the invitation it was, deepening the kiss with the sweep of my tongue. I slipped my hand under her shirt, caressing more skin as I backed her against the alley wall, and she let me, arching so I had access to more of her.

"Angel," I whispered, kissing along her jawline to her neck then back to her lips again as I rubbed soothing circles along that soft skin with my thumbs. I'd missed the feel of her against me. I never wanted to stop touching her.

As our tongues slid against each other, Mari's weight shifted so she could rub between my legs. If her skin felt like ecstasy, I wasn't sure there was a word for the way her hand felt as she stroked my straining cock over my jeans. I had a second to kick my hips into hers, to hear the soft moan she tried to hide, before stars exploded behind my eyes and I buckled.

Holy fuck, that hurt.

"Never took you for a cheap shot," I coughed as I dropped to one knee, holding my balls protectively. It'd been a long time since I'd been kneed in them, and goddamn, she got me good.

Definitely deserved it, though.

So much for going slow.

Mari stood above me like an avenging angel, the gun in her hand promising eternal damnation if I so much as breathed the wrong way.

"Don't mistake my previous affection for weakness. I'm not yours, Nathaniel Beckstrom. I never was."

I couldn't help myself. "That's where you're wrong. You'll always be mine, angel. Even if I'm not yours."

"A pity for the both of us, then." Mari sighed, stepping out of reach before holstering the gun and picking up her phone. She paused at the end of the block, where a car pulled up to grab her.

She paused with the door open, the cabbie glancing between us nervously. "Don't make me kill you, Nate."

Then she was gone, sliding into the car and disappearing down the street before I could even relearn how to breathe. But I knew that every word I'd spoken was true.

Mari was mine, even if it damned us both. And eventually, she'd figure it out too.

Until then, I'd just have to keep showing up to remind her.

Chapter 8
Mari

We were back in the conference room that starred in my nightmares. Only this time, I was in the hot seat, not Cash.

"This situation doesn't just put you at risk, Mari. It puts us at risk too. Seattle looks weak because of your decisions. What do you have to say for yourself?"

Kosas glared down at me from the other side of the table, his eyes hard and angry. Admittedly, it was likely because I wasn't paying much attention to him. After seeing Nate earlier, I was too fucking numb to care. When I said nothing, he shoved out of his chair and headed for a bottle of booze to take the edge off.

Ajilon leaned forward, elbows on the table as he worked the *good cop* angle. Or, as much *good cop* as a crime boss could be. "The only reason we're here negotiating instead of dealing with the situation ourselves is because of your family's history in the city. Make no mistake, without it, you'd be dead."

Didn't I know it.

A week ago, these men were my allies; now, they were ready to put me down and split my territory. All because of *one* mistake.

And they called women fickle.

Greyson huffed from behind me, where he'd been silent through the entirety of my verbal lashing, which was exactly why Dominic had been left at home. No way he would've kept his mouth shut. The second Kosas got on my case, it would've been a bloodbath. "You're here because Mari's proven time and again that she's a good leader. She's brought more prosperity to the city than ever before."

"More rules, too," Kieran O'Bannon muttered behind his father. The fact that he spoke at all was disturbing. He knew better than to offer his opinion when he didn't have a seat at the table.

Yet he'd done it right in front of me. What did that say about my reputation?

Christ, did I even have one anymore?

Was this what losing power felt like? Watching the men I'd cowed into submission over the years stare at me across the table like I was their disappointing daughter?

No, this was what certain death looked like.

We all ignored Kieran, though I caught Grey sliding a glance his way when no one else was looking. "This was a blip in the grand scheme of my years of service."

"Big blip," Two-Bit pointed out. The local gang leader and resident pain in my ass had said nothing while the others tore into me. Nope, secretive fuck was playing his own version of being Switzerland. Which pissed me off, because while he wasn't wrong about Nate being a huge mistake, I *knew* Two-Bit had his own mistakes he was hiding.

Secrets I suspected would get him killed right beside me if the others found out.

"It doesn't look good, Mari," Ajilon said with a disturbed frown. Out of everyone else in the room, he was the closest thing to a true ally I'd ever had, despite keeping our interactions minimal. I knew it bothered him to stand against me, just like I knew he wouldn't do it unless he had to. Now, because I'd let my pussy override my brain for once, he doubted me. It stung.

One more thing Nate took from me.

"Now, gentlemen. Let's give Mari the benefit of the doubt. I'm sure she has some way to fix this. Right?" Sean O'Bannon turned to me with that congenial smile on his face, like he was happy to help me through this mess. Even though I knew it was all a ploy—because the man had never been genuine in his entire fucking life—O'Bannon was leaping to my rescue.

Hell had officially frozen over.

I hated Nate a little more for that alone.

Reining in my urge to scream until I lost my voice, I pasted a bland look on my face. "I don't need a plan because nothing's changed."

The silence in the room said no one was expecting that. Honestly, neither was I, but I'd given them ten minutes to rake me over the coals, and I was done now. I wasn't a child, certainly not one of theirs, and I refused to let them treat me like one.

I was their motherfucking queen.

"The Beckstrom boy was in your house for months, and *nothing's changed?*" Kosas, who had always been friendly, sneered. Definitely more of a fair-weather friend since he'd turned the first second he could. Asshole.

Pushing down the initial urge to put him in his place, I forced my muscles to relax and give him my best *good ol' boy* smile.

"Have you never had a live-in booty call, Kosas? If not, I highly recommend it."

The color of his face deepened past its normal dark olive color, and I couldn't tell if it was a blush or anger doing it, but something inside me wanted to poke at him until he exploded, just so I wasn't the only one struggling. "You're telling me—"

"That Nate didn't make it past the bedroom? Yes." The lie was slick on my tongue, smooth out of my mouth, and not a single part of me flinched in the delivery, thanks to Mario Marcosa's school of life. I could feel Greyson's pride like a blanket against my back, and it bolstered me, even when I tried not to let it.

Ajilon leaned back, obviously confused. "Why was he seen out and about with you, then?"

I shrugged. "I have a high sex drive."

Kosas, who'd darkened even more at my proclamation, gathered himself again. "You want us to believe you kept him for emotionless sex for *months*?"

"It's the truth." When he guffawed, I let my irritation show. "If you think women can't have casual sex, look no further than your son. He was on my roster years ago, but I don't see my ring on his finger now."

Tyrone, the son in question, stood behind his father with a barely there grin on his face. He was married now—arranged, though he'd been single when we were together—but he didn't mind my outing him to prove a point. Then again, he was far less traditionally minded than his father, and his wife and I had lunch once a month just to chat.

Kosas's coloring was getting worrisome, while Haru dipped his head to hide what I suspected to be a smile. Couldn't verify it, though, and without proof, normally stoic Kimura would deny, deny, deny.

But I saw it.

When Haru looked back up, there was nothing on his face.

"Casual or not, it can't continue. We need our leader steady." The censure was heavy and grating in every word, but I ignored it.

I really didn't need to be told what to do.

"Nate won't be a problem."

"See to it that doesn't change. I'd hate to walk away from so much history, but the future will always be my priority."

The other leaders agreed with Haru, and when I refused to say anything else, they filed out. Kosas cuffed Tyrone when he stood, whispering furiously to the other man, who nodded solemnly. When his father turned around, Tyrone rolled his eyes and shot me a wink.

I'd have to remember to send his wife some chocolate for the headache I was unleashing on her home. Maybe some booze, too.

O'Bannon sent me a smile filled with the joy of seeing your least-favorite family member in trouble on his way out. Calling him an ally felt less accurate by the day, but at least our relationship was legally binding. Well, as legal as we could get, considering our illicit activities.

When the door closed behind him, it left only Two-Bit and me, with our seconds close by.

Griz, Two-Bit's right-hand man, looked nothing like a bear. He was long, lean, and unassuming, like his boss. It wasn't until you got to his eyes that you understood the name. History lived in the depths of those warm blue eyes, fierce and determined, like he'd rip you apart with his teeth. The stark loss that followed told me why he was the best man to protect his leader.

Griz was a man righting his wrongs, and it made him more dangerous than anyone else I knew. Power was one thing, but guilt could topple empires.

He nodded respectfully. "How are things lately, Mari?"

"Fine. You?"

"Still alive."

That was that.

"You asked to talk?" Two-Bit's eyebrow rose in question. I'd sent him a text before arriving, telling him to stay after the meeting. We needed to get something straight.

I was unsure how to answer that since I hadn't expected Griz, whose loyalties were to the organization, not to Two-Bit as a leader. I really didn't want to add *break in another Viper* to my to-do list if what I said got this one killed. I flicked a questioning glance at the bodyguard, but Two-Bit waved off my concern. "You can talk freely in front of Griz. Neither of us will tell a soul."

Even if I were still in the habit of trusting people—something Nate had broken me of, thank god—I wouldn't have believed a word out of his mouth. "As freely as one can talk in a room that's likely been bugged, to a man whose secrets rival Cash's. Is that about right?"

Two-Bit just smiled, and yeah, I was pretty sure I'd hit every part of that on the money. Fine, I didn't mind playing word gymnastics from time to time. It kept me young.

Greyson and Griz settled in at our backs, letting us have the floor. They were both well-trained in underground etiquette, and unless the bosses were pulling guns, they'd stay the silent muscle they pretended to be.

"You're a knowledgeable man."

Another grin. "I have my moments."

"Lots of them surrounding me."

"Are you surprised? You're a fascinating woman."

"Not surprised, curious." And annoyed. "You always seem to know more than you should."

Two-Bit shrugged. "My birds are everywhere. They'd be pretty worthless if they didn't do their jobs, wouldn't they?"

Ah, the translation portion of our talk had begun. This one was easy. *I have spies in every camp. Don't forget that I'm always watching.*

Given that he was a man who'd barely scraped together the power for a seat at the table, it didn't make any fucking sense that he had the information network he did.

"Did your birdies tell you about my angel?" Translation: *How did you know about my mother's family?*

"It took a lot of work to figure it out." I wasn't sure if that meant they had to dig pretty deep to get the truth or that it took them a while to get someone in the Osorio camp.

"How much work did you do involving my houseguest?" I asked. Translation: *Did you know who Nate was before I did?*

Two-Bit's smile never wavered and Griz was stoic behind him, but there was a flicker in the solemn man's eyes that gave me the answer before his boss did.

"It's smart to know all the pieces on the chessboard if you're going to play."

Translation: *Yes.*

Rage had become my constant companion since Cash dropped his little bomb, tempered only by grief so stifling, I had to pretend it didn't exist to function. But this? It twisted that rage into a torpedo ready to blow us all sky-high.

"You didn't think it was necessary to share that information with me?" I asked, done with the games already. Even on my most patient day, I didn't play them long.

Two-Bit shrugged. "I assumed you vetted your lovers. Besides, it wasn't my business."

The fact that I *did* vet Nate didn't matter. I hadn't done enough, and Two-Bit was right. What happened with Nate was no one's fault but mine.

But I couldn't say that because leaders didn't admit defeat. Not at my level. They might admit their faults to trusted guns, but Two-Bit wasn't under my banner. He was an outsider who knew too damn much for my comfort. So I'd sit and stew in my frustration until I was safe enough to let it out.

The longer I sat there debating my next move, the thicker the tension got. The air shifted, as did Grey and Griz, readying themselves for battle if it came to that. Two-Bit seemed fine, though. At ease almost, even as he poked at me. "All due respect, but don't make me a problem, Mari. You already have enough on your plate. I would hate to make things worse."

Wasn't that the fucking truth.

I had Cash wreaking havoc in my city and the Wolf on my ass, not to mention O'Bannon and the others ready to rip me to shreds for one fucking mistake. Like none of them had been caught dicking down the wrong heiress before. Since I was a woman, I couldn't make the same mistakes they did because I had to stay virginal and pure.

What a load of shit.

I debated causing a problem anyway, but Two-Bit's network was too deep to uproot. I doubted taking him out would do anything to stop them as a whole. That made him a seriously dangerous person to piss off because I had no way of learning how much he knew about my organization until it was too late. I had to take a step back, or I'd let my temper destroy years of progress and an alliance that seemed more beneficial by the day.

Deep breaths. Happy thoughts, Mari.

Centering myself wasn't working, so I smiled and spoke through gritted teeth. "In the future, if you find out something that seems like my business, I'd be glad to know immediately."

"What will I get in return?"

"My thanks," I said dryly, smiling for real when he laughed. "I'll pay you for your consideration."

"I'll think about it." He held out his hand to me, leaning over the table as we shook. "And I'm sorry about Nate. He seemed like a good guy, but I guess looks can be deceiving."

Just like that, the bubble of tension popped. Griz took a step back from his boss, shoulder dropping into a more comfortable position after holding himself at the ready for so long, and I felt Greyson shifting to do the same. I still wasn't sure whose side Two-Bit was on, but if he wasn't actively trying to destroy me, I was fine with not thinking about it for now. He could be next month's problem.

With a respectful nod my way, Two-Bit rose, following Griz's lead out the door. As his second held the elevator, he turned back with a twinkle in his eye that told me I wasn't going to be happy with him. "Good luck at your reunion."

I wasn't even surprised that he knew about the Wolf. I was just more annoyed.

"Christ," Grey muttered as the doors shut. "What do you want to do about him?"

"Nothing right now." I felt every joint in my body crack as I stood, like even they were brittle. "He's right. We can't afford another problem."

Not until my grandfather was dealt with.

Rafael had sent word that Emmanuel would arrive tomorrow morning, visiting my city for the first time since my mother had run away from home. I had no doubt that our meeting would be anything but pleasant, but I could handle that. My hope was to secure his help squashing Cash and his Aces, but as long as we all made it out alive, I'd be happy.

Greyson rested his hand on my hip as we waited for the elevator, so close to where Nate's touch from yesterday still burned that I wanted to throw up.

I hadn't told him or Dominic about the ambush or the kiss. I wasn't sure why I kept it to myself other than that I hadn't told them anything lately. I was surviving as a lonely little island because I forced myself to. To make it through the day, my feelings had to be shoved tightly into a box and forgotten at the back of my mind, even though fucking *everything* reminded me of Nate's treachery. Compartmentalizing was my friend, but I needed time and space for that, and while I was getting it now, I knew my men. They would only leave me in peace for so long, and my time of reckoning was coming quicker than I wanted.

Soon, I'd have to own up to everything, and I wasn't sure I was ready for it.

"Let's get the journals and then head back to the Celestine."

"Whatever you want, *reina*." Grey's voice was soft, measured, comforting, and I leaned into him for a second. Soaking up the warmth that only he could give me. The elevator dinged, dragging me away again, but for now, I felt whole, and that was enough.

Stepping into the mansion felt like walking into a graveyard. It had that eerie sense of emptiness and secrets and spirits roaming the halls. It felt abandoned in the same way Sevenroe had, despite only being empty for two days.

Two days since I'd lain in Nate's bed, totally at peace despite the war on the horizon. Solid in my understanding that the men I loved would be at my side through all of it.

Now, everything was different, and part of me wished I could go back to being that clueless idiot who was so besotted with a warm smile that she forgot the first lesson her father ever taught her.

Everyone lies.

"I had Tennessee's team sweep it before we got here," Greyson offered as I stood just beyond the threshold, unable to move. Captured and kept by history that hadn't even had time to seep into walls. "No one's been in or out who wasn't supposed to be home."

Home. It felt impossible for it to be real anymore when mine was shattered.

Nate had been my home, just like Dominic and Greyson were, but he hadn't been the foundation. He'd been the snake in the rafters, lying in wait to devour us whole, and I was the dumbass who'd let him in.

"Where's Amara?"

"Extended vacation to her sister's. She's pissed, by the way."

Guilt and gratitude warred in me as I tried to smile for him. I'd been so focused on my own pain that I hadn't thought about Amara or anyone else Nate's treachery had affected. I'd been so fucking blind, *again.* It had to stop.

"Thank you."

"You don't need to thank me. We're a team." He said it like he was reminding me. Like I'd forgotten.

Maybe I had.

"You ever wish you could go back, make different choices?" I asked.

"No, because then I wouldn't have you."

"I wish I'd left him to the wolves that day." Even knowing they wouldn't have done anything because Nate was an Ace like the men who ambushed me, I still wished I'd run instead. That I'd ignored the soft part of me that didn't want a kind stranger to die and left him to the bullets alone.

"No, you don't." I snorted at Greyson's words, and he stepped closer, his warmth seeping into my back and his breath shifting the hair at my ear. "That isn't who you are, Mari."

"Maybe it should be."

His noise of disagreement was barely loud enough to hear. "It's only been a few days."

"Feels like a lifetime," I muttered.

"Even so, give yourself some grace. It won't hurt like this forever."

But it would still hurt. We both knew that.

"Let's just get the journals and go. I hate it here." I hadn't before, but now all I could see were lies in the wallpaper and deceit on the floors. I didn't want to stay long enough to discover anything else. Not yet anyway.

Hell, maybe I never would. There was too much family history in the house to ever sell it, but I doubted I'd live inside again. I'd probably give the whole place to Moore and Tennessee. They could use a security outpost of their own.

The trip up to the library was silent, Grey and I wary despite his assurances that we were alone. The house just didn't feel safe anymore.

It felt haunted, and I'd never been one for ghosts.

The library was massive, the shelves packed despite most of the books never having been cracked open. When we were kids, it had been Antoni's favorite place, if only because it was no one else's. He could sit in the oversized chair by the fireplace for hours reading history books that made my eyes cross, and no one interrupted. When he met Shara, she'd join him, and they'd snuggle up like they had nothing but time.

My brother fell in love in this room. Proposed here, too. I could feel him in every square inch of it, and suddenly, I missed him fiercely. Antoni would've been the first in line to beat the shit out of Nate for what he'd done, and the first to offer me a hug for my troubles. Second in line would've been Rey, who would've destroyed Nate's car like I'd taken out Cash's before forcing me into a shitty movie marathon that ended with a stomachache and moving on.

I changed my mind. Ghosts would be fine, if *they* were the ones I got.

Greyson cleared his throat, tipping his head toward the shelves. Not trying to rush me, but reminding me we had a job to do.

The journals—both my father's and Antoni's—were chock-full of information that no one else could know. Insider knowledge that could bring everything down around me. My first order of business after taking over had been to split them up, hiding them in plain sight inside other books. My brother would've called gutting a book sacrilege, but I called it necessary.

I searched the shelves in silence, fingers tracing the familiar spines as I looked for the first journal hidden in a bunch of medical texts.

Only, it wasn't there.

"What the fuck?"

I skimmed the shelf again, pulling the books out one at a time and flipping through in case I forgot where I'd hidden it, but the hollowed-out cover was waiting for me. Empty.

Unease grew in the pit of my stomach, and I hustled to the next hiding spot to find the same thing.

Empty cover. No fucking journal.

"No."

"*Reina?*" Grey moved closer as I went to the next spot and the next, getting more frantic with each step, only to be disappointed each time.

Nothing.

"They aren't here."

Silence and then, "What?"

Grey gave a good growl when he wanted to, and it slid across my skin like the tip of a knife, leaving goose bumps in its wake. Too bad I was too far gone to enjoy it.

"The journals are missing. They're gone."

Chapter 9
Mari

The last few days had been tiring and awful and more emotional than the entire last year of my life, which was saying something since I'd buried my cousin not that long ago. Hell, maybe that was part of the problem. I was a volcano, pressure building inside me with every irritation, every pain, every second of grief I faced.

This was the last straw, the final push to set me off.

I felt something inside me—something frail, desperately clinging to life and sanity and calm—snap.

I didn't remember reaching for the first shelf or the feel of the pages beneath my fingertips. All I felt was rage. Bone-deep, blood-boiling rage.

Nate had invaded my home. He'd made me love him. He'd put everything I cared about at risk: my family, my empire, my city. And yet nothing felt worse than knowing he'd stolen my family's legacy. My brother's last remaining words.

I watched as I tore the books from their shelves and threw them across the room, like I was having an out-of-body experience. Present, but unable to stop myself as I went to the next to do it all over again. The soft tinkling of glass said that I broke something somewhere, but I didn't know what, nor did I care. I was too focused on expelling the anger from my body, and the red haze covered the entire room.

Why did I have to lose everything?

Why was nothing mine to keep?

Why did I always have to sacrifice?

Growing up, I'd given up any dreams of love and joy because my father expected me to be a tool in his arsenal, and I accepted it. When I buried Antoni, I gave up a future of my choosing to take over my birthright. I gave up ever feeling safe or living to old age.

I'd given up *everything* for this city, and all it did was bleed me dry.

Why was nothing I did good enough to keep my family—my heart—safe?

I didn't know, and the pressure in my chest said I wouldn't. So I just kept going.

Row after row, bookcase after bookcase, I dismantled the library in a fit of rage that rivaled most other forces of nature: deadly, chaotic, and dangerous to behold.

Time lost all meaning, and the rush of blood in my ears deafened me as I defiled my brother's favorite space. So I had no warning before I was crushed between not one body but two.

Struggling was second nature because I'd lost my sense of self and I didn't know these bodies, except...did I?

"Stop, Mari. You're going to hurt yourself."

I knew that voice.

Come back, I told myself. *It's time to come back.*

It took a long time to stitch myself together after a fracturing of that magnitude, but when I did, the scents of the men I loved surrounded me, soothing me.

Healing me.

"Dominic?" I asked, because I knew Greyson was in front of me. My throat was scratchy, and my eyes felt drier than sand, though I didn't know why.

Had I been crying? Screaming? Was this what a true mental break looked like? If so, I'd earned it after the last year, but fuck. Bad timing.

"I'm here, *mariposa.*" Dominic's voice was low and soft, and his skin was warm. He didn't have a jacket on, though it had been pouring rain earlier and he was completely dry. Which begged the question—how long had I been losing my shit while they watched?

"How?" I didn't need an answer to that when I already knew Greyson had called. I was really asking *Why?*

Why are you here?

Why have you stayed?

Why do you love me when I'm like this?

"You needed us," Dominic said softly, his lips pressed to my temple.

Greyson mirrored him on the other side. "And we need you."

I did need them—both of them—but I didn't like it. I didn't want to need them like this. One look at the destruction of my brother's safe space told me why.

People left. They left and they took part of you with them, and you never got it back. You just lived with a hole in your chest like it was normal. I already had too many holes in my chest.

Mama. Mario.

Antoni. Rey.

Nate.

I couldn't take another.

But I couldn't let them go either.

My men held me together as my mind whirled, catching on thoughts I didn't want to have. Circled by the ones who'd loved me longest, I realized something awful. Nate hadn't just broken my trust; it felt like he'd broken me in a way I'd never heal from. The wound itself would fade, but it would scar. And while they were reminders of past pain, past traumas, Nate had made sure his mark was too deep to ever fade.

Another one for the collection, I thought wearily.

I was tired of life shitting on me. Tired of never getting to feel whole. Tired of second-guessing everyone's motives because with power came power-seekers, and I should've learned that lesson long before Nate snuck through my defenses and laid siege to my heart.

I was just *tired.*

But I didn't have the luxury of being tired. Not yet. We had a war to win.

Clearing my throat, I withdrew from my men's arms and stood on shaky legs to face the music. Some of the books were ripped to shreds, completely irreparable, others would need some serious work, but thankfully, most were okay.

"I've got a guy who can fix those for us," Dominic said. Which was good because I didn't have the energy to fix anything in this house anymore.

It was cursed. It had to be.

Looking away from the literary carnage, I met his eyes. "Did you drive?"

He looked at Grey with eyes shadowed like he hadn't slept. Had I done that to him? Had I made him so worried he'd stopped resting, or was that the Nate effect? Had losing our fourth damaged Dominic too?

I hated that I was too selfish to ask, too wounded to care.

You don't deserve them.

Eventually, Dominic nodded.

"Good. Give me your keys."

"Mari—"

"I'm not going for a joyride. I'm going to the Celestine. No stops, no detours, no leaving the city." He still didn't want to give them up, and I sighed. "Please, Dominic. I just...can't."

Space. I needed space. It was all I'd needed since Nate's betrayal. The boys looked at each other again, and I decided they could keep their secret looks if they would just let me leave.

I had to get out of here before I burned the whole place down around us.

Snatching the keys from his pocket, which was the closest we'd been in days, I headed for the door. "Lock it down. We're done here."

For now. For a while. Forever.

Didn't matter to me. I was moving on, even if it killed me. Because if I didn't, it would kill us all.

* * *

I'd just turned onto the street outside when my phone rang.

Dr. Grant.

Fuck, please let this be good news.

"What's up, Doc?"

"Your results are back. You want them now?"

"Please."

I took a turn too fast as I waited for her to pull them up and double-check, my heart pounding. "Everything was negative. No STIs, no pregnancy. We even tested your previous implant, and it was still functioning."

Which didn't mean Nate hadn't messed with it, just that he hadn't succeeded.

She was still talking about something, but I cut her off with a muttered, "Thanks" before hanging up.

I liked Dr. Grant, which meant she didn't need to deal with my downward spiral. I'd send her an apology gift later, and hopefully, all would be forgiven.

It took three blocks for her words to sink in. Relief choked me, as well as the realization that I still didn't feel *clean*. Potential STIs weren't the problem either; it was Nate. Moments that had felt so good before were sullied now. None of it felt real. I needed something to make it sink in.

By the time I got to our suite, I still didn't know what that could be, so I stalked into my bathroom, turned the shower to scalding, and stripped. With any luck, the water would burn away the last traces of Nate, and I could move on. Start over with a clean slate.

The water burned, but it also made me feel awake again. Alive. I slicked body gel over my skin, marveling at how every part of me heated at the touch.

For the first time since Nate left, I *wanted*.

Sliding a hand down my stomach and between my thighs felt like a revelation because, *god yes*.

This was what I needed. To reclaim myself, to settle in my own skin like *he* never existed.

I slid my fingers around my clit, gasping at how good it felt. The showerhead felt even better. If I was starting over, I was doing it with the most powerful orgasm I could.

Lifting a leg on the low ledge of the tile, I let myself feel again.

The warmth creeping in, the tension in my muscles as my body climbed higher, desperately latching on to any ounce of pleasure it could. My lips parted as soft gaps of *yes, right there,* and *fuck* slipped between them.

It was incredible. It was everything.

Except I couldn't come.

Every time I got close, I remembered Nate's voice, and my orgasm disappeared like water down the drain.

The longer it took, the more irritated I got, until I ripped myself from the shower with barely controlled agitation.

My skin felt too tight, too desperate for release. I needed this. I needed to let him go. Still damp, I threw myself on the bed, pulling out my most trusted toys.

None of them worked.

Not the dildo I slapped onto a chair and rode until my thighs burned. Not the vibrator that hit my G-spot just right. Not my clitoral stimulator that held the record for the fastest orgasm at ten seconds.

Nothing. Fucking. Worked.

Every time I crested that hill, so close to ecstasy I thought I'd scream, Nate ruined it.

You feel like home.

I'll never stop loving you.

You're the best thing that's ever happened to me.

All I could see were memories I'd almost cherished and a face I wanted to forget.

You'll always be mine, even if I'm not yours.

"Goddammit!" I tossed the toy, watching it smash against the wall, shattering to pieces just like I needed to. I was desperate to come. Desperate to shatter and break so I could rebuild.

"I fucking *need* this."

Slicking my fingers in my own moisture, I circled my clit with one hand, fucking myself with the other. There was no patience, no slow buildup. It was pure, single-focused fucking. The only sounds in the room were my agonized breaths, the occasional hiss as I hit a particularly good spot, and the wet noises of my pussy.

Calling the boys was an option, but I needed this. I had to take my body back.

Nate had been the last to touch it. The last to fuck me.

No, not fuck. Make love. It made me sick.

So, I'd do this because I was Marianna *fucking* Marcosa, and I could damn well bring myself to orgasm.

I fucked myself until my clit hurt, my wrists ached and burned at the stretch, while they and my thighs were sticky with sweat and my own arousal.

And I still couldn't come.

I threw myself onto the bed, struggling through huge, gasping breaths as I finally, *finally*, let myself break down again. The sobs racked me, but I refused to curl up. Refused to cower. I let the tears trail down my cheeks and fall into my hair, the sheets, the pillows. I didn't know, nor did I care.

All that energy had to go somewhere. Apparently, my body preferred crying.

So I lay in my bed, filthy and tired and so fucking sad, wondering if I would ever feel safe enough to come again or if that part of my life was over. Would I ever feel comfortable having sex, or was I doomed to scratch and claw my way to heaven, only to be denied access every time?

If I couldn't have sex, would I lose Dominic and Greyson? Would they leave me if I couldn't give them that part of myself ever again?

I had no fucking clue, and it drove me further into my spiral until I wasn't sure I'd ever surface.

Trust them, my heart begged me. *They won't abandon you.*

Too bad my heart had already fucked me over one too many times.

If the boys couldn't handle a life without sex, I'd let them go.

They deserved happiness and fulfilling lives, even if it fucking killed me to think of them moving on. But I'd do it. I loved them enough not to want to force them to stay where they weren't happy.

But if they walked—if they left me because I couldn't heal—I was taking it out on the man who'd gone from lover to enemy in the span of a heartbeat.

Nate.

Chapter 10
Mari

If I was a queen, Emmanuel Osorio was an emperor, which meant only the best of the best for him. Lil Sal's was always my first choice when it came to lunches, even for business, but no way in hell was I bringing a potentially hostile entity there.

Over my dead body would I let the Wolf darken their door.

Instead, we sat high above the water in a fine dining establishment so pretentious, I was getting hives, and I owned the place. Everything was bright walls and bright metal. Sterile and boring.

I missed chipped tables and waitstaff who knew me by name. Maybe I'd convince the boys to stop off at Sal's on the way home. I could use a pick-me-up.

Dominic and Greyson sat on either side of me in beautiful chairs that hurt my spine around a table that was covered in a tablecloth with a higher thread count than most people's sheets. Tennessee and Moore stood against the wall behind us, playing the silent sentinels. We'd shut the whole restaurant down—hell, we'd shut down the block—because I didn't trust anyone beyond us to know who was coming. I hadn't even told Cameron what we were doing.

My empire was already on thin ice. Inviting a man who was practically a god into my city without letting the other leaders know? Yeah, that would go over well. The only person I'd told was one of the chefs, Justine, who was in the kitchen and would play server for our meal.

"Incoming," Greyson muttered, eyes glued to his phone where we had a live feed of the security cameras.

"Emmanuel?" If so, he was early.

"Worse. Rafael."

Ah.

I hadn't seen my uncle since the news came out, but it struck me last night that a man who'd worked with Nate in the past would've known who he was when I introduced them. Had he kept the secret to save his own skin or to protect Nate's?

That was *if* what Nate said about his history was true.

Operate as if everything was a lie, I reminded myself.

"*Tesorita.*" Rafael's gaze was warm and wary, and that alone told me everything.

He knew. He knew the whole fucking time who Nate was, and he said nothing. Just like Two-Bit.

And just like with Two-Bit, I couldn't afford to war with him about it.

Rafael fidgeted uncomfortably, likely because my glare was so hot I could melt metal. Too bad that wasn't one of my party tricks. "You seem to keep finding yourself on my shit list, Uncle."

He grimaced. "I can explain."

"He can explain!" I crowed with thick sarcasm, enjoying Dominic's brutal grin. Even Greyson looked ready to unleash his inner psychopath. "Explain then, Uncle. Tell me how you let me get involved with my enemy. Or how you helped him hide the truth so he could gather information right under our noses. Tell me how you gave me an *entire file of lies.* Go on. I dare you."

"I gave you what I was permitted to give you."

I wanted more than that. I wanted him on his knees begging for forgiveness, but I was also smart enough to know it would never happen. Just like I was smart enough to know he'd burned the fragile bridge we'd been building between us to ash.

Brushing off the ache of his betrayal—because, really, what was one more? —I narrowed my eyes at him. "Why are you here so early anyway?"

The meeting with the Wolf was almost an hour away. My paranoia refused to allow the building to stand empty, so we'd been holed up working inside since dawn, much to Dominic's disappointment. He hated waking up early.

"Checking your security," Rafael answered.

"Well, go on, then," Dominic drolled with that lazy wave of his that made him look like an arrogant king. "Have a look around."

Rafael looked at me for confirmation, but I said nothing. Finally, he made himself busy, getting close to every camera he could see—and some he shouldn't have—and inspecting them. I could feel Tennessee's irritation almost as heavily as I could feel Greyson's. Neither liked their toys played with.

Finally, Rafael nodded to himself and took a seat across from us to send a text. With that done, he turned his attention back to me. "Don't say no."

"To what?" The sudden conversation switch was probably to throw me off, but if so, he'd have to try harder than that.

"If the Wolf offers you aid, don't outright tell him no." I opened my mouth to answer, but Rafael held up a hand. "Please just listen. We don't have time to argue. Emmanuel will ask for something outrageous, and you'll be tempted to deny him immediately. Don't. You may not be willing to accept his terms now, but keep the option open for later."

"Tell him I'll think on the terms he's offering, when he didn't uphold his end of the bargain?"

"Yes."

"No."

Rafael sighed. "Technically, we did uphold our end of the bargain. You asked for information on Nate *Black*, and you were given what we had. Had you asked for Nate *Beckstrom*, you would've gotten something different."

The world stilled, and that red haze from yesterday crept over me.

A loophole. He'd fucked me over with a *loophole*, and the only thing keeping me from wringing his neck with it was his father's presence looming over us. The Wolf would not take kindly to his heir's death.

"That's bullshit, and you know it," I growled.

Rafael laughed, brittle and broken. "We're not exactly honorable men, *tesorita*."

"Funny, I thought you were."

The barb struck home and he flinched, but it didn't make me feel better.

I had almost no family I could trust and taking Rafael's name off that short list hurt, but I had to do it. His priority would always be the Osorios, never me. I had to accept that.

Rafael would always be blood, but he was no longer family.

"How likely is the Wolf to offer aid anyway?" Dominic asked, balancing his chair on two legs and twirling a steak knife in one hand.

"Why are you acting like a five-year-old with sharp objects?" I asked.

He grinned, wide and a little on edge. "It's fun."

Which meant he wanted to mess with Emmanuel or possibly

Rafael. I could've put a stop to it, but honestly, I didn't care to. I wasn't going to babysit Dominic today. If he wanted to fuck with the cartel, that was his business, as long as it didn't blow back on me. "Whatever."

I rolled my eyes, and he blew me a cheeky kiss. "Love you, *mariposa*."

I didn't respond, and he smiled bigger. At least Greyson cleared his throat. "Well? Is he going to help?"

There was something in how Rafael looked away that said how much faith he had that the Wolf would offer aid at all.

Namely, none.

"I don't know."

"You're too scared to get on my bad side by telling me the truth," I corrected because, frankly, we didn't have time for this shit.

Rafael stared at me, a whole host of emotions in his eyes, before he looked away. A muscle in his jaw clenched as he nodded. "You're right. I doubt he'll offer aid at all."

"Why the hell not?"

"Because I don't care about you or your father's city."

Dominic's chair legs hit the floor with a loud *thump* as all four of us stood. The playful smile on his face was gone, replaced by the serious look of a true underboss as the door closed behind the Wolf. Suddenly, I was grateful to have Dominic and Grey at my side, stabilizing me for a meeting I never thought I'd have.

Emmanuel Osorio looked nothing like Rafael. It was almost shocking how different he looked from his son and how much he looked like me. Same eyes, same nose, same fierce gaze. Though he was obviously older—close to eighty, if I had to guess—he'd kept himself strong, even with the slight paunch that said he enjoyed the fruits of having a billion-dollar empire. But there was no way to mistake the look on his face.

This was a man who had no problem doing his own dirty work.

He swept through the room like a tidal wave and, when he was close enough, held his hand out to me. I took it immediately, giving him a proper shake. His fingers were bare except for two heavy gold rings, and when his callused palm met mine, I knew I was right.

Emmanuel Osorio was death made flesh.

"Marianna Marcosa. My long-lost granddaughter."

"Emmanuel Osorio," I replied. "My not-so-lost grandfather. Welcome to my city."

"It's certainly something."

My smile stayed firmly in place, despite the urge to tell him to shut up. I didn't like people putting my city down. I also didn't like them dissecting me like a science experiment, but Emmanuel seemed keen to do that. He took in every bit of my appearance before finally looking away with the slightest tension in his jaw.

"You look like your mother."

That was a compliment. I didn't tell him that I wished I'd met her or that I wanted to know more about who she was before Mario got ahold of her. I just accepted the compliment with a grateful nod. "Shall we sit?"

Emmanuel skimmed his eyes over Rafael before he sat and turned his gaze to Greyson. "Is this your husband, Marianna?"

"Which one?" Dominic muttered. I stepped on his foot under the table, gratified by the hiss that slipped from his mouth. His hand clamped down on my thigh, far higher than was decent in my grandfather's presence.

I gave him a *don't even think about it* glare before turning back to the man in front of me. "Not exactly."

Emmanuel frowned. "What does that mean?"

"Greyson and I are together, as close as married, but there's no certificate or rings."

Disapproval weighed heavily in the air, most of it focused on me. I knew from Amara that my mother's family was devoutly Catholic and premarital sex was a major sin. "I see. Any plans to get married?"

I shot a look at Greyson, begging him to keep silent as he grew stiffer and stiffer next to me. We needed calm, collected Grey today. "Not currently."

"You're just like your father."

Even though my father had technically married my mother, I knew what Emmanuel meant. "That's not a compliment."

"It wasn't intended to be." Emmanuel sat back, his hands crossed over his belly, rings glinting in the rare noon sun. For a long time, he just stared at me, gaze heavy like he was judging us. I had the feeling he found us lacking. "I won't offer you aid."

"I haven't asked." We hadn't even gotten our drinks yet.

As I thought it, Justine swooped out with the beverage cart, taking it to Emmanuel first, as was customary. "Drink?"

He didn't spare her a glance, shooing her away with his hand like a pesky gnat. I hated when people were disrespectful to servers. I was about to say as much when Grey's hand clamped down on my other thigh, mirroring Dominic's. They'd been doing that a lot lately, following each other's lead. I hadn't even realized it until they'd all but shackled me to the chair with their hands.

"And yet my answer is still no."

Irritation rolled through me, fueled by no sleep and too much caffeine. Justine, goddess that she was, set water in front of me, and I sipped it slowly. "Why not?"

"It's not our fight. Not yet."

Just like Two-Bit. "Am I not your granddaughter?"

"In name only. We have no alliance, and I have no reason to protect your father's empire."

"*My* empire," I snapped.

Emmanuel's look was so condescending, I debated parricide

for the first time ever. Dominic's hand slid up and down my thigh, while Greyson kept his as a steady, solid pressure. Something to keep me from floating up and destroying my biggest chance at getting rid of Cash.

"Maybe so, but unless those things change...unless I have a stake in it, I'm afraid we're at an impasse."

Warning pulsed through my veins, and I knew this was what Rafael was talking about. "What kind of stake?"

"You'll marry one of my underbosses and give him control of your holdings."

I didn't even need to hear Joaquin's offer to know it would be the same. *Marry and let a man take over, Mari. It's what should've happened all along.*

Were all men as fucking clueless as my family? Were they all so blind?

The city was falling before I took over.

I gave it life. *I* rebuilt it to last for generations. *I* protected it.

What the fuck had they ever done?

Smiling through gritted teeth, I had to work hard to rein in my temper. "Let me get this straight. You'll help me save my city, but in return, I have to give it up?"

"Yes."

"Fuck no."

Emmanuel's brow creased at the cursing, and he stood, buttoning his suit jacket. "Then there's nothing to discuss."

Rafael's eyes were boring into my skull, but did he seriously think I'd ever give up Seattle? Did he think I was worth so little?

If he did, he was wrong. I was worth everything, and so was this city. I'd show them all.

I followed Emmanuel to my feet, holding out my hand for another shake. "I understand. Thank you for coming out, Grandfather. I hope you enjoy your stay."

"I won't be staying at all. I hate this fucking city."

Emmanuel turned to Rafael, dismissing me in a move so like my father it nearly stole a laugh from me. Only knowing it would make things worse kept my mouth shut. "Your *vacation* is over, *hijo*. Return home immediately."

Rafael glanced at me, then back. "Father, please. I can't leave her here. Bianca—"

"Is dead, as are her progeny."

"Still here," I muttered. Surprisingly, Dominic and Grey both chuckled, and warmth bloomed in my chest again at the sounds. They felt like home, like family, and seeing my last connection to my mother dismiss me like I was nothing had me craving them. Not for sex, but for comfort.

"One more week," Rafael bargained.

"No," Emmanuel snapped. "You will leave Seattle tonight."

"I can't do that."

"You can and you will." Emmanuel clapped a hand to Rafael's shoulder, squeezing just short of painfully. "Come home and leave the girl to burn before there's nothing for you to come back to."

Rafael stilled in his father's hold, and I knew we were all wondering the same thing. Was he threatening Rafael's position in the family or his sons? I knew next to nothing about my Osorio cousins, only that I had them, which meant I had no way to help them. If Emmanuel decided they had to die, that was it.

Rafael's head bowed, though I was sure it was to hide the hateful glare he tossed at the table. "I'll leave tonight."

"Good. In case you decide there's more you can do, here's proof that the Marcosa line is well and truly on its way to extinction." Emmanuel slapped a phone into his hand and gave me a final glance. "He's tearing the city down around your ears, girl. Better let him have it before he buries you in the rubble."

Then he turned away, giving me nothing but his back as he walked out of my life.

The whole visit was fucked, and we hadn't even gotten to appetizers.

The four of us were silent as the Osorio guards left the building behind their boss. Only when the last was truly gone did Rafael look at the phone. I wasn't sure I'd ever heard swearing quite like that.

"Uncle?"

Rafael said nothing, just tossed me the phone. One glance froze my pulse, only to send it racing to the point of pain right after.

"Motherfuck." Greyson stood fast enough to topple his chair, barking orders at Moore to stay with me while he and Tennessee did some digging.

Because the phone didn't just have pictures of my ledgers from the docks with the overages from Porter and Cash, but *all* of my ledgers.

And they'd been released to the public.

A text popped up with a link to the *Seattle Tribune*.

"Mari," Dominic warned, but I clicked it anyway. The world was hazy around me—shock, maybe—but I knew I had to see the damage myself.

Money Laundering Scheme Revealed

The article went on to go into detail about my business ventures and how I laundered my money, but it didn't name names. It didn't have to.

Anyone who was anyone in the city knew whose records those were, and they knew who'd sent them in.

Greyson rounded back to me, his hand firm on my hip. Unlike yesterday, it was grounding. Settling when I thought I was going to drift into space. The calm before the storm. "I'm already on the phone with Ronnie and Donnaghal and Sons. They'll work together to get the article removed and your name cleared by morning."

Our lawyers were incredible—and were paid handsomely for their talent at keeping us out of prison—so I wasn't actually concerned about that.

Dominic's phone went off, and one look at the screen was exactly what I was afraid of. *Troy Kincaid.*

Our clients had already heard, which meant our business was in danger. Revealing our secrets to the public meant police attention, federal attention. It meant that I couldn't smuggle shit until the heat died down.

Cash had fucked with my head first and my purse strings second. He'd cut me off from my allies and made me look more unstable by the day. He didn't even need to come after me.

A few more dominoes and the city itself would turn on me.

While Dominic and Greyson focused on their problems, I walked over to one of the floor-to-ceiling windows and stared out at the water below. The waves crashing to the shore.

Which one was I? The immovable force of the water or the easily removed sand?

A throat cleared at my side. Rafael.

"I'm sorry, Mari."

It was hard to form words when my lips felt numb. "I wish I believed you."

"I know I have things to make up for, but I promise I will. I'll fix this."

"You can't. Emmanuel said no."

"Fuck him." I jerked my head toward Rafael, and he stared me down. "Father's forgotten what family really is, but I haven't. I owe you this. I owe *Bianca* this. So even if the Wolf doesn't help you, I will if you'll let me."

I wasn't sure I wanted his help, but I'd have to take it. I'd take whatever I could to get Cash out.

Because he'd just turned on the countdown timer, and if he didn't die, I would.

Chapter 11
Dominic

Mari disappeared into her room the second we got home. She'd been silent since she'd seen the article, drowning in her own thoughts and plans. Every time I looked at her, I saw the wheels turning as she tried to figure out how to fix this. How to come back from this.

How to survive.

The silence, I expected, but everything else made me wonder if she wasn't in shock. I was about to check with Greyson when Troy Kincaid texted *again*. I fought the urge to snap my phone in half.

> I'm giving her a week. If it's not dealt with, I'm going to see how the other half lives.

This motherfucker.

Kincaid had been with the Marcosas since Mario ran the family, and now he was going to bail? Fuck that.

It's already taken care of, but I'll be sure to let Mari know you're looking at other options.

It's not personal. It's business.

Maybe to him, but I was watching the love of my life lose herself with every hit Cash landed, and I hated it. I didn't know how to help Mari.

Grey stopped next to me, and we watched her door somberly. "She's breaking."

"Are you surprised? With all the shit the last few years have put on her, I'm shocked she lasted this long."

"We have to fix her."

There was the rub. We couldn't. Mari was hurting, she was betrayed, she was in agony.

And she was the only person who could work through it and find her way to the other side, to healing.

"We have to give her a soft place to land," I corrected just before the door opened.

She'd changed into leggings that hugged her ass, a sports bra, and some sneakers, the whole outfit black with electric hints. The bright color felt more like a warning than a fashion statement. *Danger.*

Mari twisted her hair into a braid as she walked down the hall to the gym. Technically, the gym could be more easily accessed through the elevator hallway outside the penthouse, but my guess was she felt too fragile to be seen at the moment. Too close to breaking.

Too close to snapping.

While Greyson stalked her, I rushed to my room to get changed, grabbing a set of clothes for him too. I felt a knot in my chest that constricted the longer Mari's self-imposed isolation continued, the part of me that demanded to protect her and soothe her growing restlessness. I wasn't sure I could handle another night separated from her.

Then I walked into the gym and knew it wouldn't be necessary.

Mari was already attacking the bag. Her arms and legs blurred as she took out her frustration at Nate and Cash, Rafael and Joaquin. She kicked like she was knocking her enemies to the ground one by one. Considering how fast she'd gotten to work, I knew she hadn't warmed up, and I could feel the strain in her arms and wrists as if it were my own. If she didn't stop, she'd cause damage. Every punch was harder and sharper than before, aimed to kill. Her assault held nothing back, even when Greyson's veins bulged with the effort of holding the bag steady. This wasn't working out; it was fighting demons, and Mari was winning.

Except she hadn't wrapped her hands, so the bag was taking as much blood as she offered. Grey's brows furrowed when he realized she'd split her knuckles open, and I knew we were both thinking of her wrecked hands after Cash got ahold of her. Her fingernails mangled and aching.

"*Reina—*"

"Just hold the bag."

His hands tightened to keep it steady, but when he looked at me, he seemed lost. For the first time ever, Grey didn't know what to do. He didn't know how to help or where to go to get Mari back to herself.

The longer I watched her, the more I realized he couldn't.

But I could.

I had to. Someone had to direct the rodeo until Mari was on her feet again, and tonight, that was me.

"Enough."

Mari didn't even slow down, throwing another set of punches harder than before.

I could practically hear her thoughts all narrowed down to what was in front of her. *Breathe, hit, breathe, hit.*

"I said, *enough!*" Sweat dripped down Mari's neck as I gripped her arm and twisted, shoving her back against the heavy bag. Greyson snarled behind us, and I could feel him standing taller, getting ready for a fight. Even when he was uncertain, he knew when to protect, but there was letting Mari work out her frustrations and there was helping her self-harm, and he was skirting the line too motherfucking closely.

I shot him a glare that very clearly said, *stand down.*

Greyson shifted, bouncing a little on the balls of his feet so he could move quicker if he had to, and I rolled my eyes. "I'm not going to hurt her. She's doing that well enough on her own."

Indignation was a lash across Mari's drawn face. "Now, hold on!"

"No." My gaze flashed down to hers, and I saw every ounce of turmoil she was trying to hide. Her chest heaved as she tried to take in enough air to feel better, to calm down. But it wouldn't come. The certainty that she was past helping herself battered against my defenses, begging me to help, to heal, but I stayed calm. Steady and sturdy as a rock. I would ground her. I could do that.

"You have a choice. Do you want to hurt, or do you want relief?"

"What the hell are you talking about?" Greyson snapped. He hadn't moved from behind the bag, but I had no doubt he'd pull me away if it came to that. "If you put a hand on her—"

"She's fraying." My chin jerked toward Mari, whose eyes were too wide, her breathing too fast. Not that she realized it. This was Mari at her most basic. All sensation and need, none of the put-together queen we were accustomed to. "Look at her."

Grey peered around the bag and swore. He saw it now. This was the true creature we'd devoted ourselves to, this feral being with the face of our love. It was easy to praise a goddess when she was benevolent, but it was something else to worship her when she was at her most needy, her most wicked.

And worship was what I intended to do, despite how it was going to look.

"Everything that's been happening has built up, and she's got nowhere to send that energy. Fighting should have helped, but it didn't. Fucking is an option, if you're both up for it." I didn't have to ask Grey to know his answer. He couldn't hurt Mari, even if she needed it, and she did. She really, really did.

Mari spent every day making life-and-death decisions. That level of power took a toll, and some people couldn't handle the emotional accumulation. They had no way to excise the over-abundance, and it rotted them from the inside out. Mari was one of those people. We had to break her so she could heal again. In this case, we had to fuck her into submission, forcing her out of her head and into some form of subspace where she could let it all go and come back to center. It wasn't going to be pretty, but it was going to be necessary.

Greyson swallowed and looked away. "Not like this."

I nodded, and he looked relieved when I left it at that. Being unable to do what had to be done was a problem in most cases, but I didn't consider it a weakness when someone else could take up the slack. We were a family; where one failed, another succeeded. There was a reason one man would never be enough for Mari. I just had to hope two would, because Grey and I were never letting her go.

"Agreed." Mari's voice wavered like she wasn't sure about her answer, but I took it at face value. If it wasn't an enthusiastic yes, it was a no.

No fucking. At least, not yet.

"That leaves feeling. You in?" I stared down at her, knowing she was almost to the point of no return. All the shit with Nate and Cash was poisoning her from the inside out. I could almost see the blackness creeping into her gaze, the recklessness that would get her killed. We had to fix this before there was nothing to save.

"No, but if I don't try something, I'd have to resort to more destructive methods, and I don't have the time for a hangover."

As if getting drunk was the worst she could do to herself.

I let her go, stepping back to give her space as I pointed to the floor. "Lie on your stomach, arms at your sides."

"Is this a joke?"

"Do I look like I'm joking? On the floor."

Mari looked at Greyson, but she eventually dropped to her knees. When she didn't move beyond that, I clicked my tongue for her attention. "You can use a safeword."

But she wouldn't. She needed this as much as we did.

For every moment of anxiety that Mari had, Grey and I shared it. We'd felt the betrayal that rocked her. We were stressed and angry about the Wolf and Rafael. We'd been at her side through everything, and we were close to fraying too.

Tonight, everything changed. For the better, I hoped.

It took longer than I liked, but eventually, Mari lay down. The moment her belly touched the mat, she hated it. It didn't matter that the only two people in the room were ones she trusted with her life—or the fact that Grey strode over and locked the door at my urging—she felt too vulnerable, and vulnerable was bad.

Which was why she squirmed and fought like a cat when I pressed softly on her back.

"Dominic—"

"Arms down, *mariposa*. It'll all make sense in a minute."

But she was too far into her hindbrain, so she scratched and clawed, bit and tore. My arms were a mess by the time I finally had her hands shackled in my own. Grey watched closely, ready to beat my ass if she said the word, but she didn't. She needed the fight and the surrender equally.

Mari's cheeks were wet with tears of frustration, anger, and grief, though we all pretended to ignore that for the time being. She vibrated underneath me as I slowly gave her more and more of my weight until she held it all. The pressure shouldn't have felt good. She was already suffocating under the weight of everything. The last thing she needed was more, but the longer I lay on top of her, the more tension released until she was only slightly stiff below me.

Progress.

I didn't touch her beyond that. Didn't kiss her or grind my body into hers. This was about connection and release, and the longer it went on, the better it turned out.

"Why does this work so well?" She finally groaned, letting her muscles melt into the mat below. I felt the vibrations through my chest, and it soothed me as much as having her close did. Like she was whispering to the animal inside me that we were okay. Everything was fine.

I hummed above her, adjusting so I could stroke soft circles along her wrist with my thumb now that she was done hurting me. My arms were slicked with blood, but I'd wear those wounds with pride. "It puts your autonomic nervous system into a sort of 'rest and recover' mode. Pressure and weight like this help with anxiety."

Greyson cocked his head, eyes darting over Mari's face as he watched the angst slowly drain away, leaving only relief. "You're acting like a human weighted blanket."

"Exactly." I chuckled. "The other option was an ice bath, but I decided it would be too much if you were still shocky from earlier."

"I'm not shocky," Mari snapped.

I nuzzled her neck, brushing my lips against her skin. "I know that now, but it wasn't a risk I wanted to take."

After my nod at Grey, he took over. "How can we fix this?"

"You said Ronnie and the others are—"

"We're not talking about the article or the Wolf, or even Cash. We're talking about you," I said gently. As expected, she locked up underneath me, so I adjusted my weight to press her back down against the floor. "Don't bolt. Just talk to us. We're your partners. Let us be there for you. We can shoulder some of the burdens."

"There's nothing for you to do. I've got to sort through this alone."

I lifted onto my knees and rolled her over, needing her to see my face. When she was on her back, I huddled over her body, palms cradling her cheeks and forcing her to stay with me. "Maybe, but I'm not going to let you drown under the weight of the world, Mari. Use me."

"Use you?"

"Yes." I nuzzled her cheek with mine, feeling her sigh at the touch. "I'll take some of it off your shoulders so you can breathe. Just tell me what's wrong."

"I can't stand him being the last one to touch me," she whispered. I leaned back to see tears lining her eyes, though I knew she wouldn't let them fall. "I hate it. I hate him and his soft touches and his fucking words. I can't get them out of my head, and I'm so... I just... I can't do this anymore, Dominic. I need it to stop."

Her little gasp killed me. This was Mari's version of begging for help, reaching out to us and praying we'd pull her from the depths. The side she was only showing because she trusted us, because she loved us.

Of course we'd pull her out. She was ours.

Our woman. Our love. Our queen.

We'd *always* pull her out.

Greyson and I looked at each other, and though I could see the wariness in him, he nodded, reaching for Mari's hand as he made himself comfortable close by.

I stroked Mari's hair back gently and kissed her lips with the softest graze. "Don't worry, *mariposa*. We'll fix it for you."

Chapter 12
Greyson

Dominic had Mari flipped in a second, her wrists shackled over her head with one of his hands.

Looking at him, I saw nothing of the Dominic I was used to. No jokes or flirting, no sweetness for Mari. Just cold, hard determination.

Dominic undid his pants just enough to pull out his cock, leaving the rest of his clothes on. Meanwhile, he tore off Mari's bra, ripping her pants down her thighs as he straddled her ass. Hell, he barely moved to get the fabric out of the way. He held her underneath him, thrusting his cock between her cheeks and grunting like an animal. Every movement carried with it an edge of violence that set off every instinct I had as he leaned down to bite her neck.

It wasn't a love bite. It was savage, and it tore a scream from Mari's throat.

I jerked forward on instinct, ready to pull her out, but Dominic snarled at me. *"Don't."*

"You're going to hurt her."

"Only because she needs it."

"You don't get to decide that!"

"Grey, *please*." When I looked at Mari, I saw pain on her face, but I saw pleasure too. Pleasure and relief. My heart raced, and I wasn't sure I could stay in the room. Dominic was going to mount her like an animal, rut her into the mat, and even if the thought made me hard, it felt too close to real violence for me to be comfortable. It felt like one wrong move would wreck her and us and everything, and I wasn't sure my nerves could take it.

"I'll tap out if it becomes too much, but I need this, Grey. I need it. You can go, but I'd like you to stay." Tears crept down Mari's cheeks, bright in the overhead lighting, and I knew in my gut that I had to stay. I had to witness. For her. For my *reina*.

I didn't have to tell Dominic I'd tear him to pieces if this fucked Mari up, he already knew, but I glared it in silence anyway. With a nod my way, Dominic refocused all his attention on Mari. He looked at her like she was his prey, and it was impossible to ignore when she preened under him. She rolled her hips along his cock until he was laughing under his breath.

"If you wanted my dick, you should've just asked for it, *mariposa*. Is that what you need? A little fucking to set you right?"

"No. I need more than that."

He dipped and bit her again. "Ask. Nicely."

She tilted her head so she could see both of us at the same time. "Will you fuck me, Dominic?"

He shoved a hand into her hair and hauled her head back to whisper in her ear, "You're going to regret that, *mariposa*."

Then he was slamming into Mari, grunting as she clawed at the floor.

Dominic was brutal as he fucked her into the mat, fingers

bruising and teeth tearing. Sniping and snarling at her the whole time. He didn't say a word, didn't kiss her, nothing. It was almost obscene watching him conquer her, fully clothed to her complete nakedness, but the forced vulnerability that came from her nudity was part of what she needed. Dominic claimed her with his body and used her how he wanted. If I couldn't see her hips jerking back into him or hear her soft groans and the way she chanted his name, I would've killed him on the spot.

Watching it was the most difficult thing I'd ever done.

With Mari trapped beneath him, I was tenser than ever, but I couldn't help getting hard. Seeing Mari writhe, seeing the pleasure she took from Dominic, was all I needed. Even if it wasn't me riding her, Mari was my kryptonite.

Their savagery went on for a while, with Mari skating the razor's edge of pleasure the whole time. She was babbling and desperate as she tried to take over from below, but Dominic wouldn't let her. Every time she got close to coming, he stopped. Not slowing or pulling out, just stopped with his hips snug against her ass, his cock buried deep inside her. It drove Mari nuts.

She was crying again, eyes glazed and mindless when Dominic thrust forward for the last time, groaning as he came. When he'd emptied himself inside her, he leaned back, smacked her ass hard, and shoved her away like she was just another fuck for him.

I ground my teeth at the rough treatment. It was disgraceful, disrespectful, but I'd keep my opinions to myself if it helped Mari. Then he spoke, and I almost shot him in his smug fucking face.

"Your turn, Grey."

My turn, like Mari was some hole for us to use. I whipped my head toward him and glared. "She's not our whore."

Dominic's eyes were vibrant, satisfied from his orgasm but

missing nothing. He looked just as arrogant as before, but there was amusement in his face that took some of the panic from me. "I didn't say she was and I don't expect you to treat her that way, but our little butterfly's wings have been broken. Fix them. It's what you do best."

It took a moment for his words to penetrate.

Fix Mari. I'd spent my whole life helping her, protecting her, healing her.

Fix her? Yeah, I could do that.

When I looked down at Mari, she was panting and pink-cheeked, obviously desperate as she ground her hips into the mat. Dominic hadn't let her come, and she hadn't even attempted to get up and do it herself. She was still firmly in the mindless pleasure zone he'd pushed her to.

"Greyson," she begged, reaching for me. "*Please.*"

This wasn't my Mari; this was someone else. Someone in limbo, desperate for air that only I could give her. Dominic was right. I had to fix her. Pretty sure I was the only one who could, now that Nate was gone.

Rolling her over, I took Dominic's place between her thighs. Her glazed eyes watched as I stripped down, needing skin-to-skin contact. I ignored Dominic, though I knew he was watching as closely as I had, and cradled her cheeks, brushing away the tear tracks with my thumbs. I kissed her so softly it almost hurt. "Are you sure?"

"Please," she panted against my lips, her body jerking into mine. "I need this."

"Anything for you," I whispered. "Anything."

I rolled my hips, rubbing my cock against the wetness of her pussy until I was soaked and slid inside her.

If I had any doubts about where I was meant to be in the world, all I had to do was fuck Mari to know that place was here. In her arms, her bed, her heart.

Wherever Mari went, I would follow.

"I love you," I whispered, not caring that Dominic could hear me. Like he'd known she needed to be taken like that, I knew how to put her to rights again. "I'm so proud of you."

My hands roamed her body, softly easing some of the ache he'd left her with. I kissed her bruises and bites, nipping here and there to give her my own, but I kept everything easy. My hands on her waist were loose, tempting her to roll her hips with me, writhe with me.

Part of putting her back together was reminding her that she had the power here.

We were her soldiers, her knights, ready and waiting for our mistress's call.

"I missed you," she whispered as she wrapped her arms around my neck, keeping our bodies tight together. A breath of relief tore from me, and I knew that whatever this was, it had worked.

This woman under me, gripping my ass and pulling me in? This was my Mari reborn.

"I missed you too."

Mari's orgasm rose, her body tightening around me, and I ached to let it pass by, to give her what she needed without anything else, but we weren't done.

She had to let go of Nate.

Her pussy clenched around me, and her broken sob was one of relief until I leaned in and whispered in her ear.

"I'm sorry, *reina*."

Suddenly, she was crying for another reason, the ugly sobs tearing a hole in my heart. She clung to me, her fingers digging crescents into my skin, but I didn't care. She tried to roll away, but my hips kept her still. At some point, she grabbed Dominic's hand, and between the two of us, we pinned her in place with nothing but the force of our love.

Mari's surrender was harder to watch without Dominic's savagery stealing my attention. It was all pain. Every twitch screamed that she was in agony, and everywhere we touched hurt like I could feel it. I took it, though. I took everything she gave me as she finally allowed herself to grieve what she'd lost. What we'd all lost.

Nate. Our family. A future.

Dominic lifted her wrist to his mouth, pressing his lips to her skin like he needed it to breathe, and I stayed inside her, not moving, just waiting. Keeping her close. Reminding her I was there and I wasn't going anywhere. Watching as she slowly let go and following her.

My chest ached as I went through my own healing in her arms. Nate was gone, and even though it killed me to lose the man I'd trusted my world to, there was nothing to do but accept it and rebuild.

I didn't know how long we stayed on the gym floor, with Mari's tears drying on her cheeks. My body ached from being so close to her and holding back, but it didn't matter. I wouldn't come. I couldn't. This wasn't about me. Mari needed this connection, a reminder that we were hers. Always.

I should've known she wouldn't let it go, though.

"Greyson." She arched into me, rubbing herself against me and making me groan. I was trying not to push her, needing her to tell me where to go from here. "Keep going. Remind me what I'm fighting for."

Fuck yes.

This, I could do. I could hold her, kiss her, pleasure her until she remembered who she was. Until she was put back together again. Then we'd handle everything as we always should have—together.

Dominic didn't let go of Mari as I started fucking her again, his other hand creeping between us to play with her clit as she moaned and thrashed beneath me. When I felt myself getting close—*so fucking close*—I tightened my hands on Mari's waist and let go, fucking her as hard as I needed to. Dominic took the hint and rolled her clit once more before he took it between his fingers and pinched. Mari exploded, her pussy clenching me so tight I had no choice but to come too.

White exploded over my vision, and it took ages for it to finally fade, letting me see the woman underneath me who looked at Dominic and me like we'd painted the sky with stars just for her. As I blinked away the last of the fog, we all burst into laughter. I didn't know what they were laughing about, but I couldn't help myself.

The glitter in her eyes felt like the sun peeking out from behind the clouds.

Mari was back. *Finally.*

I couldn't be happier.

I dropped another kiss to her lips and pulled out, stifling the groan that came with losing her. Dominic disappeared, coming back with a towel that he used to clean Mari up before bundling her against his chest. I pressed myself against her back, hand wrapped around her hip while he stroked her hair. And for the longest time, we just breathed together.

It was perfect.

"I saw him."

Dominic and I stiffened at her unexpected words, and Mari squeezed my hands idly as she kissed Dominic's chest.

"What happened?" I asked finally.

"He apologized. Said he didn't mean for this to happen. Told me he still loves me."

She laughed like it was a joke, but I knew Mari too well for that. She was still smarting from Nate's betrayal. Pretty sure she always would. "Do you believe him?"

Silence followed, and then, quietly, she whispered, "I don't know."

She wanted to, though. I knew, and when I looked up, I could see there was no doubt that Dominic did too.

What we were going to do about that, I wasn't so sure.

"I'm sorry for hiding from you."

"We get it," Dominic said, pushing her hair out of her face. "It sucked, but we understand."

She shook her head and burrowed into us. "I won't do it again."

"Yes, you will. It's how you process." I kissed her spine and shoulders, tightening my grip. "As long as you come back to us, it doesn't matter."

"Always."

I smiled at the happy sigh she gave as she wiggled to get comfortable between us.

"No more lies, though. I can't handle it again."

"No more lies," Dominic and I agreed.

But the secrets we carried between us labeled us frauds.

Chapter 13
Mari

With Nate's reveal, I'd left one person to simmer.

Derek, the poor fool, had been slowly losing his mind, looking over his shoulder as if the boogeyman was coming. He was right.

The Seattle morning was crisp and cold, perfect for a snatch-and-grab in public. People were too focused on their first cup of coffee and getting out of the rain to pay attention to a single work van and a screaming man.

"You can't do this to me! I haven't done anything. Please!" The ranting was immediate and jarring. A nod at Dominic had Derek's hands and feet bound, his mouth gagged.

Ah, blissful silence. If you ignored the grunting.

We took him to the mansion, mostly because I needed the Celestine to be free of Cash and Nate, but also because, while we had an interrogation room set up in our new home, I didn't want to use it yet. Not for this.

I wanted to christen it with someone bigger.

Dominic and Greyson hauled him inside, setting him up in the same chair we'd put his buddy in. It felt poetic to have them meet their ends in the same space, albeit separated by time. I busied myself with the instruments around us while they worked, trying to forget all about the last time we'd been here.

How Nate had disappeared and left someone else in his wake. How I'd had to bring him back from the brink.

Or had I? Was that a lie too? He'd looked haunted, but I knew better than to assume that Nate was anything but a good actor at this point.

Treacherous, lying Beckstrom bastard.

When I was finally ready to make my little friend squeal, I'd worked up a full head of steam and was beyond ready to go.

Too bad Derek wasn't interested in my sorts of games.

"Look, I heard Cash called him home. I'll give you whatever information you want."

Him. Nate.

Dominic and Greyson settled close by, the latter with his tablet out and ready for notes.

"Why would I believe you?" I asked, getting close enough to whisper. "You're a liar and a thief."

He panted in the chair, eyes wild as he tried to find an escape. "Because he was my contact. I did this for my family, I swear!"

"Tell me, and we'll see if I'm feeling lenient after."

Derek nodded over and over like a bobblehead. "I first met Cash when I was a teenager. My father introduced us."

"Your father, Marshall. Correct?"

Derek nodded. "Yeah. Yeah, that's him. He brought me to the

docks for my first day, and on the way home, he said he had a stop to make."

"Cash."

"Yeah. Before we got out, Dad told me to do whatever he said. When I asked why, he said *we protect our family*."

I looked at Grey, who flipped through his tablet quickly. "Two sisters, both younger."

"Three," Derek corrected quietly. "My old man had an affair after Molly, the second youngest, was born. They had a baby, though she stayed with her mom."

"And instead of threatening to reveal that child to your mother, Cash threatened to kill her?" Derek didn't even have to answer. I could read between the lines and see I was right. Pulling up a chair in front of him, I settled in for a long story. "Go on."

"Cash said he'd called the meeting to meet me."

"You, specifically?" Grey asked.

Derek nodded. "Said it was time to meet the new generation."

"Was Nate there?"

"Yeah, but he was younger than me." A teenager, if my math was correct. Had Nate been working for Cash his whole life? Derek continued, unaware of where my thoughts were leading. "After they asked me a bunch of questions, they beat my dad. Told me to remember this because it was my future if I said a word against him."

Or if he didn't do what they asked. "Tell me everything."

And he did.

Derek told me about Nate being in charge of pickups, about how he destroyed Derek's apartment as a "warning." He told me all about how they made the overages work and how Porter got involved. He gave me the names of the others, even though I already knew them. Strapped to a dirty chair in my basement, Derek spilled every secret he'd ever had. And the whole time, Dominic sat in witness and Greyson typed his little notes.

I knew it was coming; I expected every second of it, but I wasn't prepared for how much it hurt. Nate was deeply enmeshed in Cash's empire. Despite the fact that his brother was dangerous, he was the man's second. His go-to guy when he was home.

How did I reconcile that Nate with the one who'd stolen my heart?

Dominic not so carefully fed Derek some water, splashing half of it down his chest. The man had talked for hours and I knew he was dying of thirst, but he didn't complain.

I'd long since stopped interrogating him, instead letting him get it all off his chest. We all knew Derek was going to die, so who cared if I was a little kinder to him than others? He wasn't going to tell. He'd fallen into this shit because his father had forced his hand. He didn't know any other way. I understood it, even if it was the wrong choice. "Nate wasn't here the whole time, though. Right?"

"No, he left for the military after he graduated high school." He looked down at his legs, eyes growing unfocused. "When Nate was gone, Cash sent his other henchmen. Let's just say, I preferred his little brother."

"Why?" Dominic asked. He looked as relaxed as ever near the door, but the tightness in his jaw said he wasn't happy with what we'd heard.

"Because he has a soul."

"What makes you say that?" Grey's silence hadn't gone unnoticed.

"Before he left, he hid my sisters. All three of them."

I jerked my head up from where I'd been watching the floor, contemplating Derek's words. "What do you mean?"

"He got them out of town, living in Idaho."

He'd moved the sisters out of Cash's reach.

"Why did he do that?"

Derek shrugged. "Said he wished someone had done it for him."

Because Cash nearly killed him once, and anyone that unhinged wasn't stopping at one attempt. How many lives did Nate have? How many deaths had he escaped? Did it make a difference to me what he'd survived, when he'd thrown me to the wolves?

I wasn't sure, and it pissed me off. "You're singing his praises, but he threatened your family before. He beat your father. Hell, he probably beat you. Why say anything good about him?"

"Because we're human. We make mistakes. But I don't think our mistakes are the sum of our souls."

If he was going to get religious, I was leaving.

Dominic scoffed. "You find Jesus, Derek?"

"No. Just self-reflection. Happens when you know you're going to die."

Oh good. A pragmatist.

"This has to do with Nate, how?"

Derek sighed, trying to get comfortable in his bindings before giving up. "Not everything is black-and-white. I betrayed you for my family, even when I didn't want to. Yet I'm telling you everything I know now. I've made an effort to balance the scales. Nate hurt me because he had no choice, yet he protected my sisters when he didn't have to. Which shows his character more?"

"What else did you do to balance the scales?" I asked, trying not to let his words sink in.

Did Nate's kindness show his character more than his treachery? Could I forgive a liar if his reasons were sound? I didn't know. I could've understood the actions of a desperate man. It was the lying I struggled with and the blatant disrespect that bothered me.

Lies were just words people said to keep you warm and compliant. I didn't want manufactured friendship or love; I wanted honesty. I wanted something real.

Wasn't I worth the truth?

"I helped when I could," Derek said. "Gave money and volunteered."

"For the family," I corrected pointedly. "I don't give a fuck about your good deeds when those people aren't the ones you betrayed."

Derek swallowed, clearing his throat. "I slipped you tips, told you where Cash would be when he stopped by for one of his reminders."

I glanced at Grey, refusing to let the surprise show on my face. He didn't even have to look at his tablet to shake his head.

We hadn't gotten any tips. Not one in all the years I'd been in power.

"Who did you tell?" Because even if it was easier to believe Derek was lying, I didn't think he was. In fact, I'd bet a lot of money that he wasn't.

"I don't remember."

Okay, *now* he was lying.

"Derek," I warned softly. "If you start lying to me, this is going to have a much bloodier end."

"I'm already going to die," he said with a shrug. "At least my siblings will be safe when I go."

He was right. I wasn't going to touch his sisters. I was a murderer, but even I had standards. We kept asking, needing that answer, but he stayed resolutely silent. Nothing we did could pry the name from his lips.

That he was willing to die with his secret told me how much power that person really had. It terrified me.

Derek's end was messy, but quick. A gift for his willingness to spill Cash's secrets, even if he had to die for spilling mine. The bloody slash on his throat was more personal than a bullet to the head, a message to Cash and his people.

Death is coming.

Dominic was in charge of the body, which would be left somewhere public. What was the point in leaving a message if no one saw it?

Greyson kept pace as I headed to the connected wet room, stripping off my clothes and placing them in a bag for incineration. "Someone in the family is keeping secrets."

He leaned up against the wall, watching me even as his mind was whirling. "Seems like it."

I mulled it over as I washed the blood from my hair and skin.

Who had a reason to take me out? Who wanted me gone and was willing to undermine my authority to do it? Who wasn't happy with their position in the family?

Joaquin.

"Do you think the other uncles are in on it, or is he working alone?"

Grey's eyes were soft with a touch of pity I hated. "They've never worked separately before."

True. My capos were a unit and always had been.

"So, they all hid the tips coming in about Cash. Are we assuming they're working together?"

The idea of a Marcosa working with a Beckstrom was insane, but there were too many signs I couldn't ignore anymore.

How had so many of my people turned? How had Cash figured out the right buttons to push to keep them under his thumb? How had they hidden under my nose for so many years, not to mention my brother's and my father's before me?

They had help. They had an insider.

I had a rat.

Another one.

"Motherfuck." I rinsed myself off, stepping to the other side of the room where a small wardrobe sat behind a waterproof door. The old servants' quarters were small, barely big enough for me to lie down in if I wanted to, but they suited our purpose fine. Slipping a change of clothes on to the sound of Grey power-washing the wet room, I sighed.

Everywhere I looked, Cash had a handhold. He'd build an empire underneath mine, ready to shake the earth and topple us at any moment.

Was it even worth fighting for? Seattle was my legacy, my birthright, but at what cost? Could I keep us safe without endangering us more? Was it worth the fight?

It had to be.

Cash had taken my brother from me, my cousin. Nate. Even if I wanted to leave, I couldn't. Vengeance was mine, and a blood debt was owed.

Cash was going to die. There was no other way.

Knowing Grey would help Dominic when he was finished, I slipped out of the room and into the hallway, fully intending to leave the house, when a noise somewhere above startled me.

I had my gun in hand in seconds, my breathing slowing as I tried to figure out who the fuck was in my house.

The lights were off in the hallway, and even though I wanted to text the boys a warning, I didn't want to risk my vision in the dark. Not to mention, giving away my location.

Creeping slowly through the halls of the home I'd grown up in, I tried to keep myself level.

It's probably just one of the men coming to check on things.

But that didn't feel right, especially the farther I went. When I crested the stairs to see light spilling out from the library, I nearly swore. I didn't want to go in there. Didn't want to see the destruction I'd caused. I wasn't sure I could handle it yet. I might've been more grounded after last night, but that didn't mean I wanted to face my actions when I was still cracked and broken.

But I had to. I wouldn't let my weaknesses hurt my family again.

Gun at the ready, I pressed the door open slowly, ignoring the pristine floors in favor of the woman curled up in the reading chair. My sigh of relief was loud enough to snap Shara's eyes to mine.

"You're here?"

"I am," I said awkwardly, looking around. The library looked the same as it had before I'd come for the journals. Every book in place, everything put together. Not a single splinter on the floor. It was as if my tantrum never had happened.

Shara crooked an eyebrow, smirking as she took in the room too. "Dominic had it fixed last night. Said you took a sledgehammer to everything. You okay?"

"I didn't take a sledgehammer," I mumbled, shuffling over to drop onto the couch next to her chair. "I just...lost it."

If I was waiting for her to scream at me for destroying her beloved's favorite place or make fun of me for my lack of control, I'd be waiting for a long time.

Shara nodded, tossing a head of short curls out of the way. She must've gotten her braids taken out recently.

"What were you looking for?"

When I jerked, she gave me a *come on* look. "You don't come in here. Ever. Hell, I don't even come here often. This place is practically a tomb, a memorial to Antoni. It's fine," she said, waving me away when I tried to disagree. "It's good for us to have a place, but we both know you weren't in here for some light reading. What did you want?"

"The journals."

"And the destruction was because you didn't find them." She stared into the fireplace, which was empty and cold, lost in her own thoughts. "Who do you think has them?"

"Nate."

Shara hummed, not agreeing but not disagreeing either. "Maybe. Were they all gone?"

"Every single one."

"Not every one." Digging in her purse, she pulled out a black hardbound book.

A journal.

"How?"

"I thought it was Antoni's, but it's not. As soon as I realized that, I stopped reading, but it didn't feel safe to leave it at my place."

"How long have you been carrying it?"

"A while." She shrugged, but she looked embarrassed. "I didn't know how to explain that I'd been reading things I shouldn't have, and then when shit went south with Cash and Nate, I just—"

Worried. She was worried that I was going to go off the deep end and kill her, brand her a traitor, kick her out. Fuck, I was doing this all wrong. "I'm sorry."

"Don't be," she said fiercely. "The people you've trusted have been lying to you, deceiving you. You're allowed to be jumpy."

"You didn't bring it to me because you were scared how I'd react. That's not okay."

"It's also not your problem. My feelings aren't yours to fix, Mari. But we're here now. I'm just sorry it took so long."

"Me too, and I'm sorry about the library."

She gazed around the room, remembered love softening her expression. "Don't be. I think it's time we both moved on.

Holding his memory here does nothing but keep us rooted in our grief. It's time, Mari."

Maybe it was. I could have my vengeance without falling victim to my grief. I could rid my city of Cash with a level head.

I could survive this.

I just had to find the right path forward.

Chapter 14
Mari

There was nothing nefarious about the journal, nothing dastardly or dangerous. It was words on a page. The entire notebook was innocuous, a black hardbound book with nothing to indicate what it was. Normal.

Yet I couldn't open it.

I stared at it on my desk, wondering what secrets it held inside. Would it give me everything I needed to end this war, or was it another waste of time? The uncertainty kept me frozen, though that wasn't the only reason.

I wasn't sure what to do if it *did* contain everything we needed to know. What would it feel like to have all the ammunition to get rid of Cash at my fingertips? It was almost too good to be true, and my bruised heart—and ego—wasn't sure it could handle that.

A knock at the door pulled me away from my one-sided stare

down. I'd taken up working in my office again, spending my days just down the hall from the conference room where Cash had obliterated my life. Not sure if it was self-flagellation or my need to keep people out of my home. The Celestine was safe, and I wasn't planning on letting another snake inside.

I found Grey peeking his head into the room, glancing between me and the journal, the tiniest wrinkle forming between his brows before he smoothed it out again. "Ronnie's here." I stuffed the journal into a drawer—out of sight, out of mind—as he rounded the desk to give me a bruising kiss, his hand tight at the back of my neck. It was possessive and controlling in all the ways I craved, and when he pulled away, I was breathless.

"You staying?" I panted.

He hummed under his breath, and I brought him back down to me, reveling in how good it felt to touch him again. The groan at the back of my throat was low and desperate, and he leaned into it and me, giving me everything I needed. Worshiping my mouth like he did my body. I loved it.

When the kiss was over, he stayed in my space to whisper against my lips, "Always."

It was about more than the meeting with Ronnie; Grey was giving me reassurance. He was still here, despite my being a less-than-stellar partner lately. He was with me, no matter what, and I so fucking needed that.

I smiled and held on to his forearms because they were close and I wanted that connection. "Dominic?"

"Stayed home to watch Joaquin."

The clench in my chest said there was more to it, but I didn't ask. Dominic had tried to bring the situation to me, and I'd shut him down. Now, I had to trust that the boys knew what they were doing. That they were making moves to help, not hurt. If I started questioning their every move, Nate would win, and I couldn't let him ruin us too.

They aren't him.

I gave Grey another kiss, though we both knew I was on edge about the situation with my uncle, then sat back. "Let's get this over with."

Greyson crossed the room and let in our guest.

Veronica LaRue looked every bit as poised and polished as usual. Hair sleek and pulled back, clothes perfect, lipstick on, but something about her seemed off. I stared longer until I noticed the blue shadows under her eyes that concealer didn't quite cover and the way the lipstick clung to her dry, bitten lips. She was anxious about what she'd found, which was highlighted when she refused to look at me like she normally would, preferring to stare out the window at midday Seattle.

"How're things going, Ronnie?" I asked carefully, finding Grey watching her just as closely as I did.

"They're...okay."

"Tell me." Because there was definitely something to tell. "Is it the audit?"

"That hasn't been fun, but no. It's the city." When neither of us commented, she continued. "People are getting restless. The Aces are meeting with your people in broad daylight and knocking down doors they shouldn't be. They're making a stand, and it's putting the security of your power in question."

"If you're worried, why don't you get out of town for a while?" Grey asked.

Ronnie snorted, turning to us with fire and resignation in her eyes. "No. If I'm going to call this my city, I'm going to stay through the growing pains."

Knowing she was loyal was one thing, but seeing it firsthand really hit me. Ronnie loved Seattle like I did, and she trusted me with it. She trusted me to fix things and to make them better. She trusted me to get us on the right track again. It bolstered me as much as having my men at my back did.

"It won't be like this forever," I promised.

"Oh, I know. You'll put that asshole's head on a platter. I'm just...wary, I guess."

"It's not a bad thing to be right now. Vigilance is a way of life for all of us at the moment, but let us know if you need anything else. We won't leave you alone, Ronnie."

She smiled in thanks, and I knew she was done talking when she moved to the small table I'd pulled over for her computer. Ronnie preferred to project things onto the wall, so while she set up her gear, Greyson closed the blinds and locked the doors. When we were ready, she took a fortifying breath and looked me dead in the eyes.

"We found the first deposit."

She clicked on her screen, and there it was. The beginning of Cash's plan.

The date hit me square in the chest, digging its way into my brain until I wasn't sure I could fully breathe.

July. *Twenty goddamn years ago.*

Two decades, Cash had his hands in my business—my father's business, Antoni's business. Beyond being fucking annoying, the implications were insane. The Marcosa empire had had more than one stream of income fall by the wayside as we expanded and grew. Had Cash been involved in those too? How many of our people were *really* ours? Could anyone be trusted? Ronnie went over everything in such excruciating detail that we had to order lunch, and by the end of it, my eyes were crossing. Cash had stolen millions of dollars from us and used those funds to finance our destruction. It was poetic in a way, and if I hadn't been on the receiving end of his bullshit, I would've applauded the psychotic bastard.

But I was, and I didn't.

After Grey and I had exhausted every brain cell we could to get a deeper understanding of the scope of Cash's treachery, we called the meeting to a halt. Ronnie packed up her things, pausing just before she got to the door. Her shoulders bunched under her shirt, and I could tell she was warring with something in her head.

"What is it?"

Another deep breath and she turned to me. "We've been monitoring the list of people we initially gave you, and although no one else agrees, I think there are more names to add."

I felt Grey's attention shift, his focus lasered in on every word out of her mouth. "Why do you say that?"

"Honestly, it's a gut feeling. These people are still using their log-ins, though more or less than they did before. Never at the same frequency. Most of them have taken last-minute leaves of absences, only to come back immediately after, like nothing happened. They haven't been seen in public in months, and some of their families haven't been seen in twice as long. It's just...odd."

Grey and I glanced at each other, both frowning. Cash didn't value human life, and he didn't care about casualties. Anyone who stood in the way of his goal was a justified loss, but was he far enough gone that he'd take out entire families? Kids? I had no fucking clue, and the possibilities made my stomach cramp.

"We'll look into it," I promised as Grey told her where to send the information and the names. We'd have Moore's team look over things and let us know if her concerns were founded. If not, no harm, no foul. If they were, then we had a problem. I couldn't leave families under my protection to suffer.

I wouldn't.

Ronnie's trust was absolute, so with a nod to me and a wave to Grey, she was gone.

As the door shut, I swiveled toward the windows, bouncing my leg as I thought. She had given us so much information that it was hard to focus on any one piece of it, but one thing had been digging at my brain throughout the meeting. "Why would he start then?"

It'd been bothering me since Ronnie had shown us the first deposit. Twenty years ago, Cash was close to my father. I knew Mario like I knew myself, and he rewarded people like Cash, the ones who were devoted to the empire. Hell, he had likely been months away from being promoted to second-in-command. What caused him to defect? To steal product and fake his own disappearance. Why sever ties when he was close to power? Hell, he could've killed my father and uncles and been awarded the seat because my brother was too young to take it. He could've had it all.

So why fight like this?

"What was going on twenty years ago?"

"Our parents."

My head snapped up as Dominic sauntered into the room, flopped into the chair at my side, and snuck his hand on my leg. He squeezed gently, forcing my absent-minded jiggling to stop. Two days ago, I would've squirmed at the feel of anyone's skin on mine, but after last night, it felt good. Reassuring. Greyson must've realized the same thing because he took the chair on my other side and did the same. I leaned into it, letting them ground me. It felt right.

When Cash dropped his bomb, I'd needed time to process Nate's treachery alone. I was too shattered to watch myself and too aware to watch them fret over me. I'd needed space, and now that I'd had it and was not good, but *better*, I was going to fall into them. Greyson and Dominic were my home, my center. I trusted them without reservation, and I was going to prove it.

I squeezed both their hands in gratitude and turned back to Dominic. "What about our parents?"

"That's around the time they got married."

And divorced.

Mario and Lucia Ricci had lasted ten days before my father pulled the plug. He'd never explained why, and I hadn't asked, too heartbroken at Dominic disappearing back to Chicago overnight. Even though we'd kept in touch, it wasn't the same, and after ten years, we stopped reaching out even occasionally. I hadn't spoken to him in a decade before he'd waltzed into my home to take over as underboss.

"You think that's relevant?" Greyson asked.

"Probably not, but we can't discount anything." Dominic seemed distracted, and I ran my nails over his hand to pull him out of it. He smiled and leaned in for a kiss. "How're you feeling today, *mariposa*?"

"Much better."

Two words changed the atmosphere of the room, and I didn't even mind it. I needed a break from politicking and trying to outthink a man who'd been working on this plan my whole life.

"Oh really? So you're not interested in a repeat?" Grey slid his hand up my thigh, fingers getting very close to my panties.

I spread my legs until I had to hook one of them over his thigh. "Maybe not an *exact* repeat, but I could certainly use some attention."

With a deadly smirk, Greyson cupped my pussy, easily sinking two fingers inside. On my other side, Dominic trailed his lips over my neck and shoulder and slid his fingers under the waistband of my skirt to play with my clit. The dual sensations made me shudder.

I leaned into Dominic, talking into his mouth as he bent to kiss me again. "Plus, I'm not sure we ever christened this office."

The boys looked at each other with wicked grins, and then it was on. Grey slid to his knees under my desk, and Dominic took my lips, swallowing my screams.

By the time we left the room, it was past dinnertime, and we were all starved.

*** * ***

The journal was in my bag, taunting me again as I poured a glass of wine and waited for Aislynn to come over, but I ignored it. Tonight wasn't about history and the future; it was about my friend. With things getting heated in the city, Cameron had been out more, following Joaquin and the other uncles to make sure they weren't trying to plan something that would get us all buried. Normally, it would've been fine, but I didn't like leaving Ash alone when Cash had already singled her out as a target.

Better to have her under my roof where I could protect her myself. When the knock came, I was ready to put everything aside and just exist with my friend, but it wasn't Ash. "Moore?"

"Got a package for you." He handed me the massive manila envelope with a grimace. I took it gingerly, knowing it had been checked at least three times between the bottom floor and here, but I didn't trust it. Cash seemed like the type to send bombs in the mail or peel the skin off an ally and have it tacked up like some kind of abstract painting. Considering everything going on, I very much didn't want the psycho's gift until Moore said, "My guy came through."

Not Cash, then. I looked down again and realized this was it. Nate's file. His *real* file. Everything there was to know about Nathaniel Beckstrom was inside this plain envelope.

And I thought the journal was a struggle to open.

"How much did he charge us?" I asked, tucking the envelope under my arm like I could hide its existence.

"A boatload," Moore said with an irritated eye roll. He didn't like people taking advantage of me, but I had a boatload of money. Generational wealth meant cash was never something I had to worry about, and I was grateful for it.

I waved off Moore's frustration, directing him to Greyson for payment if it hadn't already been taken care of. The ding of the elevator brought our attention snapping around to find Aislynn leaning against the back wall, smiling at her phone. For a moment, she seemed peaceful and free, a little naughty too. Like she was sexting her husband before she went home to rock his world.

The reminder that her husband was my cousin made me wince, but friendship won over family in this case, so I'd soldier on if she wanted to tell me all about what she was saying to Cameron.

Gross.

Then she looked up, and that happiness vanished. Well, shit. "What happened?"

"Got the intel back." I lifted my shoulder like it didn't matter, and her brows furrowed. Her eyes rocked between Moore and me until they firmed up, her shoulders straightening, and she made up her mind about something.

"Mine too. You get a pen, and I'll get the wine." She stomped past us and into the suite. Even though I already had an almost-empty bottle on the table, I decided to accept the offering. The last thing I wanted was to read the truth fully sober.

"Let me know if you need anything," Moore said quietly as I went to shut the door.

"I'm good, thanks."

After a quick stop to grab notepads and a handful of pens, I plopped onto the couch. Every part of me screamed to do this alone, but the part of me that remembered waking up with Dominic's head on my chest and Greyson curled around my back didn't want seclusion anymore. She wanted company. Friend-ship. Commiseration.

She wanted Aislynn.

So I sat down and drained my glass, holding it up for a refill before I'd even swallowed. "Keep 'em coming."

"Hear, hear," she muttered, topping both of us off. "Ready?"

"Fuck no."

"Yeah. Me either." Her look was one of pure love and devotion to our friendship, and I had to snatch up the pages to avoid telling her I loved her. If I started weeping, I'd never stop, and we had shit to do. We shuffled closer together and began. Ash had the files from her sources pulled up on her phone, and I had Gilded's employment records pulled up on mine. Together, we cross-checked each bit of information we found, writing notes on the notepads—sometimes directly on the sheets, too—with any discrepancies we found. Each page ended up on the coffee table so we could sort through it to double-check something as it came later.

When we were done, we had a much better view of who I'd let into our lives, though I wasn't sure how I felt about it.

Nathaniel Beckstrom, twenty-eight-year-old Seattle native. Younger brother of Cassius Beckstrom, mother unknown. Only child of Marjorie Black and Alec "Ace" Beckstrom. According to the files, Nate had told the truth about Marjorie being in an assisted living facility and having early-onset Alzheimer's. According to everyone, she'd been there for a while and wasn't going to leave. There was almost no mention of the father beyond his name, though I understood why Cash called his group the Aces now.

Between the ages of five and eighteen, when he'd left for basic training, Nate had ended up in the ER at least four times a year, yet CPS never removed him from his home. Probably because the danger didn't live there. The fact that he'd even been allowed to join the military at all was a surprise, considering how many *almost* arrests he had. Almost, because, though he'd been brought in dozens of times for questioning about this or that, he'd never been formally charged. I had to think that his technically clean record had everything to do with his brother, though I didn't understand why he'd left for the military when he was sitting pretty in the Aces.

I needed out of Seattle, and the military was the only way. I was just happy to be free.

That was what Nate had told me when I'd originally asked why he'd joined. I hadn't thought much of it before, but was his freedom granted by leaving the city or leaving Cash? Did he even *want* to be an Ace, or was he stuck as one in some form of fucked-up legacy situation?

Would it matter either way?

Don't put unrealistic expectations on a liar, Mari. Mental scolding done, I forced myself to get back to work.

Nate's military file was incredibly redacted, but from what we could tell, he *had* been a merc. His PTSD and the loss of his team were clear in the write-ups, too. He had more commendations than I'd ever seen in a military file, and I'd looked through my fair share. The best security came from a military background like Moore's. Everything else was exactly what Nate had told me. Hell, even his address and car were the same on all the paperwork, though he'd used his mother's last name.

Yet it all felt like bullshit.

As I drank the last of my wine, I silently mulled over everything we'd found, as if I could make it make sense the longer I did. There was so much information, and almost none of it was new. What the hell did that mean, and what was I going to do about it?

I glared out the window until Ash cleared her throat. "He didn't lie about much."

"Is it enough, though?" He might have been as truthful as he could, but he'd kept the most important thing to himself.

If Cash were any other brother, Nate's omission probably wouldn't have mattered. I'd have been upset, but I wouldn't have shut him out for having family he hated. But he wasn't. Cash was the man hell-bent on destroying my empire and me with it, and Nate was helping him. Nate, who had inserted himself into my life and the planning to keep my people safe, all while being an Ace.

It was too much.

Taking a sip from my glass poured from the second—or was it third?—bottle of wine, I pushed myself off the couch. I needed to move and take a second to think about something else. "How're things with Cameron?"

Angel that she was, Ash took my redirection in stride, looking down at her lap with a faint blush. "I think I love him."

I stopped, turning back to her with an unexpected grin taking over. "Really?"

Ash hadn't dated seriously since we were teenagers, learning the hard way the lengths people would go to for power. Her walls were high and her wounds were deep, and Cameron... My cousin wasn't interested in settling down for forever. He'd seen too much, done too much, to ever hope for happily ever after. At least, that'd been the case for a long time. Maybe things had changed. I mean, he'd been lighter since he married Aislynn. Happier, though I was sure some of the bounce in his step was from arguing with her.

I'd hoped the two could be friends, but falling in love? It felt like a pipe dream. Even if I was apprehensive about how fast she'd fallen, I wasn't going to look a gift horse in the mouth.

She smiled again, picking at her jeans while she spoke. "I don't know how he feels, but he's so sweet to me. Thoughtful and charming, too. He always warms up my blankets before we go to bed because I get cold, and he makes sure the house is warm enough for me even though he's sweating his balls off. He sends flowers and coffee, orders my favorite takeout when he knows he'll be out. Even though he hasn't been home as much, he's been so good about making sure I know I'm cared for. It's hard not to fall in love with that."

"I'm so glad to hear that." I honestly was. I couldn't imagine two better people to spend their lives together, and the fact that they'd fallen in love was everything I'd been desperately in need of. My sad, aching heart healed a little at Ash's happy smile.

Then, like she hadn't just given me her soul, she went for the kill. "How are *you* doing with everything?"

Redirection over, apparently. "I'm...better."

The night with the boys had helped tremendously, and waking surrounded by them made me feel more stable than I'd been in days. Leaning on them, even when I didn't want to, would help me work through this, and eventually, I'd heal. Though, I'd always have the scars to prove Nate existed and to remind me what he'd done, but I could handle that. With Dominic and Greyson at my side, I could handle anything.

Ash watched me carefully over her glass, like she could peel me apart and see my insides. The longer she did, the softer her face became until she was veering dangerously close to pity. When I glared at her, she didn't even flinch. "You need closure."

"Wouldn't you?"

It was a genuine question. I hadn't done relationships before the guys. When I wanted or needed sex, I found a willing partner to explore that with, and after our time together ran its course, we went our separate ways. No messy feelings needed. I had no understanding of how to deal with a breakup of this caliber, and even though she'd been off the dating wagon for a while, Aislynn had a better grip on what to do.

She nodded decisively. "Absolutely. That's why I usually do goodbye sex. It ends all the messy feelings and acts like a kick-start to a new chapter. You've never had to do that."

The words felt like a punch to the chest, and Ash winced. "I didn't mean that. Fuck, I'm sorry."

Because I had *had* goodbye sex before. I just hadn't been aware that was what it was.

I'll never stop loving you.

I squeezed her hand so she knew I wasn't mad, even if it was a little hard to breathe. Trying to fix things, Ash launched into a tale one of her spies had told her about O'Bannon and his new obsession with pigs, but her words rolled around in my mind.

What would it be like if I'd gotten the chance to say goodbye to Nate in my own way, if I hadn't had that taken from me? Would it have healed me? Would this hole in my chest be smaller?

Would it cleanse him from my soul?

"I wish I'd had goodbye sex," I said when her story ended and we were sitting in comfortable silence. The admission hung in the air for a moment. Eventually, Ash hummed in her throat as we stared out the window at the city we loved.

"Too bad there's no way to make that happen this time."

"Yeah," I croaked, taking a sip of my wine. "Too bad."

Chapter 15
Mari

Having extensive security was great until you needed to sneak out of the house. I waited until Greyson and Dominic were both out—which was almost impossible since Grey's habit of watching me sleep hadn't disappeared—before sneaking into the hall and changing.

The spare gun under the coffee bar went into my holster since I couldn't risk bringing my usual one. The moment I went near it, both my men would've been on red alert, and I couldn't have that.

Getting out of the building was an ordeal itself, and I made notes to upgrade a few areas that weren't technically blind spots but certainly didn't add any protection to us. Moore and Tennessee would have a fit, but they could get in line because Dominic was going to tan my ass while Greyson watched.

Still, I was alone, and that was what mattered. It wasn't a

good idea, but I couldn't have company for this. I needed to see this through so I could move on. I *had* to move on.

The drive across town was quick since no one else was out at the witching hour. Just me, the night sky, and a million regrets that felt like lead balloons.

By the time I pulled up to the address in Nate's employment file, I wasn't sure how to feel.

Sunshine Estates was anything but sunny. The once-white buildings were gray with grime and barely standing, with most walls and windows sporting more cracks than stone. The sidewalk was rubble, the bushes were scraggly and sharp, and the only living greenery was grass that I couldn't guarantee wasn't painted to look better. And that was just the outside.

The hallways were a mess, the stair railings so bad they practically waved in the breeze, and by the time I broke in to Nate's apartment, I was fairly certain I was going to need a tetanus shot.

The part of me that still loved Nate—because a week and an orgy or two wasn't enough time to get over something like that— was horrified that he'd lived there. I understood that for some people, it was the only option, and I understood as much as I hated that for them. But Nate had more than enough money for something better. Was the apartment a way to get in with me? To make me feel sorry for him and invite him to my place, or was it that Cash didn't want to spend money where he didn't need to? Or was it something else entirely?

I was just happy to be free.

Checking the hallway three times, I knelt in front of apartment 4-B and got to work on the lock. It clicked in no time, and even though I felt a sliver of unease, I pushed the door open. Backup would've been a smarter plan, especially if it meant letting someone else sweep the place for booby traps or hiding exboyfriends, but I didn't have time. I needed to get back to the Celestine before the boys woke up.

So, I pulled my gun, stepped inside, and shut the door behind me. *All right, Beckstrom. Let's see what you got.*

My first time through the apartment, I cleared each of the rooms, on the lookout for weapons, cameras, or alarms. Though I wasn't sure if Nate would actually kill me, I wasn't willing to risk dying in this cesspool of a building because of my gut. When I came up with nothing, I pulled out a flashlight and went back through the place, taking my time. I didn't want anyone interrupting me until I was through.

Every nook and cranny were checked, every floorboard tapped just in case, but I found nothing interesting inside. The apartment was Spartan at best, minimalist in a way that showed it was a place to sleep, not a home. Nothing inside those walls was irreplaceable, and I wondered if that was something the military had taught Nate or if it was something he'd learned from Cash.

The place seemed lonely. Two sets of dishes, though it seemed like that was only so he didn't have to do dishes as often. Only one chair at the dining table, and it was so scratched and torn I wasn't sure it would hold even my weight. The couch was lumpy from use, but not by Nate. The two different-sized indents said he'd bought it used and never made his mark.

That was all the man's life added up to. A few plates and a bed that looked as uncomfortable as everything else inside those four walls. There wasn't a single picture on the walls or tables, no color at all. It was bland and gray. Boring. It was all so *sad.*

There has to be more.

I went back to looking, unable to leave well enough alone, even knowing my window of solitude was likely ending. There was food in the fridge that said Nate still came over occasionally, so I needed to finish up and leave.

I was kneeling on the floor beside his bed, chest to the floor to make sure he wasn't hiding anything underneath, when a throat cleared.

Instinct had me rolling before I'd even registered it, a gun in my hand before my back hit the hardwood. With the lights off, I couldn't see his face clearly, but I knew who it was. I could feel it in my bones. His words only solidified it.

"What're you doing here, angel?"

I stayed where I was, feet planted and gun aimed, even though the position was decidedly vulnerable. I hated it, but I hated the idea of trying to get up while possibly losing my shot at him even more.

"Wanted to see what else you lied about."

He sighed, leaning farther into the wall, hands flat against the plaster like he was trying to tell me he wasn't dangerous. I wasn't an idiot. Men didn't need weapons to be dangerous, and now that I was in a room with Nate again, he felt decidedly like a threat. "I didn't lie about everything."

Even knowing that for myself now, I didn't believe him. I just couldn't. Words didn't mean shit anymore, his actions did, and he'd done nothing but be dishonest.

I hated him for how much that loss of trust hurt.

Saying nothing, I waited him out. Even though I'd been raised to be a bargaining chip for my mafia husband, I'd worked my ass off to be dangerous in my own right. Part of that was knowing my limits. I could hold my gun for a long-ass time if I had to, but it would turn my arms into useless noodles. I had to get out of the apartment before it came to that.

As I was creating and discarding plans in my head, Nate spoke. "You shouldn't be out alone."

Instead of rolling my eyes like I wanted to, I weighed the pros and cons of getting up and decided they were stacked firmly in my favor. Keeping my gaze glued to Nate, I carefully stood. My gun never wavered, my chin never dropped, and my hands were steady. I just couldn't lie there like a flipped turtle while we talked. I had to be on my own two feet. "Like you care."

"I do. I'm trying to protect you."

What the fuck did that mean? "Well, don't. I don't want it."

"What if *I* do?" He paused, and even in the dimness from the streetlight outside, I saw the fire in his eyes. The burning. When he spoke, his voice was wrecked. "I can't lose you, angel."

"You already did." It was instinct. Hurt lashing out to hurt someone else. Poison finding a new host. I wanted to infect Nate with whatever the fuck I had inside me so I wasn't dying alone. He started this, but I needed to finish it.

And I did. He flinched like I wanted, but I found no satisfaction in it, and that made things worse than ever.

The realization that I was in an apartment with Nate, alone and across the city from my closest allies, made my heart pound. *What a fucking idiot.*

"This was a mistake." I stepped toward the door, but Nate matched me, keeping himself between me and my exit.

"Don't go. Let's just...talk."

"There's nothing to talk about, Nate. You're a liar and a fraud. You let me love you, and it was all a lie."

"It wasn't a lie," he growled, frustration evident in his face, which I could barely look at.

You wanted closure, Mari. Close it up. Taking a deep breath, I did just that. What happened before—the kiss, the stalking—it couldn't happen again. Nate was my past, and I had to leave him there or my future was fucked. So even if I wanted him to be telling the truth, I couldn't wait around to find out. This needed to end. "Whatever it is you think you're saving, it's gone, Nate. Let it go. Let *me* go."

A moment passed in which I was sure he'd do it, that he'd admit he was wrong and walk away. It would've been the easier option for him. He could've wiped his hands clean and found himself in the arms of another woman in seconds. Fighting for a relationship when both parties were interested in keeping it going was hard enough, but fighting when the other person was actively trying to sabotage you? That was a fool's errand. Better to cut your losses and start over with someone new.

Which was exactly why I wasn't expecting Nate to cross the floor, steps quick despite their heaviness. I didn't expect him to toss my gun onto the bed before I realized he was reaching for it and shove me against the wall. I wasn't expecting him to pin me with his hips while he ravished my mouth.

Or maybe I was.

Maybe all of Ash's talk about closure sex had addled my brain.

Nate nipped at my lips, forcing his way into my mouth with his tongue and between my thighs with one of his legs until he was touching me everywhere. One of his hands gripped my hair, pulling my head back so all I saw was him. The rumble of his voice vibrated through my chest, and I was too stunned by what he said to think about moving. "No."

"What?" I was dazed and drunk on his touch as he peeled off my shirt and the feel of his thigh pressing my jeans against my clit. I wanted to come. I wanted to fuck the anger out of my body so that I could move on. The boys had done so much to help me, but a hate fuck was a good way to finish what they'd started. I'd wipe my memory of Nate Beckstrom and move forward like he'd never existed.

As if he knew what I was thinking, he pressed forward until we were sharing breaths. "What we had isn't gone, and I didn't lose you. You're still right here, about to come for me."

"Shut up." I dug my fingers into his arms, where they'd somehow ended up in the shuffle, and even though he winced, I felt his cock harden against me. I could've done more damage, could've put him on his knees, but fuck me, I needed this. I did, and I wasn't ashamed to say it—though I wasn't relishing explaining it to my partners later.

"No." Nate nipped me again, bruising me for all the world to see like I was still his. The thought pissed me off enough that I sank my teeth into his neck in return and left the perfect imprint of my teeth on him.

I tried not to think of how satisfying it was to see them.

"That's right, baby. Show everyone whose man I am."

"Not mine."

The spank to my outer thigh didn't hurt, but I yelped anyway. Mostly because I wasn't expecting it, though the sting did feel nice and glowy. "Always yours," Nate corrected. "Now ride my thigh."

He moved his hand to my hip, encouraging me to grind against him. I knew I shouldn't, knew it was a bad fucking idea, but I couldn't stop myself. Maybe that was why the orgasm came quickly. While Nate tried his damnedest to mark his territory, I detonated with his name in my mouth.

He had my jeans off and my body hauled into his arms in seconds. His warm cock slid through my arousal, and I locked up.

"Condom."

Nate froze, his hands clenching at my ass. "I haven't been with anyone else."

"I don't care. You want to fuck me, you use a condom."

He looked like he was about to punch a hole in the wall. "But we didn't—"

We'd stopped using condoms almost immediately after we'd become official. We'd both gotten tested, along with Dominic and Greyson, and since the relationships were closed and I was on birth control, it didn't seem necessary. But that was when I trusted Nate, when I was honored to have that type of intimate connection. Now, it was too close, and I just couldn't do it. "If you want to fuck me at all, I suggest you not finish that sentence. Put on a rubber, or get off me."

The standoff was brief, but I could feel Nate's agitation in every move he made. Though, I didn't know if he was pissed at me or himself. Still, the second he put it on, I felt better, and he noticed it. It might've been a thin barrier, but it was a distance I needed. He hauled me up into his arms, gentle despite the ticking in his jaw.

"Are you sure about this?"

No, not even remotely. All I could do was hope that I ended the night a little less broken, instead of bleeding out on the floor from yet another Beckstrom. "Fuck me, Nate."

"I'm not going to fuck you," he said softly. "I'm going to love you."

Please don't.

I kept my eyes on his as he slid inside me, that familiar warmth and weight of him making my pussy clench. He hissed and pulled out, keeping the pace slow and even. There was a moment when I debated telling him to go harder, but one look at his face told me he knew what I wanted and just refused to give it to me.

It wasn't until he started talking that I realized why he was doing it.

"I'm sorry."

"Don't," I snapped even as my back arched for him. I could handle the sex and the words if they were separate, but together, it was too much.

Nate ghosted his lips over my cheek. "I made a mistake."

"Stop." *Stop talking. Stop fighting this. Let me go.*

"No. I'm going to fix this." He drove deeper and harder into my body, hands holding their fill of my ass as he pulled a groan from my chest. "I'm going to fix this. I'm going to make it up to you."

"No talking."

"Angel."

Yanking his hair, I pulled his lips to mine, silencing him with a kiss while I took over rolling my hips. I fucked him hard and fast, letting his arms and the wall do all the work to keep me stable. "Fuck me, Nate. I don't want to talk."

"Later." When I nodded reluctantly, because I wasn't planning on hashing anything out, he took my mouth and unleashed himself on me. Nate fucked like he had something to prove, and hell, maybe he did, but I wasn't sure what message I was supposed to be getting.

I love you? I miss you? I'm sorry?

No part of me trusted a word out of his mouth, which made our last time together a specific type of torture because I couldn't silence the voice inside myself that wanted to believe him.

I wanted his apologies. I wanted it to heal. I wanted Nate.

But I wanted to survive more. The whole thing was bittersweet and painful, like eating the best dessert you'd ever tasted, only to find out you're allergic after the last bite. My heart pounded, and my chest was tight. I was close to crying at the same time as I was racing toward orgasm, because even though he was a shitty person and a liar of a boyfriend, Nate was very good at giving my body what it wanted. "Come for me, angel. Let me feel you again."

Then I was coming. That beautiful, bone-deep euphoria swept my body, and I let the tidal wave take me, knowing he'd be right behind. And he was. Nate powered into me, his arms holding me tight, reminding me that I wouldn't fall. He wouldn't let me.

Nate panted against my neck as he found his own release, and it felt right having us joined like that one final time.

The sex felt the same as always with Nate, like I was coming for him and coming home. It felt like I'd spent my whole life waiting to be understood and cared for and fucked like that.

But this was an interlude, not reality. Nate and I weren't real. We were a figment of my imagination, the result of a game played by the brother of a psychopath. There was no future here, and there never would be.

We were enemies, even when I hadn't realized it.

The second I caught my breath, I tapped Nate's hands, needing space. Needing distance. Needing away from *him*.

Suddenly, that condom didn't seem like enough.

"Mari—"

"*Down*, Nate."

I felt his eyes on me, even as I kept mine planted firmly on the wall over his shoulder and the door to the room. Now that our moment was over, I needed to go. It had been a mistake to come when anyone could've walked into the room while we were busy. I could've died because I couldn't just let Nate go.

Stupid.

Nate took a step back from the wall, bringing me with him, and I wondered if I'd have to fight him to get down. Then he dropped my legs one at a time, keeping his hands close to make sure I was stable before pulling away.

"Hand me that?" I asked, pointing to the bra on his bed. I could get it myself, but some sick part of me needed him to take the first step. He grabbed it quickly, squeezing it in his hands before lifting it toward me. I reached for it, but he didn't let go until I met his eyes.

I saw a fragility there that I didn't like, a vulnerability that felt too much like the hole carved in my chest for comfort.

"What was that?" His voice was raspy in that way that came from really good sex, and I forced myself to ignore it as I pulled on the bra and then my jeans so he couldn't see how it affected me.

"That was goodbye. Since you got to do it your way, I decided I needed to do it mine."

"I didn't... That wasn't what I meant... I'm sorry." Nate's voice fell off at the end, quiet and sad and a load of bullshit. I didn't believe a word he said, so I pretended it didn't matter as I fluffed my hair and straightened my shirt, even though I felt like I was leaving my heart on his bedroom floor.

Guess I was always going to bleed out tonight.

"It's fine. I got you out of my system, and now I can move on for good."

I grabbed my flashlight, not wanting to leave a single thing behind for him.

"Wait! Before you go, you should know something."

I had no doubt it was a trap, but I couldn't bring myself to walk away. I needed to know what he was going to say.

"Cash is setting up a rai—"

My phone vibrated in my pocket, and I answered on autopilot since only a few people had the new number, grimacing at the number of missed calls and texts on the screen. Greyson and Dominic were *pissed.*

"You better get down here." Cameron's voice was grim, and fear gripped my heart immediately.

"Ash?"

"No. Shara."

I stuffed my feet into my shoes, grabbing my gun and heading for the door the second her name dropped. Nate trailed me, but I ignored him. He wasn't my priority when my sister needed me. "What happened?"

"Police raided the club, said there was an anonymous tip about drugs. They found them in her locker."

My hand was on the doorknob when Cameron's words hit me so hard, I stopped cold. "Say that again?"

"They came on a tip that led them straight to Shara's locker."

My heart was thundering in my chest, my vision swimming as rage took me over. "I see. Let me call you back."

I ended the call and slid my phone back into my pocket before casually leaning down to tie my shoes.

"Is everything okay?"

"You tell me, Nate. What was it you were saying about Cash?"

He gulped, eyes averted as he told me again. "Cash is setting up a raid on Gilded. He wants to get your people in jail on drug charges."

Motherfucker. I knew it was a mistake to see him again. I knew he was going to fuck me over. "No, he doesn't want my *people*. He wants my *family*. Specifically, he wants Shara."

Nate's eyes widened, flicking down to the gun in my hand when I flexed my fingers. "I didn't know he was going to do that. I just thought he was going for the license or something."

"Bullshit."

"I swear on my mother's life, I'm not lying."

Despite knowing that his mother existed, I wasn't so sure Nate cared about her like he said he did, so I wasn't taking his vow to heart. "I meant what I said before. Tonight was a mistake that won't happen again. We're done. Go back to your brother and the Aces, and leave me be."

"Mari, wait." He reached for me, and I let the muscle memory take over. Twisting his hand away, I grabbed him by the throat at the same time that I hooked a foot around his knee. If he had been paying more attention, it wouldn't have worked, but he was distracted. The landing knocked the breath out of him, and he curled onto one side as he fought to get it back. I crouched so I was on his level, my gun at the ready without pointing at him.

"I won't say this again. Stay out of my life, Nate. I don't want to kill you, but fuck with my family again, and I will."

I didn't wait for him to answer me, just hauled ass out of the apartment. My car screamed to a halt in front of Gilded just in time to see Shara being stuffed into a cop car. She was mouthing off to the cop, who was manhandling her. Just before she ducked her head, she looked up, and we stared at each other over the asphalt.

I'll get you out of there.

With a wink toward me, she dropped into the seat, and then she was gone, locked away and firmly out of my reach.

Chapter 16
Dominic

I don't care what you have to do or who you have to bribe. I want her out now."

Mari's growl echoed through the police station, and I took note of the few officers who looked far too giddy to hear it. More than one of them had their hands on their weapons, and Greyson and I were constantly scanning the room to make sure no one got suicidal and pulled one on our girl.

"Maybe we should keep our voices down, just in case these aren't our type of cops," Lewis Donnaghal, lead lawyer from Donnaghal and Sons, suggested. When I turned to glare at him—because, really, how fucking stupid did he think we were—he blanched and turned away.

The man was a bland-made human, with everything about him lackluster and dull. He seemed competent enough, but with

Shara in jail, we needed a fire-starter. We needed a powerhouse. Lewis Donnaghal didn't feel like the man we needed.

"I've called his father. Ronan should be here any minute, and when he arrives, Lewis will be lucky to see the inside of a court-room for a year," Grey mentioned quietly as Mari slowly turned and took up Donnaghal's breathing space. He looked like he was going to pass out as she leaned in. How the fuck the man made partner without meeting her before was beyond me.

Mari took a breath, obviously trying to keep herself calm. Anyone could see it wasn't working, and I didn't blame her. Shara was inside alone. No protection, no way out. It was enough to make anyone antsy. Mari's voice was razor-sharp. "My sister is inside that hellhole. I don't give a fuck who hears me, Lewis. I want her out. *Now*. Don't make the mistake of thinking that because I pay you, you're in charge."

I was struggling with how to help. Not because I didn't know what to do, but because I was pissed.

She'd snuck out *again*. Put herself in danger, and for what?

I needed to do something.

That was what she'd said when we'd cornered her outside the police station thirty minutes ago.

No explanation about what it was or where she'd been. Just *I needed to do something*, and the fact that she wouldn't meet our eyes.

I'd been unmoored since Nate's treachery, struggling to straighten myself after he left us reeling, but this? This was too fucking much, and her bullshit answer was just that—bullshit.

I thought we'd turned a corner recently, thought we'd finally gotten back to the point where she trusted us. But obviously not, and honestly, Grey and I deserved better.

We were here, waiting for her to come to us, waiting for her to lean on us, and Mari refused to let us in. She wasn't being a good partner.

The empathetic part of me piped up with a reminder, *she just had her heart ripped out a week ago.*

Maybe, but she was ripping out ours every day. Something had to give, or Nate was going to break more than just them; he'd break us too.

The sound of a car door slamming tore my focus from the quiet man nearly wetting himself in front of my girl. He looked like a quivering dog, and I was once again surprised he'd been allowed to meet us without a fucking chaperone.

"Puppies," Mari muttered, turning away to watch the new arrival.

The man power walking down the sidewalk was the polar opposite of Lewis. Where the younger man was a wet blanket, this man had authority and substance. His suit was a perfect fit, tailored within an inch of its life so it sat like it was molded to him, his briefcase was clean and new, but it was his eyes that told the story I wanted. They were whip-sharp and cold as ice.

This was a man who could get shit done, a man who wouldn't cower in front of Mari. *He* was a powerhouse.

"Ms. Marcosa, sorry for the wait. Greyson." He shook their hands before turning to me. "You must be the new underboss, Dominic Marcosa. I'm Ronan Donnaghal, founder of Donnaghal and Sons."

I shook his hand, pleased at the instant respect he gave all of us, only to smother a laugh when he turned a furious gaze on his son. "What are you doing here?"

"Ms. Marcosa called about her friend, so I came down and—"

"I'm aware of her call. My question is, why are you standing here gabbing, instead of inside getting her sister out of lockup?"

The clarification didn't go unnoticed, and I could see Lewis's pulse jump in his throat. "The-the police said we needed to wait to talk to the commissioner—"

"On your mother's tits, I swear you're as useless as a third nipple."

Ronan made it three steps before turning back with a practiced, impassive look. "Apologies for the delay, Ms. Marcosa. If you'll wait outside, I'll get this sorted for you. In the future, you'll be meeting with my daughter, Laidan. She's my pride and joy and is much more like her Da than this one." He jerked a thumb toward Lewis's red face and sighed, though it was obvious he was going to rake his son over the coals before this was over. "How they shared a womb, I'll never know."

I thought Mari would decline, but she must've realized that the officers wouldn't give us Shara with her inside.

"Text me the second you have news."

"Of course." Ronan turned away, barking over his shoulder, "Get a move on, lad. Seems I need to teach you how to get things done."

With another glance at the hallway where we knew Shara was being held, Mari led us out the door and into the chilly night.

Habit had Grey and me boxing Mari in until we could get her somewhere mostly protected.

"I don't like being out here. It's too open."

"We don't have a choice," Mari snapped. "I'm not leaving her."

"I didn't say you would." Frustration welled inside me, and even though I knew it was because of Shara and Mari's disappearing act, I couldn't stop it. I took a breath, ready to open up the can of worms right there, but Grey's hand on my arm stopped me.

I looked over, frowning when he carefully shook his head. *Not here. Not the time.*

No shit, it wasn't the time, but fuck, I wished it were. Deep breaths weren't cutting it, so I finally just reeled Mari into my chest. Even if I was annoyed at her, I needed that closeness.

"Still mad?"

"Yep."

"Okay." The faint sound of vibration had everyone tensing as Mari looked at the text. "Shara will be out in a minute."

Her shoulders drooped, and she leaned into me, full of relief.

I wasn't much better. Not only because I could get Shara out, but because it meant I could force Mari back behind the Celestine's walls. I wasn't a controlling man by nature, but waking up to find her gone had taken ten years off my life and nearly all of my fucking patience. "Good. Grey and I will drive you both home."

"Not necessary. I have my car." She stepped away, idly tapping at her phone as she responded to Ronan.

"I don't care. You'll come with us." Her head snapped up, and I saw the urge to argue before I stepped forward and dropped my voice. "Don't even think about it, *mariposa*. You snuck out without a fucking note, and now I'm not letting you out of my sight. Moore can come back for your car later."

She would have fought me if Shara hadn't stepped out the station doors with a saccharine smile and a middle finger in the air. "See you never, assholes."

Lewis frowned next to her as they made their way toward us. "Maybe it would be best not to antagonize the police."

"Maybe they should've used their brains before arresting me in the first place," Shara retorted with a cheeky grin, though one look at Mari wiped it away. "You look like shit."

"Gee, I wonder why." The two hugged and whispered to each other quietly before Mari pulled back. "Where's Ronan?"

"My father is finishing with paperwork and threats." Lewis fidgeted with his sleeves. "Apparently, he's going to prove that they planted the evidence and take their badges."

"If anyone could, it would be him," Grey agreed before turning to get his own Shara hug.

"What—"

"Not here." Mari's pointed glance at Lewis was obvious to everyone, and the man paled again. Good lord, he was not fit to be around us.

Mari seemed to agree as she nodded toward the car. "You can leave, Lewis. Tell your sister I look forward to meeting her."

"I'm sure my father was joking, Ms. Marcosa."

"I'm sure he wasn't, but if he was, I'll fix it. Have a nice night."

Dismissed, Lewis shuffled away and out of sight.

"That boy is too fucking innocent for this life," Shara said.

"*That boy* was supposed to get you out. Thank god his father is much better equipped to handle this." Mari linked her arm with Shara's and pulled her forward. "Come on, the boys are bodyguarding us."

"You wouldn't need a bodyguard if you would stop acting out," Greyson murmured, though he glared right back when Mari turned furious eyes on him. "We're right, and you know it."

Her eyes narrowed. "We can talk about this later."

Which meant we were right and she didn't want to admit it.

Another beep came as we were almost at the car, and Mari frowned at her phone.

"According to Ronan, they dropped the charges. He's positive he can expunge your record fully, though it was made clear they're not going to stop poking into Marcosa business."

Of course not. Cash had found a weak spot in our defenses, and he was using the pigs to dig at it. Pathetic.

"What does he suggest?"

When Mari didn't answer, Shara snatched the phone out of her hand and laughed. "*Stick to the straight and narrow for a while. Keep your nose clean.* Does he know who he's talking to?"

Shara didn't seem to care one way or another, skipping ahead to slide into the car with a grin. "Can we stop for burgers? I'm starving."

"We'll order in," Grey said firmly. Neither of us wanted to be out longer than necessary tonight. There was a reason Cash had targeted Shara, and it wasn't just because the women were friends.

What better way to assassinate Mari then to get her out of her fortress?

Thankfully, the ladies seemed to realize the danger, and Mari quickly slid in, shutting the door behind her. Greyson sent a food order to a local Marcosa-owned-and-run place nearby for delivery as I climbed into the driver's seat and sent a text to Moore.

Pickup needed, SPD.

Cop or car.

Car for now.

Got it, boss.

Mari's patience lasted until we were locked in the car, doors barred from the rest of the world.

"Are you okay?" she asked Shara.

For her part, Shara seemed unfazed. "I'm alive."

"That wasn't what I asked."

"It's what I'm telling you." The women stared at each other, both waiting for the other to yield. Normally, I'd bet on Shara— I'd learned since meeting her that she was a force to be reckoned with, and Mari coddled her more than any other person in her life—but this was family business. If there was something to know, Mari needed answers.

"I have a few badges to add to your shit list," Shara finally admitted. She rattled off four names, curling in on herself with a wince.

The car's atmosphere chilled dramatically as Mari cataloged every move Shara made. "Did they touch you?"

"No. They had no qualms about the others doing it, though."

Mari's growl ripped through the car, and she leaned forward to whisper in Grey's ear, "Take care of it."

He nodded, pulling his phone back out and sending a few more texts.

As I started the car and pulled away, I knew we'd have four more bodies on our tally sheet soon enough.

The ride was relatively silent, with Mari and Shara murmuring to each other occasionally, but not much else. It seemed like none of us relaxed until we made it back to the Celestine.

I got out and opened the door for Shara while Greyson did the same for Mari. Thankfully, Shara didn't seem to mind that Mari wasn't letting her go home. Mari was in full overprotective bear mode, and the only way Shara was leaving her sight was to shower.

It wasn't until we were in the elevator that she poked Mari in the side. "Did you read the journal?"

"No."

"Chicken."

"You're right." We all turned to her in shock, but she just shrugged. "I've been letting my fear rule my life since Rey died, and it's made it too easy for things to go wrong. It got you arrested and Aislynn nearly killed. I can't afford to let it happen any longer."

"So, book club after dinner?"

"Yeah, book club."

* * *

The food arrived just as we did, so we trudged up to the penthouse, surrounded by the scent of greasy food and milkshakes. We ate quickly, and only when Shara sat back with a happy sigh, slurping her milkshake while I cleaned up the trash, did Mari tap back into the room again. When the surface was clear, we all stared at the journal in the center of the table.

"It's Mario's, right?" Grey asked, reaching for the book. He was the fastest reader—fucker taught himself to speed-read when they were kids—and Mari had decided he'd skim the pages to see if it was even worth a deeper look.

"Yeah," Mari said, worrying her lip.

Shara leaned over, dropping her head to Mari's shoulder. She melted at the touch and relaxed into the chair. The air was thick with quiet nerves as Greyson flipped through the pages. We didn't know what we'd find or if it would even help. It could just be pages of Mario blowing smoke up his own ass, but my gut said we'd find *something* to help.

About halfway through, he stopped, flipped back a few pages, then moved forward again. He kept his fingers in place, not losing the spot. When he finished, he wiped his hands on his pants and nodded. "Cash is in here."

"He is?" Mari leaned forward, staring at the journal as if she could read its secrets that way.

"Not much," Grey warned. "A few mentions here and here."

He laid the book out and tapped the pages so she could see, then he turned to me with a wince. "So is your mom."

I winced too, not wanting to read anything Mario had to say about my mom. They might not have been married very long, but they'd been together for years. If I read an account of their sex life, I wasn't going to be able to look her in the eyes ever again.

Mari flipped through the pages while I tried to decide whether it was necessary for me to look, her frown growing the longer she read. "This doesn't make any sense. Do you remember Cash around your mom?"

"No." I didn't remember seeing his face before his appearance at Gilded months ago. My brows furrowed at the implication. "What does it say?"

"Read it yourself." Mari slid the book to me and stood up to pace.

Lucia won't tell me anything, but I see the way he looks at her. Covets her. I thought Cash was going for my throne, and I don't blame him. If I was born to be a king, he was born to be a conqueror. But what if he's gunning for my queen instead?

"So, he could've stalked her? Fixated on her like he has on you?" Grey suggested. My stomach lurched at the idea of that psychopath going after my mother. We weren't close, but she was my mom. I didn't want anything bad happening to her.

"There's another option," Shara said quietly, flipping through the pages now that Mari had given her the okay. "They could've had an affair."

Everyone froze.

Marriage in the mafia world was patriarchal bullshit, with the men fucking whoever they wanted with relative impunity. But the women? If they were lucky enough to be married to a low-level man, maybe they'd get a divorce or run out of town. Some were beaten within an inch of their lives just for looking at another man.

But for the don's wife? An affair was a death sentence. Plain and simple. Mario couldn't afford for word to get out that his own wife was disrespecting him.

Yet my mother was still alive.

"We need more than this." Grey motioned to the journal in irritation, his brain obviously trying to come up with answers when we didn't have all of the puzzle pieces.

Mari hummed, turning back to the table with fierce eyes. "Then we go find it."

"Where?"

"Chicago."

My head whipped up, shocked. "You want to leave?"

"I think we need to talk to your mother, and I'd prefer we didn't paint a target on her back if we can avoid it. We could always video chat—"

Greyson was already shaking his head. "We could encode it, but with Nate's insight into the system, I'm not so sure it's a good idea right now."

"It's not safe to leave either," I argued.

"Sure, it is." Shara leaned forward, hands folded in front of her. The picture of innocence and a bald-faced lie. "Donnaghal said we all needed to lie low this weekend anyway. Make it seem like we're holing up here for the weekend. I'll stay and make it legit. You have room service, right?"

She winked and stretched out her legs, looking beyond comfortable in our home, and I could see the gears turning in Mari's head. "If we plan the conversations with Shara's new *friends* while we're gone, it should look like we're still here."

"What about the airports? It'll be impossible to hide if we go commercial. We'll have to charter a plane."

Mari snorted. "Or we can just use ours."

"We have a plane?"

Her eyes glittered. "We do."

The words *Mile High Club* whispered in my ear, and I grinned. "To Chicago, then."

"To Chicago."

Chapter 17
Dominic

By the time we landed, I was already itching to get home. It'd been less than a year since I'd found my way back to Seattle, to Mari, but it held me more than Chicago ever had. I'd been born there, had grown up there before my mom got with Mario Marcosa, and I'd returned there when it was over.

I'd become a man on those streets, was born to rule them by blood and by rights, and yet I didn't feel even a tinge of homesickness inside me for the place that had birthed me.

I wanted overcast skies and rainy days on the couch more than I wanted to return to a past that didn't fit me anymore.

That was all Mari. She was my home, my heart. She was the center of my universe, not a city that didn't care about me. Even Greyson felt more like mine than this place ever had. My brother, my friend.

Fuck, when had that happened?

"We're here." His voice pulled me out of my thoughts, and I blinked up at the gated mansion. It was closer to the Marcosa mansion than the O'Bannon one, with old money seeping out of every crack in the stone. Stained glass on some of the large windows was visible from the gatehouse, where I gave my name. He didn't even have to check it to immediately let us in.

Greyson pulled the town car to a stop in front of the door, pocketing the keys so no one could try to move it in case we needed a quick getaway. We'd come as incognito as possible, leaving a seething Moore and Tennessee behind to keep up appearances of us staying home. Despite staying in Seattle, they'd arranged everything from the car to the private security that followed us through the streets. Considering we were at the home of a House representative—my mother's fourth, or was it fifth, husband—people probably assumed that we were visiting dignitaries or other representatives, and that worked fine for us. The blacked-out windows meant they could guess all they wanted and still never know.

Not unless they knew Grey's face, at least.

The wrong people would, but they'd keep their mouths shut. My mother held some serious sway over Representative Doug Patterson, and he'd bring the law down on them the second they hinted at revealing her secrets. Ironic that my mother would use her federal lackey husband as a guard dog, considering Lucia Ricci was a mafia queen just like Mari.

Or she would've been if my father had survived.

My father's family had been in charge of Chicago longer than the Marcosas had ruled Seattle. It was part of the reason my mother had married Mario in the first place, to unite the two families and expand his reach across the country. Despite how young she'd been, my mother was a smart woman. Without my father, my position as heir had been tenuous at best. I had been too young to rule and too ornery to care about it. She'd tried to hold on to the seat as long as she could, but eventually, another family came in with an offer she couldn't refuse. The Lords of Chicago, the ruling faction at the time, let me live as long as I denounced any possibility of coming back for my position. I could live here, grow old here, and die here, but I would never rule.

Amnesty deals were few and far between, so my mother took it. One of many.

I helped Mari out of the car, careful to keep myself between her and anyone else until Grey boxed her in on the other side. She stiffened immediately, not liking being guarded so closely. But we were in unknown territory, and even if my mother held her husband's leash tightly, I wasn't risking my girl for anything.

I'd leash her myself if I thought I could get away with it.

The door opened before we knocked, and my mother filled my vision.

Lucia Ricci was nearly sixty and looked half her age. Only the faint wrinkles at the sides of her mouth and her eyes betrayed her secret, and no one who looked that hard at her would care. Her sheath dress was new, just like the diamond necklace at her throat, and only the kitten heels on her feet told me she was dressed up with nowhere to go.

No less than three-inch heels would do for leaving the house. Mama Ricci's rules.

She hadn't always been so put together, but after my father was murdered, she fell into the routine of being a mafia wife. Always on, always perfect.

I missed the woman she'd been before. When she'd just been my mom, not Lucia.

"Dominic." Her wide-eyed expression went from happy to

worried the second I shifted to the side and Mari stepped forward, holding out her hand to shake.

"Lucia. It's lovely to see you again."

Mother shook it robotically before her eyes flicked to Grey and then beyond us all to the street, though it was impossible to really see from here. "Why don't you all come in?"

I could see the calculations in her eyes, wondering if I was bringing trouble to her door, while also trying to make sure the neighbors didn't get a good look at who was coming in. Most likely, she'd spin a story that I was some billionaire wanting to put his money into politics to help Doug's career.

"We'd love to." Mari stepped in first, casually looking around as she did. "You have a picture-perfect home."

It was not a compliment. The inside looked like a magazine and felt about as warm as a hospital room. Even our place at the Celestine was more comfortable than this.

"Tea, coffee? I think we've got some of those butter cookies you like, Mari. They're Dominic's favorite too, so I keep them in the cupboard."

They were my favorite because they were Mari's, and from the sly, sweet look on her face, she knew it too. "No, thank you. We've just got a few questions, so we won't take up too much of your time.

"We were going through some of Mario's things recently, and we came across your name mixed with an...adversary of ours. Considering his history, we wanted to get the story from the source."

"Adversary?" Mother asked, but she knew. Her hands crept to her throat, clutching the necklace there with shaking fingers and a firm grip.

"Cash Beckstrom."

The name felt like dropping an atom bomb in the middle of the room. My mother's face twitched but didn't move, and that alone told me she had more history with Cash than I wanted her to. Fear soured my stomach, and I prayed like I never had before that he hadn't hurt her. He was already a dead man for what he'd done to Mari, but if he'd attacked my mother too, there wouldn't be enough pieces to identify his remains.

Lucia's eyes flitted around the room, barely stopping on one thing before moving on to the next. "I'm sorry, I don't—"

"I should've been more clear," Mari said, leaning back in the cushions as if to show how comfortable she was. "We aren't leaving until you give us everything you've got on him."

My mother's eyes flicked to mine. "Dominic."

It was a plea, a desperate, bone-deep cry for help, and I couldn't give it. "Tell her, Mother."

A long, tense moment passed, during which the only thing breaking the silence was the roar of the wind outside. The house was sturdy, but it creaked and moaned as all old houses did. My mother stared into the empty fireplace, tracking the marble like it would give her the answers she wanted.

When she spoke, her voice was barely loud enough to hear. "We had an affair."

Christ. "You and Cash?"

"Yes." She turned to us then, eyes brimming with tears. "You have to understand, I didn't want to marry Mario."

"But you didn't have a choice," Mari guessed. She was versed in the ways of mafia women in a manner Grey and I never could be. "What happened?"

Lucia shook her head. "I met Mario at a gala with Alonzo, my second husband. It was a few years after Dominic's father died, and I was just starting to get back to normal. Happy, even. Alonzo was older but sweet. He took care of us."

By older, she meant ancient. My memories of my first stepfather were of puffy white hair and a crinkled smile. He had been old enough to be her grandfather.

"Mario found me the second he walked in, and he was, for lack of a better term, besotted. He followed me around the entire time, even cornered me by the bathrooms at one point to explain why he'd come to Chicago. He offered me a place at his side immediately. *Love at first sight*, he'd called it, and even after I explained that I wasn't available, he wouldn't walk away. He asked for a drink, a dance, a night. I refused.

"When Alonzo came over to take me to the dance floor himself, I could see that Mario didn't like it. He'd come to Chicago looking for a wife, and just because the one he'd found was married didn't mean he was going to take no for an answer."

She stood on shaky legs, heading for the bar cart in the corner. She came back with a full glass of bourbon and didn't even realize she hadn't offered us any. It was as close to off-kilter as my mother got anymore.

After half the glass was gone, Mother continued. "He played nice the rest of the night, being friendly with Alonzo like nothing had happened. Turns out they were old friends, and my husband had been the one to suggest expanding the pool of potential wives to our city. Mario played on their friendship, teasing and joking about extending his stay until it felt impossible not to invite him to do it. We couldn't slight him, and Alonzo was just happy everyone was getting along.

"Mario showed up for dinner every night that week and the week after, bringing me flowers and treats each time, even when I said it was unnecessary. Alonzo thought it was sweet that Mario thought of me, but I knew better. He was testing the waters and finding the protection around me lacking. I told Alonzo I didn't like him around so much, but they'd been talking about marrying the two of you together, uniting the bloodlines. Until the decision was made, we couldn't say no."

Ice slid down my spine as I cautiously looked over at Mari,

but she was focused on my mother. "How did you two end up together?"

Lucia looked at me then away, her ears burning. "Alonzo and I had an arrangement. He wasn't interested in sex, but he knew I was young and I wanted more children. We agreed that I could have affairs, as long as I kept them discreet."

None of us flinched. It wasn't uncommon in our world, nor was it cheating when she had full permission of her spouse, but Mother was from a different, less accepting time. Hell, Mari was dating two men. It wasn't exactly stereotypical monogamy in our lives either, but Mother wouldn't agree. She'd grown up with that as the example and expectation, and anything outside of it was perverse.

Like she knew she had to tread carefully, Mari's voice was gentle. "Mario was one of those affairs."

"Initially, yes, but only because Alonzo convinced me it was a good idea, and just while he was in town. As soon as we worked out your engagement, Mario would go home, and our relationship would be over. I knew immediately that Mario wouldn't accept the terms of our arrangement for long. He was the type who needed to own someone, not share them." Another sip and a deep, shuddering breath. "The affair lasted three months. Then Alonzo died."

"Mario killed him," Grey guessed because we all knew how obsessive the asshole had been. Honestly, I was surprised my stepfather had survived that long with Mother in Mario's sights.

"I was pregnant at the time, his baby, obviously. The second he found out, he got rid of Alonzo." The glass clinked against her teeth as she took a shaky sip. "I told him I wasn't interested in marrying him, even after the mourning period was over, but Mario didn't care about that. He blackmailed me with photos and videos he'd taken from our time together. I either married him and brought you to Seattle, or he'd tell everyone and let the Lords of Chicago take care of us both."

She reached forward and snatched my hands, clinging to me. "You have to understand, they would've killed you. I couldn't let that happen."

"So, you married Mario." I'd always wondered how she'd met him, but I'd accepted her excuse. *We run in the same circles.* Apparently, I should've looked into the situation sooner.

"Eventually, yes," she answered, looking at Greyson. "I think he would've done it immediately, despite the mourning period, but the stress of it all made me lose the baby. He wanted to give me time to heal so we could try again, but there were *complications.*"

The way she said it made it obvious that those complications were entirely intentional. Mari sat back, staring at my mother with newfound awe. "You got sterilized."

My mother looked over her shoulder, fingers trembling in mine, and I squeezed them.

"Yes," she whispered. "Your mother—"

She didn't need to explain more than that. Everyone knew that Bianca Marcosa's story was a warning. My mother had given up her chance at more children, which she desperately wanted, just for a chance to survive long enough to raise me herself. For the first time in years, I saw a glimpse of my mom inside her, and I wondered what else she'd sacrificed for me.

Had she ever done something for herself?

"When did the affair with Cash start?"

"Almost immediately after we got to Seattle," Mother admitted. "I was lonely and reeling from everything, and Mario didn't trust me with his men. He kept me locked in our house and only let me out enough so that people could see I was alive. For a year, the only men Mario had guarding me were the ones he thought too loyal to break." She huffed in annoyance. "Like it was my fault he'd pursued me so hard in the first place."

With the last of the booze drained, she sat back. "Cash started doing nice things, leaving me my favorite treats in my room, sneaking me books and movies, taking me out on long drives when he had to leave the compound. I told him I couldn't be with him, not when it risked Dominic, but he promised it wouldn't. He'd keep things quiet, and Mario wouldn't kill me because then he'd never get another chance to make more heirs. No woman would touch him willingly if he killed two of his wives, and he was all about the willingness of his partners. He got off on us saying yes, even when it was the only way out."

"But my father found out about you two. How?"

"Cash told him just after we got married. On our wedding night, Cash convinced me to meet him and we..." She looked at me before her eyes darted away again. "He took photos, taunting Mario that he'd had me on our wedding night too. I'd already known that our affair was more about power than anything, but I didn't realize that Cash didn't care what happened to me. When Mario found out, I ran for Cash, but he wasn't there. I thought I was going to die."

"But you didn't."

"Cash was right. Mario knew that getting rid of me would bring questions he couldn't afford to answer—about his sanity, his virility, his control over me, and his people. His very hold on Seattle was at risk."

I glanced at Mari, realizing she was dealing with the same destabilization of her power base now.

"Things would've been different if Cash had still been in the city, but he'd left in the middle of the night, taking Mario's product with him. After he burned the evidence, Mario offered me a quiet divorce if I signed the deal and left Seattle until it was time for Dominic to return. Once Dominic fulfilled the deal, everything would be forgiven."

Mari sat back, tapping her fingers on the couch arm as she tried to piece together the puzzle. "What deal are you talking about?"

My mother's brow furrowed as she looked between Mari and me, and my stomach dropped. "The marriage deal. You and Dominic have been engaged since you were sixteen."

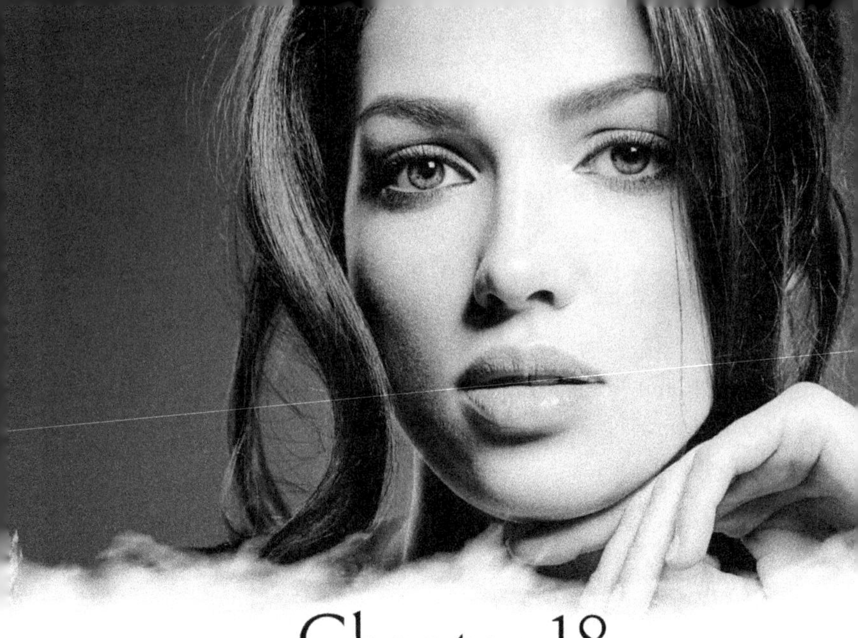

Chapter 18
Mari

I tried to bring myself back to the conversation after that, but my brain was stuck trying to figure out what the hell had just happened.

You and Dominic have been engaged since you were sixteen.

There was no fucking way. Right?

I tried to remember if my father had acted strangely after his divorce, but nothing stuck out. Other than not pushing another match on me as I grew up, regardless of how old I got. It was pretty unheard of for me to get to sixteen without a match. Hell, Aislynn was engaged to her first beau before she was in school, though that obviously didn't take. Men in our world were notoriously short-lived.

As if that wasn't confusing enough, Mario never talked much about Dominic or Lucia after the divorce and their return to Chicago, nor did he attempt to woo anyone else to his side. By all accounts—though I didn't keep track of my father's sexcapades—he kept things casual after that. Nothing serious, nothing personal. In fact, his only real change after Lucia left was that he preferred escorts over attempting to find someone organically, and yes, I wished I didn't know that.

He just went on with life, existing and ruling as if nothing was wrong.

Then he died.

That was the part that stuck with me as I sat on Lucia's couch, mulling it all over. The pact would've ended as soon as Mario died, unless Antoni chose to uphold it. My brother hadn't mentioned Dominic either, nor did he have any use for expanding our reach. Mario was the ambitious one; Antoni just wanted to survive his inheritance. He wanted to take Shara as his wife and grow old in Seattle with their children and grandchildren running around them. He wanted a pipe dream, but he hadn't sold me out. I was as sure of it as I was of my own name.

If Antoni had asked, I'd have married Dominic in a heartbeat, but he didn't. He wasn't planning on honoring jack shit.

So why didn't Dominic tell me?

I wasn't sure and wouldn't be until we talked, but did it really matter? Intention had always been the crux of Dominic's and my issues. He wanted to bundle me up and keep me safe, protecting heart and head in every endeavor. I wanted a partner who trusted that I could handle myself.

Was the reality that we were just too incompatible? I didn't want to believe that because losing Dominic for good felt like a fate worse than death, but I wasn't as sure about us anymore.

Nate's treachery had taught me one thing: I couldn't be with someone who lied to me. Small things like whether they took out the trash or huge things like this, I couldn't take it. I needed transparency or the trust was gone, and in both of their cases, I wasn't sure we could get it back.

Greyson cleared his throat, reminding me where we were. Regardless of how I found out about it, Lucia was right. It had been the only way out for them, the only choice to ensure their survival. I could hate the situation all I wanted, but at least they were alive. That was better than most could get, and I was glad for it.

As the others talked around me, I felt this ache in my stomach. At first, I thought it was pain, but it felt like something else. Something urging me to be impulsive. To act.

But on what?

"Was there anything else you needed to know?" Lucia said some time later, startling me back into the room. Christ, what was wrong with me? I looked over at Grey, but his little headshake said it was nothing new or necessary for me to pay attention to. Thank fuck for that.

"No, that's it." Deciding to give Lucia the same honesty she gave us, I leaned forward. "You should go underground for a while."

She sucked in a breath, clutching that necklace again. If she'd had another glass, I had no doubt she'd have emptied it. "So, the rumors are true."

Dominic had mentioned soon after he arrived in Seattle that rumors had made their way to Chicago, but I didn't realize that Cash was part of them. I glanced over instinctively before I tore my gaze away. Keeping my shit together meant I couldn't look at him. Not now. Not yet.

"They are. He's back and out for blood. I'd prefer not to give him an easy target."

Lucia nodded. "Doug and I were planning to go on our yearly vacation next week. I'll extend it."

That infernal pressure pushed on my chest, making every breath a chore.

Engaged. We were fucking engaged. Had been for years.

Out. I need out.

"Good." I stood, nodding Greyson to the door. If I didn't leave the room, I was going to lose it. "We'll let you say goodbye. Be safe, Lucia."

As we headed for the front door, I heard Lucia's whispered apology. "I thought she knew."

Dominic's silence was its own answer. Yeah, I should've.

I shoved open the front doors like I was breaking out of jail, sucking in huge lungfuls of air, even when I looked the epitome of calm. God bless Mario's training; it was stupidly useful. Grey kept pace with me, eyes wary and sharp as he took in every shaking leaf around us while we moved.

"Do you think I'm destined to pick men who lie to me?" I asked, wincing at my tactlessness. Turning, I grabbed Greyson's hand. "I'm sorry."

His fingers swallowed mine, squeezing in that easy comfort that made my eyes prick with tears. "I understand, *reina*, and no, I don't think so. I think the men you choose need to strive to be better."

"Even you?"

His lip quirked, but it was tinged with sadness. "Especially me."

I didn't ask if he'd known about the marriage pact because it wasn't his responsibility to tell me even if he did. It was Dominic's or Antoni's or my father's. Grey wasn't innocent, but he wasn't in the hot seat either.

That was all on my *other* boyfriend.

Leaning against the town car, I let the wind ruffle my hair and sweep my thoughts away. We waited there until Dominic came outside, leaving his mother in the house. I slid into the back seat, hating that because our focus was stealth, I couldn't sit in the front. I needed space to get my head on straight and to see if that piercing pain in my heart was something we could even fix.

Dominic came after me, laying his hand on my thigh. "Mari."

I moved as far away as I could, desperate to keep some distance between us. Touching him hurt when I couldn't even look at him. He'd lied to me for years, and I honestly didn't know if I had any more grace to give him. My head was so jumbled, and my heart was already a bleeding, torn-up mess. This wasn't something else I was prepared to endure. I needed to heal, not hurt.

"Not right now, Dominic."

"Baby, please—" He reached for me again, and I slapped his hand away, even as it killed me to do it.

Looking at him, I felt like we were the only people in the world. There was no Grey, no Lucia, no Cash. Just me and my lying partner. *Christ.* "Don't touch me. I asked for no lies, and you gave them to me anyway."

"I know." He swallowed, looking at where his hands sat limp in his lap. "I just didn't want to lose you over something we couldn't control. I was selfish and wrong, and I'm sorry."

"You should be." I saw those three words land, and it did nothing to soothe the ache. In fact, it made it worse. I hated him and I loved him, and I didn't know which one was going to win in the end. The entire situation was a special kind of purgatory for me.

Turning to the window, I gave him my back before my pain made me lash out in more permanent ways. "I'm not interested in talking. Leave me alone until I've wrapped my head around this."

From then on, everyone gave me a wide berth. In the car, on the tarmac, in the airplane. Hell, even the flight attendants were wary to offer me anything. I couldn't blame them. No doubt I looked fit to kill, and Dominic's moroseness was oozing through the cabin. Only Grey was acting normal, and he was glued to my side, a silent sentry.

Normally, I'd head to the gym to work out my frustrations, but by the time we made it back to the Celestine, I was exhausted. Opening the door, I felt both men on my heels, ready for whatever I needed. Dominic because he wanted to make things better, Greyson because he knew I wasn't doing well. "I need to sleep," I said, moving down the hallway to my room.

"I'll come with you." Dominic followed on my heels, and I felt my hackles rising the closer we got to my space. Blocking the door with my body, I glanced up at him. "No."

His face was the picture of regret and surprise. "You're pushing us out again?"

"No, Dominic. Just you." I ignored the wounded look and pushed the door open farther, raising an eyebrow at Greyson. He didn't hesitate to slide into the gap, taking over with Dominic as I went to shower the airplane funk off me.

Proving he knew me best, Grey left me alone to wallow in my shower. I scrubbed myself raw, trying not to fall into the fatalistic mentality I always did, but the hurt festered. It clung to the wound that Nate's treachery left and dug its claws in.

Was this it for Dominic and me? Would I ever be able to trust him again?

Did he think the lying was worth it?

I wouldn't know until I talked to him, but that was tomorrow's problem. I needed to regroup; I needed to remember that Dominic's actions weren't my fault, and I knew just the person to help me see that.

I felt a thread of something inside me, something that had been there for a while, slowly picking up steam. It felt like inevitability, fate. A piece of me screaming for its match. For home. And the louder it got, the more necessary it felt to act. To move. To do.

When I was dry, I changed into one of Grey's shirts, needing the extra comfort to get through the night, and finished getting ready for bed. The murmured conversation by the door was still happening, but I ignored it. That wasn't for me.

Dropping my phone on the bedside table, I cringed when it buzzed loudly. I was in no way ready to face the world, but I flipped it over with a sigh anyway. My job meant I didn't get a break, even when I needed one. Still, nothing could've prepared me for the name on the text.

Nate.

> Stay home for a while. Cash is gunning for you.

For the longest time, I just stared at it. The wounds he'd left were open and raw, and I wanted to drag him through them with me. If I hurt, he should hurt. But I also knew I wasn't ready to open that part of me up to him again. That vulnerable section of me was locked away, where it needed to be.

In the end, I didn't respond because it wasn't like it was new information. Cash had been gunning for me for months, and he wouldn't stop until one of us was dead. I knew that, he knew that, the entire fucking city knew that, and they were placing bets on the victor.

Grey finally shut the door, turned out the lights, and curled up in bed, saying nothing as he wrapped himself around me. It felt like he was trying to imitate Dominic's actions in the gym, but I didn't need a weighted blanket; I just needed him.

My Greyson. My heart.

My most trusted friend.

That *something* in my stomach pushed me again. *Do it.*

"I love you," I said quietly as I let my eyes adjust to the darkness.

"I love you too, *reina*. I'm sorry about today."

"You're always having to apologize for the others. Doesn't it get frustrating?"

He hummed, the sound vibrating against my body. "Maybe, but it's not about them in the end. It's about you. I want you to know that you're safe with me, that I'll take care of you, even when I'm not the one who's broken something."

How did he know exactly what to say to my fragile, bruised soul? I knew the uncertainty wasn't forever, that I'd probably find a way to forgive Dominic again, but for now, it felt impossible to regain our footing. I was too thick in the pain to see past that, but one thing was becoming perfectly clear.

"I think you're the only one I trust." Snuggling deeper into his embrace, I realized this was the place I felt the most at home. That was the thought that struck the match.

Grey had always been there for me. When we were kids, he was the one who held me when I needed it, who picked me up when I fell, who kissed my boo-boos and wiped my tears. As adults, he was my shadow, the other half of my brain, my everything.

I didn't want to live without him for a second.

"Baby." He pulled closer, trying to squeeze his love into me with actions instead of words, but he didn't need to. I knew he loved me. He showed me every fucking day, even when I didn't deserve it.

Now, it was my turn to show him something.

"I'm serious. Dominic has already proven he'll keep things from me to get what he wants and—" I cut myself off before I talked about Nate. I couldn't talk about him right now. Not when I wasn't sure what was happening. "This isn't about them, though. It's about you. You've always been there for me, even when I didn't deserve you. I don't want to lose you."

"You've always deserved me, *reina*. I'm not going anywhere. Not unless you're with me." He said it so fiercely that I felt it in my chest, but he didn't understand.

That need in my stomach was growing with every second and had been for days, weeks, months. Years, if I was honest. Maybe I'd spent my whole life with it coiling and writhing in my belly.

All I knew was, it was time to do something about it. Time to claim what was mine.

Do it.

I twisted, lifting my head so that we were facing each other. His brows furrowed, and he ran his fingers over my cheeks gently, soothing me. But I didn't want to be soothed. I had to do something. It was time. "I'm serious, Greyson. I can't lose you. Not now, not ever. I can't survive without you."

"Mari, I'm not going anywhere."

"I know that. I do, I just want to make it official."

"Official?"

I pulled him closer, wrapping myself around him this time. Giving him every piece of me that I could. I didn't want Greyson every day; I wanted him always. When I tipped my head back to see his face, Grey wrapped his hand in my hair, supporting my neck so I didn't hurt myself. It was so simple, so full of love, that I smiled. It was just one more example of how in tune we were.

I never wanted it to end.

"Marry me, Grey."

Chapter 19
Greyson

N o."

In every dream I'd ever had, every fantasy of making Mari my wife, I'd never expected my answer to be that.

"No?" The rejection hit swiftly, and her voice shook as she pulled away. It was hell trying not to grab her back, but while I needed her closer, she needed distance. She'd always been the type to run away and gather her thoughts before she came back to discuss things. She needed solitude and peace to process, but that wasn't going to happen this time.

I sat up, and even though she was only a few feet away, arms wrapped around herself as if they could hold her together, it felt like a canyon.

"I don't want you like this."

"Like what, Greyson? Begging you? Because I can guarantee that's not going to happen again," she snapped.

"Scared."

Silence fell thick and painful around us.

"You think I asked because I'm scared?"

"Yes," I admitted. The look on her face when Lucia had dropped the marriage pact on her...it had been just as devastated as when she'd found out about Nate. Honestly, it was probably worse. "I don't want you as my wife because I'm the only choice. I want you as my wife because we love each other. Because it's the most rational step forward. I want you because you want me as much as I crave you."

For a moment, she just stared at me like she had no idea who I was. Then she huffed, and the shock quickly wore off, transitioning to something almost warmer. It was unexpected. Mari's fear of rejection tended to react with snarky barbs and sharp words. Instead, she climbed on my lap.

"Why do you think I asked you to marry me?"

It felt like a trick question, but I couldn't help answering. My queen commanded, and I obeyed. "Because you're upset with Dominic and Nate. You think I'm the safe choice."

I didn't mind being the safe choice when we all knew I'd never hurt Mari intentionally, but it stung that she'd used it to decide something as important as this.

Unexpectedly, Mari laughed, head thrown back and loud. She was so fucking beautiful like that, unencumbered by the world and its problems, and I wanted her in my lap, on my cock, always.

When she quieted, she took my face in her hands. "You've never been the safe choice, Grey. You've always been the one most likely to break my heart in two."

I clenched my hands at her hips. "I would never."

"But you could. It's always been you, Grey. Even with Dominic and Nate, and the others before them, you've always been my forever. I *did* ask you because I was scared, but not for the reason you think." She slid closer, running her hands through my hair so softly it was almost heartbreaking. "I cannot lose you. Not to secrets or life or this fucking war. If I don't have you by my side, at my back, I can't breathe. I asked because I need you and I love you. I know now that there isn't a future where I exist without you wearing my ring. Don't make me live it."

I cleared my throat, trying not to show how much her words meant to me because I wasn't sure I could believe them. Not truly. I'd been without her for so long that some part of me still expected her to walk away, to choose someone else. When I told her that, she frowned.

"Why do you think I'll leave you?"

Shrugging, I tried not to show how much the idea of it hurt, but Mari was my everything. My blood and bones. Losing her wasn't losing a limb; it was losing my existence. But I didn't know how to tell her that, so I just said, "Forever is a long time."

Mari had always understood me better than anyone else, even Antoni. He'd seen the surface, but Mari had always seen to my heart with ease. She brought our foreheads together, whispering against my lips. "You think I can't love you enough for forever, Greyson?"

"I'd understand if you couldn't." Some days, I wasn't sure I had anything substantial inside me, and it wouldn't surprise me if it wasn't enough for her. If *I* wasn't enough.

She pulled back to stare at me until, finally, she climbed carefully off my lap. The disappointment was staggering, but I kept my hands where they were and didn't call out to her. She didn't need me chasing after her right now, not on the heels of so much bad news. When I expected her to head for the door, she walked farther into her suite, and I watched unsurely as she moved over to the ornate dresser and pulled open the top drawer. She dug around for a minute and brought out a package I'd never seen, still in the mailer.

Keeping it in hand, she climbed onto the bed and gave it to me.

"What is this?" I asked warily, unsure what was making my heart race so much. For the first time in ages, my hands were shaking.

It was like my body was telling me something was happening. Something important.

She tipped her head to one side and smiled. "Open it."

I pulled off the mailer, surprised to find a jewelry box inside the size I'd expect for a necklace. When my hand hesitated over the flip lock, Mari laughed at me. "Be brave, Greyson."

Three rings sat on the velvet, similar but not identical. As I looked at them, my eyes caught the one on the far right. It was a charcoal gray, shined to near sparkling. A single line of bright silver broke up the bottom edge. It was sophisticated and smart, basic without being boring. I loved it. When Mari gave a pointed nod, I tilted the band and saw something incredible.

The inside of the band was etched with a single word. *Always.*

"That one's yours."

My eyes snapped to hers, disbelief dropping my jaw even as a sense of rightness dug into my bones. I'd known it the moment I'd reached for it, hadn't I?

"I had them made a while ago. They came in recently, and it just hasn't seemed like the right time to give it to you."

Because there were three rings in the box and only two of us left.

"Why tonight?"

Mari climbed back onto my lap, circling my neck with her arms, cradling me in every inch of her warmth. "Because I don't want to spend another second without you wearing my ring."

When I couldn't speak, she plucked the ring from my hand, holding it between us, though our eyes were locked together.

"Marry me, Greyson Andrews. Be my husband. Live with me, fight with me, love with me. Always."

Always. "Yes."

Mari wasn't asking because of Dominic's secrets or Nate's; she was asking because of me. Her lifelong best friend, her childhood protector. Her soul mate.

Just me.

And I would love her forever. Always. A day beyond eternity.

The metal was cool against my skin as Mari slipped it on my finger, but I'd never felt anything more right than the weight on my hand.

The second it was on, I grabbed her by the hips and tossed her off me. She startled, barely catching herself as I got up and headed for the door.

Her huff was uncertain as she yelled at my back. "I have to admit, I expected more than a runaway groom from that proposal. This better not be a warning sign."

Smirking to her, I said nothing as I slipped out the door. Dominic was waiting in the hallway, legs spread wide on the floor, head tipped against the wall.

"Is she okay?"

"She will be," I said before hustling to my room next door. I probably should've told him, but it didn't feel right. Tonight was ours—Mari's and mine. Tomorrow, they'd sort things out and he'd be back in the fold, but for the first time ever, she was mine. Just mine.

For a few hours, at least.

It took me seconds to find what I needed and cram it into my pocket, and a few more to get back to the bedroom and lock the door behind me.

Then I pulled out the box and dropped to one knee in front of the bed. "Marianna Marcosa. You're the love of my life. My heart, soul, and breath. I don't want to live a day without you. Marry me."

She slid out of bed, eyes bright with happy tears. "You weren't supposed to counter propose."

"If you think it's necessary for me to wear your ring, you have no idea how much I need you wearing mine. Say yes, *reina*. Be my queen forever."

"Yes. Of course."

I slid the ring on her finger, happy when we looked at them together and they matched. A one-carat upside-down pear-cut diamond sat in the center, and the rest of the ring was all filigree and diamonds around the top edge. It looked like a crown, the perfect ring for my queen.

Mari's eyes were wide as she took it in. "It's beautiful, Grey."

"I've had it for ages. Found it in an antique shop one afternoon and just knew it was yours. I wasn't sure if I'd ever get the chance to give it to you, but I kept it just in case." I'd stored it in a safe-deposit box in a neighboring town for years. But after Cameron's and Aislynn's wedding, I'd moved it into my room, wanting it close in case I got up the nerve to ask.

Seeing it on Mari's finger felt like a full-circle moment.

We stared at it for another beat longer, then I tossed her on the bed.

I could hear those happy squeals every day for the rest of my life.

Our first kiss knocked me off-kilter. It felt like it always did with Mari, like coming home, but there was something else too. For the first time ever, I believed that I'd get to keep her. That she was well and truly mine. Yeah, I'd share her with the others, but she wasn't going to wake up one day and wish she hadn't chosen me.

She asked for forever because she wasn't going to change her mind.

We were nothing but grasping hands and lingering lips as we tore off each other's clothes like we were both in a hurry. I needed her naked and mewling under me, needed her pussy stretched around my cock, warm and wet and real.

I needed to claim her the only way I could.

My cock throbbed as she wrapped her hand around it, the glimmer of the ring bright against my skin, and I groaned into her neck. "Don't tease me right now."

"I'm not." She swiped my head through her slick lips before lining me up and tilting her hips until just the tip of me was inside her. "Remind me what I have to look forward to for the rest of our lives."

Done.

Cradling her close, I slid all the way home, not pausing for a second to let her catch her breath. She'd have all the time in the world for that later. Right now, I had to imprint myself on her body. With each thrust, I whispered all the things I loved about her, hoping my words embedded in her skin so she'd never doubt them, obsessed with how her body clenched with each one.

Mari loved me dirty, but she loved me soft, too.

Sneaking a hand between us, I circled her clit, knowing we were both close. "Greyson," she warned.

"It's okay, baby. I've got you."

When she came, clenching around me, she took my breath away. Head thrown back, mouth parted on a sigh, and fingers digging into my arms. It was the sight of that ring on her finger that sent me over, pushing myself as deep as I could go, as if I could brand her from the force of my orgasm. Mark her like she'd marked me so long ago.

For a moment, neither of us moved. Then I realized I was going to crush her and rolled us, not willing to let her move even an inch. Hell, I was still inside her and desperate never to leave. As we caught our breath, I brushed her hair back, needing to see her face. When she waggled her eyebrows at me, I thought I was going to combust. "I'm going to love you forever, baby."

She grinned at me. "Always?"

"Always."

She rested her head on my chest, letting me stroke her hair as we both came down from the endorphin high that I knew we'd be repeating soon enough. The longer we lay there, the more I wanted to come clean. "I knew about the deal."

"Antoni," Mari guessed, tipping her head up to see me. I nodded and she sighed. "I was too harsh with Dominic."

I hummed, not agreeing or disagreeing. "He knew better than to hide it."

"He did, but still. I promise to fix it tomorrow."

"Secrets are only good if we're keeping them from everyone else."

She paused. "I have to tell you something. I'll tell Dominic tomorrow too, but...I saw Nate. We...talked."

"Just talked?" Because her voice sounded anything but sure.

"No."

Ah. I waited to see if any residual jealousy surged within me, but other than concern for her safety, I felt nothing. The longer I spent thinking about Nate's lies, the less the entire situation made sense. Sure, I'd initially been pissed, but I saw the way he looked at Mari. I'd watched him interact with her, and I'd checked every single second of his time at the mansion while she'd isolated herself from us. He'd never taken a step out of line.

If he truly was a spy, he was a fucking terrible one.

But Mari wasn't ready to hear that yet.

"That's where you were last night? With him?"

She nodded, and I pulled her closer, letting her rest on my chest so she knew I wasn't mad. She hummed in her throat, a happy sound that made me smile, even if the situation sucked. "I needed closure."

"Did you get it?"

It took her a long time to answer. "I don't know. He says he loves me, that he made a mistake and he's going to fix it, but I can't get over it."

"Do you believe him?"

"How can I? He's a liar. All he did was lie to me. To us."

That wasn't all he did, but I could understand his lies being the most pressing thing for Mari. "Maybe."

Because the more I thought about it, the less the lies made sense. Especially knowing that he rarely lied about anything at all.

And the love he showed Mari, the kindness? That couldn't be faked. Not the way he did it.

No, I had a feeling Nathaniel Beckstrom had been all too honest with my queen, and one day, she was going to realize it.

"I'm sorry I didn't tell you."

"I'm not mad at you, *reina*. I can't understand what you've been through, and if that was what you needed, then so be it. All I ask is that you keep me in the loop." I tipped her head up, pressing a gentle kiss to her lips. "I'll follow you into hell any day, without question."

"I love you."

"I love you too." With a grin, I smacked her ass and kept her still. "Now, rest up. I've got plans for you tonight."

Chapter 20
Mari

The next morning came too soon, but it came with a burst of happiness I wasn't expecting.

I was engaged to Greyson.

Regardless of all the other shit going on, it felt like a dream come true. Greyson had always been my person, and I got to keep him forever. I got to wear his ring and call him my husband for real.

Now, I just had to get the other half of the romance equation sorted out.

"Are you ready to face it now?" Grey's sleep-heavy voice asked. I turned to him with a smile, loving how utterly worn out he looked. His hair was a mess from my hands, and his neck and shoulders had more scratches and bites than I'd ever seen before. We'd gone so many rounds, I'd lost count, neither of us willing to go an hour without touching. I'd had him in every part of my body, and I felt thoroughly claimed in all the best ways.

"I don't have a choice."

"You do," Grey corrected. "But I'm glad you're choosing this."

With another kiss, I slipped off the bed, grabbed his shirt and a new pair of panties before I stepped outside. I was prepared to go searching for Dominic, thinking he'd probably gone to our gym, only to find him sprawled in the hallway, legs askew and hair a mess.

"Have you been here all night?"

He startled awake, forcing himself upright and running a shaky hand through his locks. "Please let me explain. I know you're mad, but I can't—I don't— Please."

Looking over the red-rimmed eyes lined with dark circles and the wrinkles in his clothes, I knew he hadn't slept, and a pulse of empathy took away another part of the edge that had spurned him yesterday.

"Come to the kitchen. I'm making breakfast." He looked surprised at first, but also concerned.

"Are you going to poison me?"

"I can make pancakes," I said hotly, knowing he wasn't asking about actual poison. Breakfast was about the only meal I could make, but it was still something.

Dominic grinned at me, uncertain and a little shy. "Pancakes sound great."

"Good, you start the coffee, I'll make the dough."

Grey choked as he exited the room behind me. "Batter. It's pancake batter."

Fuck. "Whatever."

I could feel the boys exchanging glances behind me, but I didn't care. Just having us all in the same room made me feel more level, and I realized that even if I was mad, I couldn't kick

Dominic out anymore. Everything felt wrong when he wasn't here.

I blamed the engagement for the sappiness.

As if he knew I was thinking about him, Grey pressed a kiss to the back of my neck. "Why don't I make breakfast, and you two can talk this through? I'll have coffee out in a second, too."

Nodding, I motioned Dominic toward the living room. It would've been easier to go into the bedroom, but it felt wrong to invite turmoil into that space right now when it was so full of joy. We settled on the couch next to each other but not quite touching, and we waited until Grey brought us our cups and disappeared again before we got into it.

"Explain."

Dominic set down his cup, his hand shaky, and turned fully toward me. "What my mom said was true. We've been engaged since you were sixteen."

"You knew the whole time?"

He grimaced. "Yes. It's why I kept the name, despite the divorce."

And why the capos had been gunning for him to usurp me. Joaquin knew about the marriage pact. "Mario wanted you to take over."

Dominic shook his head, scratching the scruff on his cheeks as he thought. "Mario's intentions were always his own, but I think he truly intended for Antoni to run Seattle and for us to take Chicago."

"Then he wanted us both dead." Dominic's brows furrowed, and I smoothed them out with my thumb instinctively, unsure why it felt so good to touch him today, when yesterday I hated it.

"You told me a long time ago that you were only allowed to stay in Chicago because you promised *not* to take over. If my father really wanted us to seize the city again, he was ready to watch us die."

"Maybe, maybe not." Dominic snatched my hand off his face, cradling it between his. "Mario probably had a few different paths for us to take to get to the top again, and who even knows if that really was the plan. Maybe he just wanted to connect the bloodlines."

I thought about it, letting Dominic's finger rubbing over my knuckles relax me. "Maybe it wasn't about us, but our legacy. *You* couldn't go back without risking your life, but did your amnesty deal with the Lords mention heirs?"

Dominic startled. "No. You think he was going to put our kids in charge?"

"I think it's easier to usurp a throne when you have twenty years to do it without damaging the entire infrastructure of a city than to try to get it done in just a few and rule over a broken kingdom."

It was exactly what Cash was doing, though he was too impatient to avoid breaking Seattle.

"So you knew about the pact the whole time, yet you didn't come home. Why?" I had to know, even if I wasn't sure I'd like the answer.

"I wasn't intending to follow the pact," he admitted. The sting in my chest made no sense. I knew he hadn't been planning to come for me. All I had to do was look at what he'd done since he left Seattle to know that. For fuck's sake, his extracurriculars rivaled mine, and I certainly hadn't been celibate.

"You were going to stay." And never come home. Then again, had Seattle ever been his home?

He ran his hands through his hair again, cringing at the feeling of them there. "I'm not sure. I was looking for something I couldn't find and searching in all the wrong places."

There were so many places, too. Though I'd tried to avoid it, Dominic's exploits in Chicago always made their way to me over the years. I knew all about the women who passed through his bed, but one of them had always stuck out.

"How does Rose play into this?"

Her name dropped like a boulder between us, and I realized that even though we hadn't talked about her—hell, maybe because of it—she'd been a sticking point in our relationship. He said he wanted me, but he'd wanted her once too. What the hell was to say he wouldn't change his mind with me like he had with her?

Dominic swallowed, tightening his grip on my fingers before he spoke. "Rose and I met in college. We were together for three years, engaged for one, before I eventually ended not just our engagement, but our relationship as a whole."

I knew that. Had heard all about the scandal through the grapevine. What I didn't know was, "Why?"

He looked at me then. Held my eyes like he needed me to know what he was saying was the truth. "Because I was never meant to marry anyone else."

"Because of the pact."

"Because of you." Dominic watched me before he moved toward me until our knees were pressed together and his hands were in my hair. "All the pieces I loved about Rose were pieces that reminded me of you. Her strength, her resilience, her...innocence." He had the grace to wince. "I'd been searching for someone who felt like home, only to realize that home was never in Chicago. It was with you, wherever you were. Rose was the unfortunate consequence of that. I never should've agreed to marry her."

The jealous part of me clung to the fact that he didn't marry her. I wanted to ask, wanted to dig out every detail of their relationship, but I wouldn't do that. It wasn't my place and, honestly, asking felt more harmful than guessing. Besides, Dominic felt terrible about what had happened, and the more I asked, the more the wound would hurt him.

And I didn't think I wanted to hurt Dominic Marcosa anymore.

"You didn't set out to hurt her."

"But I still did it. I'm very good at hurting the people who love me." He looked up at me, gaze weighty. "I'm so sorry, Mari. You deserve more than another apology, but it's all I've got for you other than my assurance that it's going to happen again."

I jerked. That wasn't what I was expecting him to say. He tightened his hands in my hair, keeping me still for him.

"I don't want to lie to you. I'm a fuckup, we both know that. I'm going to make mistakes, I'm going to step on your toes, I'm going to make you angry. There's no doubt about it, just like there's no doubt you'll do the same. But I'm always going to apologize. I'm going to prove that I'll fix whatever I break. I promise you that. I just need you to trust me."

He grabbed my hand in his, pressing soft kisses along my fingertips. "Give me another chance, Mari. Tell me I haven't lost the only thing I care about."

Dominic's eyes were so impossibly hopeful, yet tinged with defeat, like he expected me to walk. Maybe he felt that way because I'd proven that I couldn't handle conflict well. Instead of staying and fighting, I ran and distanced myself. I isolated. Maybe we both had work to do.

"I should've let you explain last night."

Relief lowered his shoulders, and he kept kissing my fingers, one knuckle at a time. "I get why you didn't. You needed time to think things through and get past the initial shock. I just—don't kick me out again. Be mad all you want, ignore me if you have to, don't touch me if it feels wrong, but don't cut me off from you. Not completely. I can't take it."

Considering I'd felt the same this morning, I had no problem agreeing. "I need you to tell me your secrets, Dominic. I'm trying to understand that you had a life before me, but I can't build a life with someone I don't know."

"I know. I'm sorry." He swallowed thickly, keeping his eyes on my hands. "Are we okay?"

I stole my hand back, only to press it to his cheek, pulling his gaze to mine. "We're okay."

"Thank fuck." His hand pushed mine harder into his skin, and he leaned forward. The kiss tasted like apologies and new beginnings, and I had the fleeting thought that what Nate had done wasn't all that different from Dominic. Hell, Dominic had kept his secret for far longer.

So, if I could accept Dominic's apology, what was stopping me from accepting Nate's?

When we pulled away, Dominic hauled me into his lap, trapping me in his arms like he wasn't planning to let me go. "I haven't forgotten about your disappearing act."

"I went to see Nate," I admitted, hating how his arms tensed around me. "We—"

"I don't need to know."

"But—"

"I trust you to make the right decisions for our family and for yourself, whatever those decisions are." He gently pushed a piece of hair behind my ear, though I could feel the anger coursing through him. He might trust me, but he hated Nate. I couldn't really blame him either. "I love you, *mariposa*."

I clasped his hands in mine, and that was when I saw his attention shift, the laser focus darting to my hand. "Grey proposed?"

There was a lilt to his voice, and I didn't want him thinking Greyson had taken advantage of the rift between us.

"Actually, I did. It was time."

Dominic ran his finger over the ring, silent.

"Are you upset?"

"No. I'm good. This is good."

"It is?" I wasn't sure I believed him, but he nodded and softly kissed the ring.

"Grey's a good man. He'll take care of you."

"He is, but so are you."

"I know, and I fully intend to show you I can be good too. But first, you owe me something."

He flipped me over in his lap, so my ass was bared to the room. "You disappeared on us."

"Yes," I panted. I was a little sore from all the sex with Greyson, but that didn't make me want Dominic any less.

He hummed, sliding his finger along the length of my panties until I squirmed. "I should make you fuck me without coming as punishment."

A bark of laughter came from the kitchen that we both ignored, though I grinned against Dominic's thigh. "I'm pretty sure that's impossible for me."

These men had all my buttons memorized; there was no way I could stop myself.

"You're right. So, let's do this." He hauled me up with a hand in my hair until he could whisper in my ear. "You come until I tell you it's time to stop."

Oh fuck.

"You're so wet I can smell it. Let's see if I'm right." He shoved me farther down so I was nearly face first in the carpet, and he ran his tongue along the damp spot of my panties. "Fuck, you taste good."

Even the heat of his breath against my covered pussy was too much and not enough. "Dominic."

"Hush, baby. I'm going to make you feel so good that you'll think twice before leaving me behind next time."

Before I could even brace myself, he ripped the panties to the side and got to work. His tongue circled my clit, his fingers speared inside me, and he forced me into an orgasm faster than I'd ever had one before. I was barely able to keep my balance, trying—and failing—to rock my hips, as if that would make it any better. Lightning-quick, I came, and Dominic didn't stop. He pulled my clit into his mouth and sucked, pushing one orgasm into two and then into three. His fingers never relented.

It was painful to come so quickly and not nearly as satisfying as it was when I worked to come, but Dominic didn't care. He kept me going until my pussy was truly swollen and we were both drenched in come.

"Enough," I rasped. "Enough."

"Say you're sorry, *mariposa*."

"I'm sorry. I'm sorry. I'll tell you next time. I promise."

"Even if we're sleeping?" he asked, his fingers circling my worn-out clit.

"Yes! I promise. I promise."

"Good girl."

He flipped me over again, holding me steady when the blood rushed back to my head. Then he unzipped his pants and pulled out his dick. "Now, sit on my cock."

I blamed the orgasms for how long it took me to respond. "What?"

"You got me all worked up."

The implication was clear: *You started this. You finish it.* I stared at him, trying to make my brain work faster. "If I do this, we're good?"

"We're already good. You'll do this because we both need it." He was so fucking sure of himself, I hated that he was right.

Rising onto shaky knees, I hooked my panties to one side and rocked my hips along his length, soaking him until he growled and grabbed me by the throat. "Now, *mariposa*."

I lined him up and sank down on his cock before he'd even

finished whispering my name.

"Fuck, this is where I belong," he groaned, holding me captive as he thrust into me from below. "Inside you, all the time."

"You'd have to share," I said hoarsely, trying to move my hips, to do something other than come again because I had a feeling it would wreck me.

"I can work with that," he said, pulling me forward by my throat. "You've got two holes we can use."

Oh my god.

A pan clattered in the kitchen, but neither of us turned to look. I knew for a fact that Grey had finished cooking ages ago and had been watching us ever since. His gaze was a cool breeze along my heated skin, and suddenly, I wanted both of them. Dominic's heat and Greyson's ice. The juxtaposition of two men who hated each other for loving me, only to find peace in loving me together.

I wanted them inside me at the same time so we could truly be one unit.

Dominic's growl sent shivers over my spine. "That's a good girl. Squeeze my cock just like that, and I'll fill you up like you want."

I did want it. I wanted to be owned by both of them, just as I was meant to be. Tapping Dominic's hand, I rested mine on his shoulders and took over, moving my hips over him until he was speaking gibberish and wound tighter than I'd ever seen him.

"I have to come. Fuck, make me come, baby. You can do it."

Despite how nervous I was to do it, I was close too. So I kept going, kept pushing until we were both on the brink of insanity, and then it was over, the tidal wave of pleasure bowing my spine and making me cry out. My voice mixing with Dominic's as he clutched me closer and thrust himself as deep as he could go.

And when it was over, I rocked my hips again.

He winced at the sensitivity, but he didn't stop me. And soon enough, it didn't matter anyway as he was rock hard and ready inside me.

Because I didn't want a piece of Dominic, I wanted all of him. Just like I had with Greyson.

Time was irrelevant as we remade ourselves together. We forgot all about Grey in the kitchen and Cash outside our walls. It was just the two of us enjoying each other, losing ourselves to pleasure, until Grey's phone burst our little bubble.

I startled, looking over with hazy eyes. He stood in the doorway, eyes heated as they ran over me in Dominic's arms, his hand tight against the doorway and his cock hard enough that I could see it all the way from over here.

Dominic's laughter against my throat made me squirm, and Grey's eyes darkened. "I'm sorry to interrupt. I could watch you all day, *reina*."

"What about me?"

Greyson snorted. "You were adequate, but we both know I don't watch because of you."

Then he dug his hand into his pocket and pulled out the phone. "Andrews."

He didn't have it on speakerphone, but his eyes kept me captive, spurring me into the stillness that came from prey being spotted. I wasn't prey normally, but if Grey and Dominic were going to hunt me, I could get on board with that.

"Stop thinking lusty thoughts," Dominic admonished, spanking my thigh.

"Never," I promised.

"I see. We'll be right there," Grey said, turning back to us.

Dominic cursed under his breath and clung to me a little tighter.

"Sorry to interrupt your fun, *reina*, but there's been an attack."

Chapter 21
Mari

There were aspects of my job that I loved. The money was nice, the toys were fun, and the respect was addictive, but the other side was far less enjoyable.

Staring down at the dead body of an old woman was certainly not how I preferred to spend my day.

"What happened?"

"They drove a car through the front window. Mama Ophelia was…" Grey looked at the ground, only to realize the body was at our feet, and sighed. "She was right there."

Which was why she took the brunt of an attack meant for me.

Mama Ophelia was pushing eighty and a widow. She, her family, and their little bodega had been under my protection since Antoni died. In fact, she was the first person who'd asked for my protection. Her husband had just died, and she wasn't sure how to keep everything going. She'd had some of the local gangs sniffing around, pushing her to sell the place so they could turn it into a dealing spot.

I'd sent them running myself.

That first taste of responsibility had set me on the right path. That reminder that I protected mothers and daughters, sisters, and wives humbled me.

Mama Ophelia had changed everything.

And now she was gone. Dead on the floor of the bodega she and her husband had saved for a decade to buy.

All because Cash wanted to prove a point. Just because he didn't try to run me over didn't mean he didn't do this to get back at me.

"She was, and where were you?" Siska, Ophelia's teenage granddaughter, snapped at me. "You're supposed to protect us, and what have we gotten? Huh?"

"Years of peace," her mother said. Aliska took her grieving daughter in her arms, wrapping her tightly in a warmth I'd never experienced. It looked comfortable, and for a moment, I ached for it so fiercely I wanted to turn away. Aliska turned soft eyes to her daughter and wiped her tearstained cheeks. "It isn't her fault that Mama's dead, Sis. She didn't drive the car."

Maybe not, but I was still to blame. If I had taken Cash out sooner, their bodega would be safe. They wouldn't be facing thousands of dollars in damage and lost wages. They wouldn't have to see their life's dream up in flames.

They wouldn't be burying their matriarch.

Aliska tightened her hold on her daughter when I stepped forward, that mama bear instinct out in full force, but I just grasped the girl's shoulder gently.

"I will fix this," I promised, staring directly into red-rimmed blue eyes.

"You will?" She sounded more like a kid than she had the

entire time I'd been there, and it killed me that she had to deal with this so young.

"Yes. I'll make them regret this. Mama Ophelia deserved a better end, and I'm sorry she didn't get it." Turning to Aliska, I nodded to the glass-covered floor that had come from the car slamming into the building. Fuck, the building itself probably had structural damage. The guy had been doing double the fucking speed limit before he'd crashed.

They were lucky Mama was the only one dead.

"We'll pay to get you up and running again and cover any bills you have in the meantime."

Aliska shook her head immediately. "Oh, that's not—"

"It's very necessary. You paid for our protection. This is what that looks like." I moved my hand to her shoulder, squeezing gently. "We'll pay for the funeral too. I want Mama to go out in style. Money isn't an object."

"Mama didn't care about things," Siska said softly.

"No, she didn't, but she was traditional. Bury her according to the customs she preferred. It's the least I can do."

Aliska wanted to argue again, but I stepped away, unwilling to hear it. Mama Ophelia deserved the best, and I wasn't going to let her family worry about a single thing while we sorted through the aftermath of her death.

"Grey will be in touch tomorrow to get repairs started and settle the funeral costs. I'll send over a guard to watch the place full time until it's fixed enough to lock up. Until then, we'll have our people over here more often, but let us know if you need anything else."

We left to soft thanks from both of them, and every word grated on my nerves.

They shouldn't be thanking me. Not when I was the reason their family member had just died. "Hey, wait!" I turned just in time to watch Siska skid to a stop behind me.

"If you're going to knife me, you've got to be quieter next time," I joked. Grey growled beside me, and I was suddenly grateful that Dominic was outside. He wouldn't have enjoyed the joke either.

"You promised you're going to make them pay. Did you really mean it? Because I want a trophy."

"Siska! You are not asking Ms. Marcosa to bring you back a *body*." Aliska's horrified voice carried until everyone in the vicinity stopped.

To Siska's credit, she didn't even flinch. "I didn't ask for a body. I asked for a trophy."

Okay, that was funny.

"She's like you as a kid," Grey whispered, and I seriously had to work to keep the laughter in.

Aliska muttered under her breath—swear words, I was pretty sure—before pointing toward the back hall. "Upstairs, now!"

Siska glanced between her mother and what I assumed was the stairwell. "Is it even safe up there?"

More muttered swearing. "Fine, go to Lena's. Just get out of here."

"I still want that trophy." Siska ran out the door. If I had to guess, I'd say she was desperate for some time with her friends and a moment away from the sorrow.

Aliska walked us outside, her face marred with grief. "I'm sorry about that. She and Mama were close, and she's—"

"I get it." I rested my hand on her shoulder, knowing I couldn't do anything else besides ease their burden. Their matriarch was gone and had left behind a hole too big to fill.

All I could give them was closure. If that meant bringing one of Cash's fingers in a jar for Siska, I'd do it.

Grey wrapped his hand around my shoulder as he squeezed, not to pull me away but to offer me support. I leaned back just enough that he could feel my gratitude before I straightened up and stepped away. "We'll be in touch."

With another nod our way, Aliska went inside, and we headed off to find Dominic.

"They never should've gotten that close," I said softly.

Grey hummed his agreement. "No."

Grey and I made our way over to where Dominic and the others were looking at the car. The man inside was already dead, a gunshot to the forehead the reason he careened into Mama Ophelia's. At least, it would've been, if he hadn't already been heading this way.

"Anything?"

I knew who'd done it, but part of me desperately wanted another explanation. A madman with a grudge just wasn't sitting well anymore.

"Ace." Dominic didn't say anything else, but what was there to say? Cash had done this to undermine my protection, to make the people we took care of fearful and easy to manipulate. As with everything else he was doing, he was making me look inferior while building up his own group to be the better option. He wanted people questioning who to trust. It didn't even matter if those people picked one of the other territory leaders, as long as they didn't stay with me.

And one of my protectees dying like this? It was going to cause some ripples in my pond.

"Do you think there was a reason they went after Mama?" Dominic asked, sitting back on his heels as he looked over the inside of the car again.

"If Cash has really been around as long as we think, he might know that Mama was our first official client after I took over. He could've done it for that reason, or he could've just picked a random place. There's really no way to know."

"Maybe not, but it doesn't seem like a coincidence that he

goes after Shara and Mama Ophelia in the same weekend. This feels personal."

The truth struck me so hard I nearly stumbled. "You think this is Nate, not Cash."

"I'm just saying that if they've got eyes on us, you may have pissed off some people." His gaze dropped to my engagement ring, and I scowled.

"That happened last night, Dominic. No way it has any bearing on Mama's death."

But the text on my phone was a stark reminder that Nate might have said he was sorry, but he was still Cash's boy. *Stay home this weekend. Cash is gunning for you.*

Had he done it? Had Nate been the one to put Mama down? Did he shoot the driver?

Was this some fucking flag they were waving in my face?

I wasn't sure, but I couldn't discount it, could I? Nate wasn't mine, and I had no real idea what he was capable of or what he'd do for Cash.

Swallowing that uncomfortable realization, I nodded to the car. "Let's get this cleaned up and get the windows boarded. The family deserves some peace."

I was a fucking idiot. That had to be why I stepped into Shady Oaks Assisted Living that evening. Not because I missed Nate, liar that he was. It certainly wasn't because, after the day I'd had, I wanted to believe the fantasy he'd fed me so I could fucking breathe again.

Truth was, the longer this went on, the more I needed to know if he was like Cash—like my father—or if the Nate he'd shown me was really somewhere inside him. I had to find out if there was anything worth saving, because after watching my people wheel Mama Ophelia's body out of the store she'd spent her life in, I wasn't so sure I could afford to let him live if there wasn't.

The part of me that still loved Nate with everything I had didn't want to hurt him, but if he'd helped put Mama in the ground, I was going to go scorched earth. Cash was already a dead man, but I would send Nate with him if I had to.

With Greyson stationed in the car, grumbling about staying behind, I signed in at the front desk as Nate's partner, cringing inside at how right it felt to call myself that still, then made my way to his mother's room.

The difference between how Nate's mom lived and how Dominic's did was astounding. The only similarity was how sterile and cold the rooms were, though in distinct ways. The hospital was perfunctory, while Lucia's sprawling mansion held the chill of abhorrent wealth.

Marjorie Black looked peaceful as she rested in her armchair by the window, her eyes unfocused as she took in the trees outside. She seemed too small to me to be Nate's mother, too frail from what I could see, but looks were deceiving. I'd learned that lesson well.

"Marjorie?" I asked softly, not wanting to startle her.

She turned, and it was like getting sucker-punched. They had the same eyes, the same nose. I bet they'd even have similar smiles, if she was inclined to let one loose. It fucking hurt staring at her because she was all the good parts of Nate. The parts that haunted me in my dreams.

"Do I know you?" she asked, tilting her head to the side. I thought I saw recognition in her eyes, but knowing we'd never met helped me brush it off.

"I'm Nate's friend," I lied. "Can I come in?"

She motioned me toward the chair at her side, and I took it carefully. I wasn't sure how to ask questions and get the answers I wanted. From Nate's admissions and his files, her Alzheimer's was severe. How would I know if she was having a lucid day?

Turned out, I didn't need to worry about it.

"You're not his friend." I glanced up and saw her eyes trained on me, bright and aware.

"I'm not."

"Last I heard, you were his girlfriend."

I blinked, trying not to let the shock show, but Marjorie noticed. She laughed, wobbly and unpracticed. "You didn't know he told me."

"No," I admitted, letting myself sink into the chair more fully. She didn't seem confused or upset, so I had a feeling we were in a moment of lucidity, and as shitty as it felt, I had to take advantage of it. "We aren't together anymore."

"I know that too. He said he made some mistakes with you."

"He did. Big ones. Ones I'm not sure I can forgive."

"But you want to."

I didn't answer that, but she nodded to herself anyway, looking back out the window. When she didn't speak again, I tried not to let the disappointment drown me. All the research I'd done said that focus could disappear in a second, leaving the patient confused and struggling. If that was the case, I'd lost my chance for more answers.

"He's a good boy stuck in a bad life," Marjorie murmured. "He's been paying for my mistakes since he was five, and I don't know how to fix it."

"What mistakes?"

"Falling for the wrong man." She shook her head, her fingers twitching in her lap. "If Nate had had anyone else as a father, he wouldn't have had *him* as a brother. He'd have been safe."

I didn't know why I did it, but I couldn't handle her beating herself up over everything. I laid my hand on hers gently, trying not to flinch when she looked at me with those eyes that were so close to the ones I loved. "This world isn't kind to anyone. I don't mean to be cruel, but he never really would've been safe."

It was a shitty consolation, but it seemed to do the trick. She patted my hand gently, holding on to me when I tried to let go. "You know, when he told me about you, I thought it was history repeating itself. I thought, *there's no way he gets out of this alive.* But the longer you were together, the more *alive* I saw him. He'd never shone that brightly for anyone or anything before. He's been lost for so long, but I think you brought him home."

"He brought me home too," I confessed, feeling like I'd just carved myself up and handed it to her.

Another pat on the hand and Marjorie's attention went back to the window. Even though I should've asked her more, I didn't. I just sat there, holding my ex-boyfriend's mother's hand in mine and watching the trees shake in the wind.

That was how he found us five minutes later.

"Mari," Nate breathed, his eyes wide and terrified as he looked between us. I could see the war inside him, the urge to step into the room and separate us. He wasn't sure if he should be protecting her or not, and I reluctantly added another point in his favor. It was obvious Nate cared about his mother, and when her eyes brightened again, I knew she loved him just as fiercely.

"I didn't think you were coming." Marjorie motioned him over, pulling him down for a cheek kiss when he was close enough, and I could see that he was as shocked at her lucidity as I was.

"Hey, Mom."

"What, no hello for your friend?" she joked, though her smile was more uncertain than it had been a moment ago. We were losing her again. Nate's joy dimmed, and I suddenly felt awful for taking that time away from them, even if he hadn't been there.

Nate kept his eyes straight on me, like he was trying to read my intent. For my part, I gave him nothing but blankness. There was no intent here. Finally, he swallowed thickly. "Please don't hurt her."

Before I could say anything else, she tossed her hand in the air as if shooing away his worries. "Your friend and I were just talking. She's a good girl. She deserved better than what you gave her. Hell, she deserved better than what the world gave her." Her grip was weak, but she clung to me again. "Don't worry, darling. It'll get better one day. One day, those boys will see exactly what you deserve and give it to you."

Heat pricked the backs of my eyelids and I tried to swallow back the sudden tears, but in the aftermath of Mama Ophelia's death, kindness felt like too much for me to handle.

"Thank you, Marjorie."

Nate and I kept staring at each other until I could feel Marjorie getting agitated, like she was falling victim to the tension between us, and I couldn't handle it. Finally, I relaxed in my chair.

"We're just talking, Nate."

He sagged in relief, and a part of me hated that he truly thought I'd go after his mother. It poked at those fresh wounds and dug in until they bled anew. With a practiced smile Marjorie's way, I stood. "I'm going to give you some time alone. It was wonderful to meet you, Marjorie."

"You too, Mari. Come back anytime."

I didn't agree to that. No way Nate would appreciate me getting closer to his mom, not when she could easily be used against him. Instead, I gave her shoulder a gentle squeeze and left.

"Mari!"

I walked faster, not wanting a direct confrontation with Nate.

Just make it to the car, I told myself. I could break down with Greyson, but I would not do it in the halls of this place.

Because I'd come for a sign, and I'd gotten one. The problem was, I didn't know what to do now.

"For fuck's sake, Mari. Wait!" Nate caught me by the arm and kept me close, voice low enough to make my stomach clench. "If you want to kill me for everything I've done, fine, but leave my mother alone. She really doesn't have anything to do with this."

"She's the reason you came back, isn't she?"

"Cash would've come for me either way, but yes. I wanted to be here for her in case..." In case she died. I stared at him, letting myself actually look at his face again. A little empty, a lot exhausted, and a kind of weary I felt in my soul, but still somehow hopeful. Like a conversation with his mom would lift him up again. He looked so fucking beautiful, it killed me.

"Were you at Mama Ophelia's today?" I asked abruptly. I focused on every part of him, desperate for a reaction, and I got one.

Confusion.

He looked at me from under furrowed brows. "Am I supposed to know what that is?"

"No. Why did you tell me to stay home?"

He looked around and crept closer, hiding me from view as a man wheeled a medical cart down the hall. I felt Nate nod at him, but other than a cursory glance my way, he didn't stick around. Nate's voice was barely higher than a whisper when he spoke. "Cash didn't like that you got your girl out so fast. He had plans for her inside. He was pissed and wanted to do something bigger, something you couldn't avoid."

So he'd gone for my people instead of my family.

"Would you ever order a strike against an innocent family?" I was pretty sure I knew the answer, but I had to know for certain.

Nate's eyes darkened, the pain in them so noticeable it made my chest ache. "No." He looked away, clearing his throat. "Do you really believe I could do that?"

"Do you really think I'd go after your mother?"

We stared at each other, all heartache and mourning, the words unsaid but so fucking clear I could practically read them in the air. When neither of us took that first step, toward reconciliation, toward peace, I slipped under his arm and down the hall.

No, I didn't believe Nate could condemn innocents to die. That was the problem.

If he wasn't what I thought he was, and he wasn't like Cash, who the fuck *was* Nate Beckstrom?

Chapter 22
Nate

I'd never been to the Celestine, but I certainly hadn't been idle when I was in Mari's home. The security system was near impregnable, but I'd found a small blind spot on the penthouse floor.

Telling Moore hadn't been a huge priority since it was twelve stories up, and I doubted anyone in their right mind was going to climb twelve fucking stories to get to Mari.

I was not in my right mind.

From the moment I walked into my mother's room and saw Mari there, everything had shifted. I'd been sitting there for longer than they knew, watching the ease she had with Mom.

The kindness she showed her. Despite everything I'd done, Mari hadn't taken it out on my mother.

It wasn't just my love blinding me to her faults either. Mari's character was the reason I'd changed my mind about pursuing her in the first place. Like me, she was someone good who was born into a world that didn't like her for it, and this had gone on too long.

Besides, the love I had for her was different. I'd never been in love before, had no business trying when I knew my brother would destroy it for himself, but this felt like more than first love. This was soul-deep, lifetime and beyond shit. There wasn't a world where I didn't try to keep Mari forever, but I didn't know if she felt the same anymore, and I couldn't stand it. I'd given her space, but knowing she'd gone to my mother to check she hadn't been wrong about my character stung. She deserved the truth if we were going to find a way forward like I wanted, and she needed it now. Hence my midnight climb.

Honestly, it wasn't that bad since I started from a neighboring roof to get onto the Celestine then climbed down, but it was slow going. Trying to avoid detection was more important than speed. This was a one-chance operation. If Moore figured out I could get to Mari, he'd lock this place down in a heartbeat, and I'd have to wait around until I could get her alone again. Something told me we didn't have time for that.

It was laughably easy to get inside, and I settled into the pristine apartment to wait for my moment. Though it was almost midnight, I could hear Mari and the others in the kitchen. The clang of pots told me Greyson was cooking a snack as Dominic and Mari ribbed each other. The hole in my chest grew as I realized I should've been there too. I would've been poking at Dominic and making fun of Mari. The hole I should've fit in was empty, and they'd closed ranks around it. The reminder that they'd been a family of sorts before me was stark.

Just because they'd invited me into it didn't mean they mourned my loss.

I was so distracted by the pain of it that I almost missed my chance. Mari's soft footsteps were so quiet under Dominic's and

Grey's voices that they were hard to make out. I caught them just in time, waiting until Mari stepped past me to make my move. All it took was a quick glance to make sure the others weren't looking, then I reached out and snatched her.

I had her pressed against the wall, one hand on her mouth and the other restraining her hands before she even realized what happened.

"Don't scream."

I don't know if it was my scent or that she recognized my voice, but the way she melted at my whisper made my pulse race. She instinctually leaned into me, that touch easing some of the agony I'd been living in without her. Having her in my arms made me feel like I could breathe again.

She was mumbling against my hand, and I didn't need to hear the words to know what she was asking.

What the fuck are you doing?

"I think it's time we talked. Properly."

Her snort made it obvious that an ambush fifteen feet from her partners wasn't exactly a proper conversation, but it was the only way I could see her.

"I don't want to hurt you. Not now, not before. If you still hate me after this, I'll go. I'll leave you alone, but I need you to hear this. Hear me." The lie slipped out slick as silk, but I didn't dwell on it. If Mari didn't realize I wasn't letting her go, then she hadn't been paying attention. If I could've walked away cleanly, I would've done it already. She was inside me, body and soul, and there was no exorcising her. Not anymore.

My pulse raced as I counted the seconds, praying the others stayed where they were. From our position in the hallway, we were hidden, but the moment they rounded the corner, they'd see, and I really didn't want to shoot my way out of her apartment. Especially because I didn't want to hurt Dominic and Greyson if I could avoid it. I'd never get rid of the guilt.

Finally, Mari nodded, a tiny, almost imperceptible move that lifted my spirits as much as holding her did.

Thank fuck.

I swallowed, pressing myself closer to Mari, stealing her warmth. I hadn't realized how hard it would be to start. "The first time my brother tried to kill me, I was five. I guess he was jealous that our father had another son. He's Cash's idol, and Cash hated that he had to share anything with me. Cash continued his attempts on my life on and off throughout the years until he realized I was worth more alive than dead. I was a good fighter, scrappy and smart, despite being a lot younger. That meant I was small enough to get in and out of places his men couldn't. When he realized I'd also do whatever it took to keep my mom safe, he had me right where he wanted me.

"I started sneaking into houses, stealing whatever he told me to. If I did, he'd reward us. Food for the house, bills paid, whatever. If I didn't, he'd hurt her. Our dad was already in jail at that point, so there was no one to rein Cash in. By the time I turned thirteen, I was already inducted as his enforcer."

Mari had long since stopped struggling, and I leaned my face into her neck, sucking in deep breaths of her scent. I'd never done this before, bared every part of myself to someone, but we needed this. She needed the truth, and I needed the outlet. If we had a future after this, we needed to walk into it clean.

"I killed my first man a few days before my birthday that year, some guy who tried to stiff my brother in a deal. I remember the blood on my hands, sticky and warm. I threw up all over the body. Cash nearly beat me to death because of it. Said my mistake made it harder to cover up the crime."

Mari wiggled her hands, and when I carefully let them free, she snatched mine, wrapping me around her like she could feel how much I needed her. Taking my chances, I let my fingers slip under her shirt. When she didn't buck me off, I traced the warm skin, letting the tactile feel of it ground me, even as I ached for more.

The story would be a lot easier if I had something else to distract me.

As if she could hear me, Mari slid our hands into the waistband of her sleep shorts and pushed both of our fingers inside her.

"Christ," I whispered into her neck. She was so warm and wet. "I didn't come here for this."

She shook her head until I pulled my hand away, leaning against my shoulder so she could whisper in my ear when I did. "You don't want it?"

"I didn't say that." I'd always want her. "But you need to know the truth."

"I need something else too."

Her voice was greedy and desperate, and every protest on my lips stopped. I'd do anything for Mari. No questions asked. If she needed me, I was there. Even if it was just for a quick fuck.

Stretching my thumb up, I played with her clit while we finger-fucked her pussy together. "Did they leave you wanting, baby?"

"No. I'm like this for you."

Christ. "I love that about you."

She stiffened a little at the comment but ground her hips into my hand anyway. "Keep going. I want to hear it all."

"I was an enforcer for three years before an officer came to my school. Cash wanted me to drop out to work with him, but Mom and I convinced him that it would look too suspicious. The kid of a career criminal needed to keep his hands clean, especially when the cops were already sniffing around. If he wanted to keep the heat off us, I needed to graduate. He didn't agree, but he didn't push either because he was *this close* to a life sentence beside our father.

"The officer came by every week for months, and I slowly started to talk to him when I knew I wasn't being watched." I sighed. "Officer Tate was the first person to ever help me."

"He got you out." Mari's voice was all breath, barely even audible, and I was as close as I could be. Her heart was pounding so hard I felt it through my chest, and her hips were restless as they chased release. She pulled her hand out, grasping my wrist with sticky fingers that I quickly replaced with my own, not wanting to lose our momentum. I was rock hard and grinding against her ass, and I didn't even care. This moment felt like everything we'd never had and everything we needed.

It felt like possibility, and I wasn't going to stop for anything.

"He did. I asked if they could keep my enlistment quiet somehow. I didn't tell them about Cash, but Tate was a local and he'd heard the rumors. He personally drove me to the hotel the night before we left for basic and promised to keep my mom safe too."

"How'd you get Cash to let you go?"

"I told him the truth. Officer Tate had his eye on me and was asking me about potential for special training, training I could use when I got back. If I agreed to come back to the city when I was done, Cash promised to leave my mom alone, especially when it became clear she needed a facility. It was a no-brainer."

"More," she sighed, and I couldn't take it. My hand stilled and she whined softly, trying to move even as I kept her hips captive.

"You want me to fuck you, angel? Want me to slide my cock inside you while your boyfriends are in the other room?"

"Yes. Fuck yes."

I shoved her shorts down around her thighs, unzipped my pants, and pulled myself out. The first squeeze was painfully good, and I just knew I was going to have to fight not to come early. Yanking her hips back, I rocked myself between her thighs, slicking myself up. She mewled quietly below me, and I bit her neck gently even though my jaw ached to mark her more. There was no way she'd be able to explain things to the others if I sent her back out with a huge bruise. "Beg me, Mari. Say you want me. Say yes."

"I want you, Nate. Fuck, *please*."

"Such a good girl for me. Now, stay quiet." A shift of my hips and I was home, sinking inside Mari's pussy like I didn't ever want to leave.

I kept each thrust slow and deep, wanting to savor every second of contact even when it wasn't a good idea. I shifted my hand around to circle her clit before dropping down to feel where our bodies met. The slickness of her moisture against my fingers and her pussy stretched to take me were almost too much.

"You feel so good," she whispered. "Keep going."

So I did, with everything. "When I got back from the Army, things were different. Cash had spent years setting the dominoes in place for the city and they were finally ready to fall, but you were a wild card. He needed a plan to neutralize you, so he sent me in."

"The ambush at my car."

"Yeah," I sighed, dropping my head to her shoulder. Mari grabbed my hands again, pulling one up to wrap around her shoulders, pressing just barely into her neck. Our bodies meshed tighter together, and her little sigh of relief told me that's what she wanted in the first place. To feel closer even as I explained my duplicity. "I was supposed to get close to you, find whatever information I could to get rid of you and get out. Assassination was also an option, if I could do it without leading your family back to Cash. Instead, I watched you."

"Why?"

"He told me you two were the same. That he'd seen that same depravity in you that he had himself, and it made me wary. I didn't want to do what Cash wanted, but if the city was better off without you, I had to do whatever it took to keep my mother safe. He was wrong, and so was I.

"You were so different. Strong and powerful but down-to-earth. Kind to your friends and family. You did what you had to do to keep your people safe, but you weren't like Cash at all. You cared about who died because of you. You cared about the consequences of your actions. You cared about me, a total stranger."

I picked up my thrusts, not wanting to drag this out anymore, and Mari's nails dug into my skin. I didn't care; she could scar me all she wanted. I wasn't stopping. Not until we were both set free.

Needing to see her face, I wrapped a hand in her hair and pulled so her head dropped back to my shoulder, peppering kisses all over her skin while I fucked her harder. It was hell not being deeper, but I couldn't risk alerting the others yet.

"You took me in when it wasn't really safe because you felt honor bound to do it. You felt like you'd ruined my life, and you wanted to fix that for me. No one but Tate had ever done anything that nice for me. It fucked with my head. I wanted to pretend you were like him, to keep my distance, but I couldn't. You called to me, and my brother noticed. Cash kept asking for intel, but I lied. Said your systems were too advanced or I was too closely guarded to help. He didn't buy it, but he didn't press either, and I thought I could get away with it. I could have you, get rid of him, and keep Mom safe at the same time. Then he took you."

Her body jerked, and I stroked a thumb over her collarbone, reminding her that I was here and she was safe. "Shh, don't be loud, or they'll interrupt."

When she steadied again, I continued, picking up momentum now that we were close to the end. "When you disappeared, I nearly killed Sabine. I was mindless with grief, and the thought that she was responsible for delivering you to

Cash when I'd been so careful not to was agonizing. When you came back alive, I knew I didn't have much time. Cash started calling more, and the nurses let me know he was trying to visit my mom. I knew I could've told you—I *should have*—but the arrogant part of me thought I could fix it all before you noticed. I was wrong, and I lost you in the process. I'm sorry for that."

Mari's eyes were glassy as they looked my way. She was close to coming, but both of us were holding out even though it was obviously a struggle. My arms were shaking with the need to shove myself deep and come inside her, but I held back. *Not yet.*

"Why'd you leave?" she asked softly.

"He'd wanted me home for weeks, but I kept deflecting, saying I was close to getting into your systems. The night we torched the hospital, he told me he was paying my mom a visit the next night and whether she survived was up to me. I had to go, even though I hated it."

"So you fucked me and said goodbye."

"Yes." I saw the hurt on her face before she turned it away, and I kissed the glimmer of a tear I knew she'd never let fall. "I'm so sorry for that. It wasn't fair to you. I regret it."

"You regret telling me you loved me?"

"No." Instinct had me hauling her closer, reinforcing my claim. "Never. I'm just sorry I did something so shitty to someone I love. It wasn't right. None of it was right. If I could do it all over again, I'd change so much, but I can't. All I can do is promise it won't happen again and beg you to forgive me."

Dominic's voice slithered over us, asking Greyson if Mari was okay, and I knew this had to end. Our time was running out. Sliding my arm tighter around her shoulders, I picked up the pace as much as I could without making too much noise. "I need you to come, baby. Let me have it."

She shook her head, and I kissed her cheek sweetly as I

circled her clit again and again. "Yes. You can do it. Come on, angel."

When she squeezed around me, her eyes rolled back, and I fought not to do the same. I had to commit this look to memory in case I never got it again. My final thrusts were shallow since I desperately didn't want to leave the deep warmth of her body, and when I came, we were as close as two people could be.

"I love you," I whispered into her hair.

She didn't say it back, but that was okay. I knew she wouldn't.

For the longest time, we soaked in the press of our bodies against each other and the warmth of my come deep inside her.

Mari was the first to break the silence. "Cash killed an old woman yesterday."

"He did." I wanted to explain that I knew all about Mama Ophelia, but Dominic and Grey were getting restless in the kitchen. "Please trust me when I say I took care of it."

"She was hit by a car."

"She was high as a kite when it happened."

"What? Why?"

The visit to Mama Ophelia's had been somber and sad, but in the end, the old woman had made the choice. She loved Mari and she loved the city, but she was tired. She was older than dirt, and with no signs of her body giving out, she was desperate to be with her husband again. I gave her death a purpose, because it was the only solution.

"It was her or you, angel. She chose herself."

"Did you send the Wolf the ledgers?"

"No." I wanted to ask about the meeting, but I knew she wasn't ready to trust me with those answers yet.

"Do you know who did?"

"Not for sure."

"Give me something, Nate," she begged. "I want to believe you're not a heartless bastard."

That wasn't all. She wanted to believe me, but I couldn't tell her who the spy was, not without putting all of us in more danger than we could handle right now. That was an endgame move, and we weren't ready yet.

"My brother is obsessed with our father. He wants to emulate him. It's a sick sort of hero worship to Cash."

"Why?"

"Because Alec was set to take the city before Mario got to it, but he wasn't as strong, and when the Marcosas came in, he knew it. He gave up quickly, so he got to live, but he was still sent to prison for murder."

I wanted to explain more, but I couldn't. Not yet. Mari was still too stiff in my arms and I wanted that softness back, so I kissed her cheek again and again until she seemed to lose some of the steel in her spine. "Do you still hate me?"

"No." But she still wasn't sure about us. I hated that I had no way of fixing it except having patience.

"That's okay. I've got time."

Her arms fell to her sides, and I took advantage, swooping in for a hug and a searing kiss. It wasn't until she laid her hand on my cheek that I felt the chill of metal on my skin. Pulling back, I saw what I'd missed.

An engagement ring.

It was beautiful, exactly what I would've picked for Mari, but a deep part of me hated it too.

She was supposed to wear my ring.

One thing at a time, I reminded myself. If I could get her to stop hating me, to give us another chance, I'd happily play boyfriend for the rest of our lives.

She watched nervously as I gently rubbed the ring with my thumb and pressed a kiss to it. "I want this one day."

Obviously, Mari hadn't been expecting that. She jerked, ripping her hand away by accident. "Nate."

I just smiled, diving for one last kiss. "I have to go, but if you need me, call and I'll come. Okay?"

"Okay."

I hoped I'd done what I set out to do, but I couldn't stick around to find out. Dominic had finally lost his patience and had come looking for her. "Congratulations, Mari. Grey's going to be a good husband."

Then I slipped out the window and away from the love of my life.

If I wanted forever too, I had a war to stop and a psychopath to put down.

Chapter 23
Mari

My head was still reeling from Nate's confession and the unexpected orgasm he left me with when I finally slipped back into the kitchen.

Nate had infiltrated my home, my family, because he'd had no choice. Either he did it, or he condemned his mother to die. I wouldn't wish that ultimatum on anyone, but could I forgive him, even if I would've made the same decision?

And that was only part of the problem. Even if I forgave him, could I ever forget? Could that trust we'd built be mended, or had we lost everything we needed to repair? If anyone but Nate had betrayed me, I'd have killed them on the spot, but I didn't. Nate was different. He'd always been different, but that didn't mean I knew what to do.

Slinking into the room, I wrapped my arms around Greyson

while Dominic was grabbing a shower. Dipping, my fiancé kissed the top of my head. "You smell like sex, *reina*."

Oh fuck. I'd run to the bathroom to clean up a little since I couldn't exactly walk in with come dripping down my leg, but I hadn't wanted a full-blown shower. I needed Nate's scent on my skin for a little longer.

Note to self, stay away from Dominic.

When I stiffened, Grey kissed me again and pulled me tighter against him. "I take it we have a visitor?"

There was no anger in his voice, and I didn't realize I'd been nervous about his reaction until then. With a happy sigh, I melted against him, grateful once again that Grey was there for me through everything. "He's gone."

"For now."

Not knowing how to answer that, I took the mature route and ignored it. Dominic came back, making it much easier than I expected. "I thought we could watch a movie tonight."

It'd been so long since we'd all just relaxed together, and I missed it. Despite the chaos looming, I wanted to enjoy my partners. The situation with Nate taught me there was no guarantee that tomorrow came with all of us alive.

We needed to celebrate every minute we had together.

Admittedly, it felt shitty to celebrate life when someone had just died, but Mama Ophelia had made that choice for herself. I had to believe that.

"Sounds great, baby. I'll get the popcorn."

In minutes, I was plopped between them on the couch, popcorn in hand and bickering over which movie to watch.

"We're not watching some B-list mafia movie when that's our entire life." Grey rolled his eyes, and Dominic mimicked him back like a child.

"What's wrong, Andrews? Worried you're doing it wrong?"

"Oh, fuck off." Greyson threw a pillow, and the two of them laughed.

"Are you going to start a naked pillow fight like at a real sleepover? If so, I want to be the judge." I grinned, leaning back so I could have the best view. Both their eyes darkened, and like they planned it, each of them dropped a hand on my thigh.

"If you want us naked, baby, all you've got to do is ask." Dominic leaned in for a kiss, but the shrill tone of my phone cut him off. "Motherfucking cocksucker."

He leaned back and snatched it off the coffee table where we'd thrown all our devices in hopes of a quiet evening, scowling at the display. "It's Cameron."

Grey sighed, sitting back. "If it were anyone else, I'd say we could play, but he could have news about Joaquin."

Ah, yes. My asshole uncle who'd been planning my demise as boss bitch of the Marcosas. Couldn't wait for that update.

"We'll play after."

Dominic grinned, slipping off the couch and putting his big body between my legs. "Better hurry, *mariposa*. I'm getting hungry, and I'm not sure I can wait to start the feast."

Hell yes.

I lifted the phone to my ear, wondering how fast I could get my cousin off the phone so our evening could continue. "Yeah?"

"There's a fire!"

For a second, I was paralyzed, then I shoved Dominic out of the way and ran for the nearest shoes I could find, smashing my finger into the speakerphone icon. "What?"

"The Aces set my house on fire. Mari—" My cousin's voice broke, something like desperation and resignation soaking into it. "Ash and I are inside."

No. I stilled with one boot tied and the other's laces wrapped around my ankle. This wasn't the time for slip-on sneakers. Thankfully, the boys were hot on my heels as I worked the laces into the boot, shoving their feet into shoes and grabbing guns, all while barking down the phone at people. "Excuse me?"

"I was outside when I saw them running away like cowards, and I knew she'd be asleep. I went in for her, but we got trapped." He paused, and I could hear the crackle of flames through the speaker. "I can't get us out, Mari."

Snapping out the address to the boys, I grabbed a gun and bolted for the elevator. "Why did you do that?"

"Because she's my wife." That was it, and really, there was no other reason needed. Ash was his, no matter what. Of course he went after her. *Fuck.*

"Cameron Marcosa, if you die—"

The call dropped before I could finish, and I felt the screen crack under my unforgiving hand. Grey replaced it with his, and I dialed up a number I'd never used before.

"Chief McDaniels, it's Marianna Marcosa." Yes, I had the fire chief's personal number, and I damn well used it. He promised to be there right after us, and I hung up as we raced to the car and through the silent streets of Seattle, but I wasn't sure if we would be too late.

How far had the fire spread?

How long had Ash been inside?

Was she even alive?

Was Cameron?

A wave of grief tried to crush me, but I refused to entertain it. Until I was staring down at their bodies, we had time.

On impulse, I threw a text to Nate, knowing it probably wouldn't do anything.

Cameron's house is on fire. 4486 TeeTree Road.

I didn't tell him we were going in; he already knew that. I just had to hope this was a rescue mission and not a recovery.

* * *

For once, I was grateful to be at the Celestine. If we'd still been at the mansion, we never would've made it in time. We'd blown through every light and stop sign we passed and cut the ten-minute trip in half, planning on the way even without any idea what we were walking into.

Grey and I took the time in the car to get ourselves as prepared as we could be, even working on Dominic while he drove. Damp clothes, gloves, snowboarding goggles left over from last year, and cloths around our mouths and noses. We didn't have oxygen masks like the firefighters would, so we had to be quick and strategic. We had no room for error here.

Pulling into the driveway was like walking right into hell. The fire roared, and all I could hear under it was the groaning of the wood and the snapping of beams. Some cars were here already and I could hear the distant sirens of the fire engine, but no Cameron. No Aislynn.

The boys and I shoved out of the car, gathered what we needed and headed toward the inferno.

"The fire department and the rest of our men should be here soon. Grey, you're out here coordinating. Dominic, you're with me."

Greyson didn't argue; he just hooked an arm around my waist and pressed our foreheads together, clapping Dominic on the shoulder to keep him close. "Be safe."

I didn't promise to try. He already knew I would. My brain whirled as we got closer to the house, and the heat scorched my skin, so hot it chilled me. *That's not good.* "Cameron said Ash was asleep when the fire started, so we'll head to the east wing and start looking. Work our way down from the top."

"We'll be lucky to get up there without the ceilings collapsing," Dominic said with a grimace.

243

"Then we'll be lucky," I said firmly.

I was almost to the door when he pulled me back. "If we think the house is going, I'm pulling you out, with or without them."

There was no compromise in his eyes or gentle platitudes of *we'll go back in after* on his lips. He was as unforgiving as the fire raging in front of us. Nodding stiffly, I bolted for the door and into the house.

Inside was like nothing I'd ever seen before. Everything was fire and smoke. There was no air, no safety. Just chaos and danger in every corner. The idea that anything had survived felt foolish as the flames curled wallpapers and destroyed curtains.

Refusing to give up, I motioned for Dominic to follow me when we finally hit the third-floor landing. Breathing as shallowly as possible was difficult, and rushing three flights of stairs in the stifling heat had both of us out of breath. The smoke was thick and acrid, seeping into my lungs and making me desperate to cough, to choke, to get the fuck out. But we were so close.

Almost there. Almost there.

Got it.

"Back up," Dominic barked before I could try the door to their bedroom. I moved just in time to see him heft the ax he'd strapped on before we'd headed in, swinging for the door. The wood cracked near the hinges, and he took advantage, kicking the whole thing down.

The sight of the bedroom engulfed in flames was one I'd never unsee.

Nothing was untouched. The curtains were gone, fluttering to the floor in wisps of fabric, the closet was nothing but kindling, and there on the bed was a person-sized lump.

Tears pricked my eyes, but I blinked them away. There was no room for grief in hell.

"Cameron!" Dominic and I moved carefully, trying to be

aware of the floor as we went, but we found nothing. The room was empty. "Cameron Alonso Marcosa, get your ass out here!"

No response.

"Where would they go?" Dominic asked, pulling me farther out of the room. Tears streamed down both of our faces despite the goggles, and my head was getting woozy. We had to get out soon or the smoke would get us before the fire did. "Mari, focus. Where would you go if you were in this?"

I tried to think like my cousin, tried to put myself in his shoes. My soaked shirt warmed to the touch, and I gasped, regretting it instantly when the smoke scorched my throat. "Bathroom."

Cameron would've tried to get Aislynn ready to brave the flames, and that meant water.

Dominic stormed across the room and kicked the door in with no warning. It was a lot easier this time because the frame itself was barely standing. We had to get out. If the foundational points of the house were that easy to tear down, the house was going to fall apart around our ears.

"Here!"

Rushing in, I took stock of my cousin in the bathtub, rocking his soaked wife in his lap. Ash's eyes were closed, her face a little gray, though I couldn't tell if that was from the soot or something else. "Is she—"

"Take her." The rage in his eyes was barely tolerable as he held Ash up to me. I tried, but I was too weak already to carry her, so Dominic took her instead. Without Ash on his lap, I saw why Cameron hadn't been able to get out.

His legs were a mess of angry skin and burned fabric. The burns looked bad, and given the number of them, I knew the clock to get him help was ticking fast. "Come on. We have to go."

He grabbed on to my hand, hauling himself halfway out of the tub before collapsing. "I can't."

"You can. Try."

"I can't."

I couldn't pull him with us. He was too heavy. He had to get out on his own. "*Please*, Cameron. Try harder."

"Mari!" Dominic's voice cut through the screaming in my head. I was going to lose my cousin because I wasn't strong enough.

"I'll come back for him," Dominic promised, but we all knew the house wouldn't stand that long.

"No! Get up!"

Cameron grabbed me by the wrist and shook me. "Please get her out. She doesn't deserve this."

None of us did, and that enraged me more than anything. We hadn't done anything to deserve this. My father had. Cash had. And we were paying the fucking price.

"Mari!" Dominic barked, and I knew if I didn't move, he'd drop Ash where he stood and take me out instead. I couldn't let that happen.

Looking back at Cameron, I felt my heart break. "We'll be right back."

"I have no doubt. Love you, cousin."

"I'm not saying it back."

Cameron smiled, something bittersweet and aching. "Okay."

Forcing myself to turn away, I saw Dominic waiting for me at the edge of the room. "Go!" He hoisted Aislynn higher in his arms, and I had to force myself to look forward as we ran. Cameron would either be alive when we got back in or not, but Ash was our priority, like he wanted.

I had to believe that the universe wouldn't take my final cousin from me like this.

I stayed on Dominic's ass the entire way through the house and down two flights of stairs before the house gave up. It groaned a deafening noise, and the stairs collapsed with Dominic and Ash on one side and me on the other.

Chapter Twenty-Three

"Mari!" He twisted around, arm outstretched to reach me as the stairs wobbled.

"Go! I'll be right there," I promised, already trying to figure out a way down, but the gap was too big. There was no way down. Not without going up. "I'll find a window. Just go!"

I was begging, and I didn't care. He and Ash could still make it if he hurried. He could save her.

Please don't stay and watch me die.

"I'm coming right back," he promised, his voice dark with agony. With grief.

"I know. I love you." It felt shitty to say it to Dominic when I'd refused my cousin, but I couldn't let him walk away without it.

"Don't you fucking dare," he snarled. "You get out of this house alive, or I swear to god, I'm burning the city you love down."

"I will. I promise."

The house groaned again, and Dominic took a step back. "I love you, *mariposa*. I'm coming back."

Then he ran out of the house with my sister in his arms.

Going down the stairs was impossible, so I went back up. A jump from the third story was a death sentence, but if I could find a soft place to land, I could make it out of the second story with some injuries. At least I'd be alive.

Bones healed; body bags didn't.

Rushing through the second floor, I picked through the rooms, trying to stay as low as I could to avoid too much of the smoke. I'd already been inside too long and I knew it, but I was so close to getting out.

You can do this.

When I turned the corner, I realized I was right by Cameron's office. Knowing him, he'd left a secondary exit just in case things went sideways.

I was right.

The window opened easily, and I had just hoisted one leg onto the ledge when the wall crumbled and the floor went out from under me. For a second, I thought I could hold on. I wasn't strong enough to carry Cameron, but I could do this. I could get myself out that window.

But my gloves were soaked, and my grip was too weak.

It was a short, sweet fall to the floor. My hip ached at the landing, and the breath was knocked out of me, a dangerous thing when I was already struggling to breathe.

Disoriented wasn't the word as I tried to get to my feet amid the flood of papers and books at my feet. The world felt underwater, and all I could think was, *How did they get here?*

Focus, Mari.

I could drag myself out, but I was sure I'd end up under the debris pile if I tried. Still, there was no way I'd give up, so I clawed forward as much as I could, fighting the light-headedness that threatened to sweep me away for good.

When I finally couldn't move anymore, I flopped onto my back in a relatively clear area of the room, staring at the ceiling that looked like it was ready to come down on me. Every breath was a struggle, my eyes were barely open anymore, and I couldn't catch my breath at all.

Maybe he'll make it in time. If anyone was going to beat the odds, it would be Dominic.

Still, the possibility of death felt fitting that it would be like this. Maybe the fire would burn away the sins I'd committed in this life so I could be happy in the next.

My eyes closed, too blurred to be any help, and as I took another stuttering breath, arms came under me, hoisting me into the air. My head lolled into a broad chest as the sweetest words I'd ever heard floated over the chaos.

"I've got you, angel."

Chapter 24
Mari

"Y ou're here," I said softly.

Nate. He'd come. He'd saved me when I was too fucking tired to save myself.

"I'm here."

"Cameron." I tried to tell him, but I fell into a coughing fit that made everything hurt.

"You first, baby."

"No. He's been in here longer."

"I'm not arguing with you, Mari. I'll get you out, and then I'll dig him out." Nate didn't wait for me to respond, picking his way through the debris, dodging hot beams and wobbling sections of floor as he went.

I reached to feel his face, needing him to ground me, and found a mask instead. At first, I wasn't sure why, then I realized, right now, he was the enemy. An Ace in a Marcosa house that was just set to flame.

Dominic wouldn't be the only one to pull a gun if Nate was seen. "It's not safe for you."

"I don't give a fuck. You texted, I came."

That was that. I hated it, but I had to trust that Nate knew what he was doing better than I did at the moment. Resting against him, I drew strength from his steady heartbeat, forcing my lungs to breathe with him. It hurt, but by the time fresh air filled them, I felt better. That might not have been a good thing, though.

We moved around until, suddenly, I was being set down, cold grass at my back. The fabric around my mouth and nose was stripped off, and when the chill hit, I twisted and coughed until I thought I'd puke. Those arms that had cradled me so sweetly disappeared, but I reached a hand out to keep them close even though I was flailing around blindly. He couldn't leave. "Wait."

"I'm going back for your cousin, angel. Do you have her?"

I thought he was talking to me, but Greyson spoke. "Of course. You should stay."

"I can't. I've got a job to do." He brushed his lips against my forehead. "Love you, angel."

"Wait!" I croaked, but he was gone. Suddenly, I regretted asking him. I wanted him with me, even if it cost me my only cousin.

Was that love or obsession? Was it greed? *Was it wrong?* It felt wrong. I didn't want to lose either of them, but I wasn't sure I could lose Nate again.

Cool hands wiped a cloth over my eyes, fingers caressing my cheeks. "He'll be back, *reina*. Have faith."

I'd had faith once, but it had all been burned out as surely as the walls of Cameron's house. Faith was for people with the luxury of believing, but I could hope—and I did.

Grey worked on clearing my face, telling me all about Ash while he did. Apparently, she and Dominic were in the ambulance. Aislynn woke up just long enough to refuse to leave until Cameron and I were out. Dominic had passed out almost immediately after he'd dropped her on the gurney. The smoke inhalation and the strength it had taken to get them outside would have him out for a few hours. Long enough for Nate to disappear again without risking Dominic's wrath.

A small miracle. I listened to Greyson's rambling, but my focus was on the house in front of me. Every second that passed made my hope flag a bit more until I was certain I'd just lost Nate for good.

When he walked out, clothes steaming and my cousin held in his arms as securely as he'd held me, I thought I was going to die. My heart pounded in my ears as he walked closer, laying Cameron at my side.

"He's alive, but he needs a hospital."

"I've already called Dr. Grant. She's waiting for us," Grey offered.

Wanting to thank him, I turned back to Nate, only to realize that his clothes weren't just smoking because he'd been inside. "You're hurt."

His shoulder was a mess, the skin red and angry. He looked down at it, and even if I couldn't see his face, I knew he winced. "I am, but I can't stay."

"You can't let that go untreated," Greyson said, stepping closer. "You'll get an infection or something."

"If I stay and he finds out, we're all dead. My mom, the three of you, me. You have no idea how unstable he is."

"So, tell us." It was an olive branch, but one he'd earned.

Nate didn't have to save us. He didn't have to go back in to get my cousin, but he did. For me. Actions spoke louder than words, and while Nate may have been Cash's, he'd proven he was mine where it counted.

He sighed, rubbing his sooty thumb over my fingers. "If he finds out I was here, Cash won't care what his plans are. He'll blow the city sky-high. He'd rather be king of the ashes than nothing at all."

He leaned over and moved the mask high enough so he could brush a kiss against my lips. "I have to go. I'm so glad you're okay."

"Wait!" I sat up, struggling until he slid his arm behind my back and helped me. "This can't go unpunished."

Nate sighed. "I know, but...he's unstable, angel. I don't want you anywhere near him. Not without me, and I can't go with you. Not yet. Not until I'm done."

I wanted to ask what he was waiting for, but I was realizing that I needed to have more trust in my men and Nate. He needed me to try. We both did. "Give me a target I can hit that he'll care about."

"The Cardinal."

What the hell? "That's Marcosa territory."

"Not the second basement."

Motherfucker. Deciding not to comment on the *second* basement in my building, I asked, "Why is it important?"

"Our father used to live there before you took it over."

I remembered what he'd said, about Cash's obsession with Alec and Mario taking over where their father was trying to rule. Knowing that, it made sense that Cash had a home base his father used. He was trying to emulate him. "We'll take care of it."

Nate clenched his hand around mine, forcing me to focus. "Mari, I need you to be careful. Cash isn't just unstable because he's a psychopath. He's unstable because he's an addict."

Grey cursed under his breath, and I felt like doing the same. Addicts were unpredictable, and one who was already as off-kilter as Cash was bound to be deep in his sickness. It would've been good to know ages ago, but I wasn't going to harp on it now. "What's his poison?"

"Coke."

Well, shit. That made a lot of sense. I'd bet half of his decisions were made when he was out of his mind, which was why he was so erratic. He was following the high and the power it gave him. "How long?"

"Decades. It's bad."

At this point, he probably couldn't function for ten minutes without a bump, which meant he was constantly straddling the line between survival and overdose. His body couldn't take it much longer, and if I had to guess, that was why he kept coming at us. He was running out of time.

"I'll be careful," I promised.

Nate leaned back down, and I kissed him, mask and all. "I'll call you when I can. I love you."

"Be safe," I whispered. "And thank you."

He glanced over at Cameron, who was still unconscious, and turned back with a smile for me. "Anything for you, angel."

Watching him walk away without knowing if he'd be okay was one of the hardest things I'd ever done, and I knew it would only get worse from here.

✳ ✳ ✳

The Cardinal looked different after dark, or maybe it was just knowing that it was going to burn.

Cameron and Aislynn had been transferred to Dr. Grant's care at Seattle General, but Dominic had shoved his way out of the ambulance just as they were about to leave, hacking and coughing and refusing to go home. I'd balked, trying to get him to go in to get checked out, until he pointed out that I'd been inside much longer. If I wasn't going, neither was he. No amount of cajoling or convincing could get him to agree, and Grey hadn't even attempted. Probably because he thought Dominic was right.

Giving up, the three of us drove back to the Celestine long enough to grab what we needed and to have Tennessee lock down the building.

No in or out until we know what's going on.

I already knew what was going on, but I had to bide my time. Once I knew if my cousin was okay, I could make plans. But the punishment had to fit the crime, or I'd invite more than criticism into the ranks.

We got out of the SUV, not bothering with stealth. If the Aces didn't know we were coming, they were fucking stupid. Besides, this wasn't about killing them, like Sevenroe had been. This was about destroying something Cash was attached to because he'd gone after my cousin. Because he'd gone after Ash again.

Fuck with my family, I'll torch the memory of yours.

Greyson stood watch at the car, listening to the police scanners and checking in with our own security team. Knowing Cash had almost gotten Shara into jail made me leery, and even though the officers in charge of that shitshow were now deceased, thanks to a visit from Cameron, I didn't want to risk it. The police weren't ours anymore, and that made them enemies. Plain and simple.

"Are we going to burn it down or level it?" Dominic asked, coughing into his arm as he crouched beside me. We both sounded like pack-a-day smokers, but the EMT I'd finally convinced him to see—as long as I did too—said it would go away with time. We already had an appointment with Dr. Grant when she was done sorting out Cameron and Aislynn.

"Level it. I want it wiped off the map." I could feel his eyebrow rise as he watched me place the first of many explosives.

"This isn't just about him irritating me. It's a message for his little spy too. No one messes with my family."

"And when he retaliates?"

That was the question. Cash would come after us—that was a given—but how would he do it? What would he take that he felt was equally as important to me as the Cardinal was to him?

"We deal with it when it comes."

Now that I knew Nate was on our side, I had a feeling the playing field was going to be much more level. If we could get Nate out without losing him, he could turn the tide.

Dominic followed as I circled the building, checking in with Greyson occasionally. Just after two a.m., the area was silent, not a single soul around. Crazy to think a few hours ago we were sitting down to watch a movie, and now we were demolishing a building that had been in my family for almost longer than I had. With the explosives laid, we had nothing left to do but get out of range and trigger it to blow. Dominic coughed again, and I grabbed his hand, eager to get out of here so I could force him into bed. He looked exhausted.

"All clear?" I asked as we caught sight of Grey again.

"Clear," Grey confirmed, opening the back door of the SUV. "Get inside, and we'll—"

"No." I needed to feel the heat, to let it sink into my bones in a way I'd been too frazzled to allow the fire at Cameron's house.

"You'll be a sitting duck for shrapnel," Dominic snapped.

We were well out of shrapnel distance, but I could see how worried and tired they were. No way was I going to fight them on it. "We'll go on the other side of the car."

I would still feel the heat and see the destruction; I'd just be less likely to die because of an errant brick or something, and they wouldn't have a coronary. Compromise was a lovely thing.

"You want to say anything?" Dominic asked.

Not really, but I thought it. *This is for you, cousin.*

Then I set off the bombs.

The building went down with a bang that shook the car and fucked our hearing. A gust of air blew my hair back in streams as level upon level dropped like tipping dominoes.

It was beautiful.

I'd always liked destruction, the chaos of pulling something to the ground to make way for something new. This time, it was just joy that I'd taken something from the man who had stolen so much from me. It felt a little like justice.

No one said anything as we watched. We couldn't stay long, but I wanted to see what the aftermath was like. I wasn't surprised when no Aces came out of the building and no one drove up. The place was abandoned by Cash's men, but the destruction was meant to be an emotional wound. I didn't need bodies everywhere to make a point. I ignored my phone the first time it rang, but when it started up immediately after, I knew something was wrong. Seeing that it was Nate made everything feel far more dangerous.

"Nate. Are you okay?"

Dominic's head whipped around, and I swear to god, if he could've shot fire out his eyes, he would've. "Give me the phone."

"Fuck off!" I hissed, turning back to my call. "Sorry, what did you say?"

"I said I'm fine, but you have to get out of there."

I batted Dominic's hand away when he tried to snatch my phone and glared at him. "Why? Is he coming?"

"Worse."

What the hell could be worse than Cash coming for me personally?

The flare of red and blue lighting up the darkened street was my answer. *Cops.* "Seriously, he brought the police? It's my fucking building."

"Angel, listen to me. These are not *your* cops. There's a

reason Cash wanted Shara in jail, and if he gets you in there, I'm not sure you'll come out." Nate's voice was desperate, and he panted like he was sprinting somewhere.

"I have protection in jail." Not a lot because my people didn't end up behind bars, but enough. I'd gotten even more after the incident with Shara, but considering I had *just* thought about the pigs being on someone else's payroll, I listened. I hauled Greyson and Dominic behind a small group of trees, hoping that it would give us enough cover to hide in.

"Not for this. Run. I'm begging you."

"I can't." It was already too late. One of the cruisers flicked on their spotlight and shone it our direction. The only thing hiding us was the car, and once they got out of their cruiser, we were all fucked.

Our only hope was they were clueless about who they had at the end of their leash, which was obliterated when someone called my name over the loudspeaker. "Marianna Marcosa, come out with your hands up."

"Don't even think about it. We'll hand ourselves over to the cops. You get your ass up and run," Dominic hissed. "I already left you once today. I'm not doing it again."

"You have to." I pressed my fingers to his lips, speaking quickly because we definitely didn't have time. "Someone set Cameron's house on fire. Only three people knew where it was. Him, me, and Joaquin. That's it. They tried to kill Aislynn, which would've set O'Bannon on the warpath. These idiots need a scapegoat, and our people need a leader they can trust. Right now, that's you two. Keep Joaquin on ice, take care of Cameron and Ash, and get me out as soon as you can."

"Mari—" Grey looked beyond horrified.

"We can work with this," I said fast, hearing more cruisers stop. "People need a reminder that I'm on top, and we'll give them one. I'll make jail my bitch."

Dominic growled. "No."

"Dominic."

"I said no." He wrapped a hand around my throat and brought his lips to mine, biting until the bottom one split. "I'm not losing you again, temporary or otherwise."

With a shove, I was in Greyson's lap as Dominic slunk toward the car and stepped into the light.

"No!" I lurched for him, but Grey held me back, slapping a hand over my mouth as the cops screamed at Dominic.

"Hands in the air!"

I scratched and clawed at Greyson, desperate to get out, but he had me locked in his lap. He dropped his head to my shoulder, whispering, "You can't go out there, Mari. You know you can't."

I never wanted to be the type of leader who required their people to make sacrifices for them, and this was something I couldn't condone. "I can't let him do this alone."

"You said it yourself, your people need a leader they can trust. That's you."

"But Dominic—" My voice cracked, and I hated it. I needed us safe. It was too dangerous to be separated right now.

Greyson squeezed me tight, though it was more comfort than restraint this time. "Is doing his job, Mari. Trust him to get out quickly. Trust him to come back to you."

"Taking the fall isn't his job or yours."

"Yes, it is. We're here to support you and guide you, but we're also here to shield you. Let him do it."

Not like I had any choice but to sit front row as every gun in the vicinity—and there were a lot, considering four fucking police cars were on the scene—turned Dominic's way.

"Who the hell is that?" someone asked.

"The guy who set fire to this building," was Dominic's flippant reply. *Fucking idiot.*

The confusion continued until someone else said, "He's a Marcosa. I saw him when they brought the girl in."

All at once, the other cops seemed to get the memo.

"Get on the ground!"

"Hands above your head!"

"On your stomach!"

They all yelled their own commands, most of them contradictory, and I could practically see Dominic rolling his eyes. I just had to hope that he wasn't going to cause any issues. There were too many to fight off, and I wasn't willing to risk hurting him in a shootout. The Donnaghals would get him out of jail quickly or I would make them regret their choice in career.

"Rogers, go check the car."

My heart went into overdrive, and I pulled out a gun. We weren't hidden well enough for someone to come snooping around nearby. Unfazed, Greyson squeezed me tighter. "Don't."

I didn't drop the gun. We weren't going to die because of a cop on Cash's payroll. Not in this lifetime or the next.

Heavy footsteps smacked the pavement, getting closer by the second, and when they were close to the front of the car, I raised the gun, finger poised to squeeze the trigger.

"You're a bunch of cocksucking assholes." Dominic's voice echoed in the relative quiet, and the footsteps ground to a halt.

"Excuse me?"

"No, I won't. You're a sorry excuse for a cop and an even sorrier one for a man. You're whipped and not in the fun way. Seriously, how do you live with yourselves? The second Master calls, you go running. Fucking pathetic."

"Is he out of his mind?" I hissed.

"No, he's trying to get them away from you."

It worked.

Men with any semblance of power had the biggest egos

around, and Dominic had poked a hole in theirs, rendering them a slowly deflating balloon.

The cops converged on Dominic. Nothing felt right about letting them cuff him, especially when they kicked him as they did. I felt every single hit like it was on my skin, and I was ready to kill each and every one of them. Someone called him a scumbag as they spat in his face, and I wanted to creep out from behind the tree and destroy everyone who touched him.

"Later, Mari," Greyson promised. "We'll take care of them eventually."

We would *destroy* them later. I'd make sure they died bleeding.

Watching them drive Dominic away was so reminiscent of Shara that I thought I was going to throw up. Instead, I pulled out my phone and sent a text to Laidan Donnaghal.

> Dominic arrested. I want him out.

We waited for ages until the cops all left, feeling like they'd taken part of my heart with them.

Chapter 25
Dominic

Despite the family I'd grown up in, I'd never been to jail. Not beyond a holding cell anyway. The fact that the Seattle PD got me booked and changed into the fucking red uniform before Mari got me out was wild. I didn't mind, though. I was fuming mad and ready to take that shit out on anyone who came my way.

Cash set my girl up to die. There was no doubt about it. He wanted Mari in here, away from all the protection her position granted her, so he could orchestrate a hit on her. He probably would've succeeded too.

We'd managed to get some protection in the jail, but not nearly enough for a fucking kingpin to stay safe. If she'd gone down for this, Greyson and I would've had to do some serious work to keep her alive. I was talking about jailbreak-type work. This whole situation screamed of a setup, but what did I know, other than Cash was a psycho and my girl was apparently talking to his brother.

We'd be having words about that.

Walking to my cell was fascinating. At first, everyone whistled. Catcalls and yells about the "pretty boy" were ignored, only for the men to ramp up, shouting offers to get me anything I wanted if I bent over. It was all exactly how I expected it to be, so I kept my mouth shut, my eyes forward, and my vibes gearing toward *back the fuck up*.

Then the whispers started.

I heard Mari's name and then Cash's, and the voices at the bars got hungrier, darker, and I knew that even if she had *some* protection, Mari definitely wouldn't have survived. Not because she wasn't powerful or strong enough, but because there were just too fucking many people in here who weren't on our side, and I had no doubt the women's section was just as split.

In fact, it was probably worse since Cash had been planning to get one of our ladies in there for a while.

The guard tapped my cell, A31, and shoved me inside it. "Here you go, Killer."

Refusing to rub at the bruised ribs his asshole friends had given me, I smirked like a dick. "Thanks for the nickname, but it's not really my style."

The guard looked at me like I was an idiot. "I wasn't talking to you. Enjoy your new bunkie." He jerked his head to the shadow at the back corner and grinned, laughing his ass off as the doors clanked shut behind me.

It wasn't until the shadows moved and I was against the wall, a sharpened toothbrush at my throat, that I realized *I* was not the only killer in the room.

The man was lean to the point of almost being too thin, but those wiry muscles were strong. Most of him was still shadowed, but I caught a halo of dark-blond hair and a flash of brown eyes.

His skin was a dark tan and a little ashy, like he was desperate for some water and a bottle of lotion.

My eyes peered to his side of the room and the near-empty bottle of lotion near the head. I cringed. *Maybe he already has some.*

"You got a name, pretty boy?" He shook me when I just stared silently, bringing my focus back. "Well?" I blamed the fire; it'd zapped all my strength to get Ash out, knowing Mari was inside.

"Dominic."

"You got a last name?"

I thought about my answer for a long time, knowing that if he wasn't a sympathizer, I was as good as dead. This shitty-ass room would be the last thing I was going to see.

Yeah, fuck that.

I wanted to die buried in my girl, not sharing space with some six-foot-something asshole. If he wanted to play, I'd play all fucking day.

Straightening up, I said, "Marcosa," and hoped for the best.

Silence weighed heavy between us, and I could practically see him making calculations that I hoped were the *How can I make this work to my advantage* variety instead of the *How do I kill him without getting another lifetime in this shithole* kind.

"You're the underboss." I nodded, and he stepped back, finally giving me some space. "I'm shocked to see you. Thought it was a rumor you got pinched."

"It was a calculated risk," I said carefully, not knowing if he was really on my side or not. People would say anything to make you believe them.

He nodded like he understood and held out a hand. "Montgomery, but I go by Killer."

Keeping my eyes on the shiv, I shook. He looked down and startled, as if he'd forgotten he had it in his hand. With an apologetic grimace, he tucked it away under his bed and came back.

"I'd say it was a pleasure to meet you, but I don't know if that's true quite yet. Is Killer an accurate nickname?" He smiled at my question, and it changed his whole face, making him look way younger than I'd expected.

"Fuck me, how old are you?"

"Twenty-one and, yes, it's accurate."

Christ, he was a kid *and* a murderer. I mean, it wasn't a surprise in our lives, but still. He should've been in college or going to bars, more focused on getting laid and setting his life up for success. Instead, he was in jail.

While I grappled with that, he lifted up the gray T-shirt he wore and flashed a tattooed chest at me. I stepped back, holding my hands between us. "Look, man. I'm not interested in—"

"Fuck off." He laughed as he tapped the skin near his hip.

I had to get way too fucking close to his junk to see the insignia, but there it was. The filigree M that all Marcosa men had. "You're one of ours?"

He nodded, then shook his head. "I was initiated, but I got picked up almost immediately after. No time on the ground."

"That doesn't mean anything." If he'd been asked to initiate, especially as young as he was, it meant Mari had a reason to ask him to. "What's the protection like in here?"

He dropped the shirt and settled against the opposite wall. "Not much, but it keeps us alive. Most of it has been in place since Antoni was in power."

He said the name with such reverence that I reevaluated him. "You one of Antoni's boys?"

There had been whispers even in Chicago of Antoni taking street kids and initiating them early, giving them a chance to get their lives in order. They were desperate and foolish, but Antoni wasn't the type to play fast and loose with someone's life, and he didn't mistreat them. If he initiated them, he thought they had a chance at something better.

The kid nodded, and I could admit, I was shocked. I'd assumed most of the kids had died early trying to prove themselves. Apparently not.

"How long?"

"Was I in the family, or how long have I been here?"

"Both."

"Seven years in the family, six in here."

Christ, he was fourteen when he blooded into the family, and he'd been arrested just before Antoni had died. That was young. He was either stupid, desperate, or seriously good at his job.

"Tell me what I'm getting into here," I said, taking a chance that he really was on our side. He was still in here, still alive, but who knew if he was loyal to our queen. Jail changed people; I didn't have to be in here to know it.

He ran me through the basics. The food lines, the commissary, the way cell checks went. He also told me which guards were more lenient to contraband than others. Killer or not, he was a fucking gold mine of info. He'd just spelled out the current gangs and their holdings inside the jail when he explained that there'd been some strange dealings lately.

"Guards who've been clean are turning their heads at beatings, longtime rivals suddenly working together to smuggle shit in, best friends killing each other in their sleep. No rhyme or reason to any of it, man."

"How long?"

"About six months ago."

"Around the time Rey died." Mari's former underboss had been feared and revered in equal measure, and his loss had rocked the foundation of the Marcosa name.

Killer hummed. "There's always chaos when power shifts, even in here, but this was worse."

Sitting on my bed, back against the wall, I wondered if it had something to do with not just Cash, but Nate. How long had he been out of the Army? How long had he been in the city?

Was he the catalyst for all this?

Not knowing how much time I had, I decided to utilize Killer's information and put the fear of god back into the Marcosa name. But first… "Have you heard anything about Cash in here?"

"Only that he's a fucking psycho." I raised a brow, and Killer blew out a breath. "Honestly, it's his people who make me nervous."

Dread pooled in my stomach, and I thanked every deity I remembered that Mari wasn't in here. "You have Aces in here?"

"Yes, and they're insane. Genuinely, certifiably insane. None of them should be in gen pop. I have no clue how they weren't hospitalized instead of jailed."

A shitty justice system, probably, but I didn't say that.

A loud bell preceded a guard's voice echoing through the cellblock. "*Inmates, on your feet. Time for chow.*"

Killer walked with me to the now-open door, holding me back before I left the cell. "I've got your back out there. The Aces have been out for blood."

As we stepped into line, I thought about what Mari had said and realized she was right. We needed to remind people that we had power everywhere, even in jail. My job was to take care of problems that didn't need her attention, so I'd send a few messages while I was inside and get back to the real world before I caught a knife in the back.

Easy.

The mess hall was uncomfortably quiet. There were low conversations, but the tension was thick enough to snap. "Is it usually like this?"

"No." Even his voice was tense, and I could see his eyes darting everywhere.

That's comforting...not.

We edged forward a bit more in line, with Killer nearly plastered to my back. It was honestly as safe as possible. Or, I'd thought it was.

I stepped up to get my food, when two big bodies shifted beside me. "What the—"

They moved quicker than I expected, snatching me away from Killer and shoving me into the kitchen, where another man waited. The move was so smooth and practiced, I wasn't surprised not a single guard had noticed.

It definitely wasn't their first time.

"Dominic Marcosa, underboss to that bitch. You're worth a lot of money."

My fists clenched at the disrespect, but I held myself back. Taking two of them down wouldn't normally be a problem, but the third was an added difficulty, especially when my eyes and lungs were still fucked from the fire.

Did I show them any of that? No. I was Mari Marcosa's underboss, and I didn't cower for anything. I threw my arms out to the side, cocky as always. "Well, let's go, then."

I held my own fine for a while. The first guy went down in a shower of bloody curses and broken teeth. The second went down in silence with a right hook to the eye, but as I went to finish the third, I made a critical error.

Never take your eyes off your opponent.

My focus had shifted to the third asshole, so I didn't see the first one get back on his feet. Didn't even know he'd moved until the flash of movement caught my eye. I twisted, avoiding a straight shot to the kidney, but he still stabbed me.

Motherfucker, that hurt.

Grunting, I angled my body so I could see all three of them, berating myself for the mistake. "You think that's enough to take me out?"

"Maybe not right away, but it'll get you eventually. Unfortunately, the boss said we had to make it messy."

Of course he did.

I straightened, ready to take them all on, when the door slammed open to reveal my pissed-off bunkie. He took one look at me, eyes narrowed on where I held my side, and the nice kid from my cell was gone.

Killer charged in, face tight and fists flying. "I told you they were out for blood. If you don't kill them, they pop back up like roaches."

Feeling the blood seep through my fingers, I had to agree. "Figured that out, thanks."

With Montgomery's help, we quickly killed the three men, not even bothering to drag them farther into the kitchen where they couldn't be stumbled upon. "Any idea how to get these guys out of here?"

I didn't know much about prison, but I knew bed check was a thing. If I ever wanted to leave, I had to make sure the bodies couldn't be traced back to me.

"We've got a cleaner in-house."

"What?"

He grinned, but before he could explain, four more Aces stepped into the room. I was exhausted, my side was burning, and I just knew we weren't getting out of this. One glance at the kid said he felt the same, but I didn't see a hint of remorse on his face. He didn't seem to care if he died here because he'd never really lived.

If I get out of here, I'm getting him out too.

They rushed us, jumping over their fallen comrades until they were throwing fists left and right. One caught me on my sore cheek and another to my stomach. I fought not to groan when they hit the stab wound, but my opponent—an older meathead well past his prime—doubled down, readjusting his grip on my shoulder so he could pound his fist right into it. I threw my own punches as much as possible without giving him access to more deadly spots, but I didn't have much I could do. I was in bad shape, and Killer was across the room battling the other three as my already-dismal energy levels flagged.

I was seconds away from dropping when someone hauled the guy off me and into a trio of bodies ready to pound the shit out of him. They punched and kicked with laser precision, while I did nothing but watch. When my attacker was finally done for, they turned on me, and I realized I might have just traded one devil for another until I noticed they didn't move closer.

"Are you all right?" I spun, arm flying, but Killer caught my fist before it landed. The move twisted my stomach, and I groaned under my breath.

"You're hurt."

I was up and in front of the kid before the other man finished, and he cocked his head. Taller than me by at least four inches and older, something about the way he held himself screamed *military*. The people who went in never seemed to be able to release those taught mannerisms, even after they got out.

"Who the hell are you?" I asked.

"A friend."

"A Marcosa friend?"

"No."

Well, that was direct and not at all what I wanted to hear. "I don't take help from people I don't know."

Killer shot an elbow to my side, grimacing when I doubled over with a pained cough. "What the fuck!"

"Sorry, just...take the help."

As I glanced up at the kid, he looked both grateful and wary, and I wasn't sure what to make of that. For his part, the newcomer ignored me, focusing on Montgomery instead.

"Take him to the infirmary. We'll get rid of these idiots."

Montgomery nodded, carefully wrapping a hand around my back. "Come on, I'll take you the back way so no one sees."

"Thanks." The last thing I needed was an audience to my injury. The strong always hunted the weak, especially in places like jail.

We were steps away from the door when the leader called to me. I turned back warily, and his eyes seemed to lighten some. "Give the kid our best."

What kid? I said nothing as we walked out, leaving the trio and the bodies behind. As soon as they were out of sight, I ripped myself out of Killer's grasp and glowered behind us. "What the hell was that? Were they Marcosas?"

"Aces."

Aces helped me? That didn't make any sense.

Killer looked over at me and grinned. "They're not like the others, though."

"How so?"

"They stay out of shit. Most of them are too mental to be messed with, but those three stick to themselves. They never get into fights."

Then why were they messing around protecting their sworn enemy? It didn't make sense. My side throbbed, reminding me I had bigger problems to worry about.

"Fuck," I hissed, holding my hand to the bloody wound. "Mari's going to kill me."

"The queen? Why?" Killer kept his distance, and I walked my happy ass to the infirmary. These assholes wanted to see strength, well, here it was. I wasn't going down without a fight. If they wanted to jump me again, they'd better bring more men.

She's my girl, was my first thought, but I wasn't just Dominic in here. I was Dominic Marcosa, underboss, and the way I phrased things mattered. Mari had to hold the power, always. "I'm hers."

"What about the other one? Greyson. Dude's been her shadow her whole life."

I snorted, knowing the kid had probably heard that from someone else. "He's hers too."

He jerked to a stop. "And you're okay with that?"

I shrugged like it didn't matter. "She's the queen."

"Fuck me, I want that job."

I cuffed him on the back of the head, groaning when it pulled at my wound. "Don't be disrespectful. It's an honor to be hers. We don't take that shit lightly."

The kid lifted his hands, though that lecherous look was still on his face. "I bet you have the best orgies."

I was seriously going to take his nickname from him if he didn't shut up.

The visit to the infirmary was quick and painful. No numbing drugs for me, but the stitches weren't awful, and I hid the bandage under a new shirt that Killer got for me. We were about to head out when I peeked toward the hallway and saw one of the Aces posted in front of the door.

"Have they ever helped a Marcosa before?"

"No."

Give the kid our best.

Nate. He'd been on the phone with Mari when the cops pulled up, and I knew they'd talked since he left. Had he done this? Had he given me extra protection? If so, why?

It would be easier for him to get Mari if I was dead, either to kill or keep.

Even though I despised him, I couldn't see him as the type. Not when it was obvious that he wasn't letting Mari go. I'd take the protection he offered, but it didn't mean I had to like him.

After I was fixed up, we went back to the chow hall, hoping to get something to eat. Our cellblock had already cleared out, but no one told us off, so we got in line, grabbing things we could take back to the cell. I was waiting for Montgomery, idly watching the heavily armed tables with a frown, positive there were more guards than before when the voice rang out.

"Beckstrom, back in the cage!"

My head whipped around, and I caught the eyes of a man who looked so similar to Nate, it was uncanny. There was some of Cash in him too, but Mari's boy toy was front and center in the man's face. He sneered at me, spitting on the floor, only to grunt when the guard clipped him in the kidney with the butt of his gun.

"Ace Beckstrom. He was in gen pop when I first got here, but he killed three prisoners and two guards after his son came to visit him, so he's been in isolation pretty much ever since."

"Which son?"

"The eldest."

Cash.

Made sense. I wanted to ask if he was unhinged too, but a guard barked my name next. I turned, making sure the only one who got my back was Killer. "Yeah?"

"Get your shit together. You're out."

Oh, fuck yes.

Chapter 26
Mari

Controlling myself was a struggle, and the second Dominic and I were locked inside the car, I launched myself at him.

"Fuck, it's good to see you. Are you okay?" My hands were roaming his body, desperate to make sure he was in one piece. All was well until I touched his side and he hissed. Anger froze me. "What. Happened?"

The idea that Dominic had been hurt outside of my care had me *this* close to homicidal rage. "We'll talk about it later, but there's someone we need to get out of there immediately. Can we do that?"

We'll talk about it later wasn't the answer I wanted, but I knew the stubborn set of his jaw. He wasn't budging. Fine, I'd wait and badger him tomorrow. "I'll make it happen."

"Thanks, *mariposa*." He readjusted me on his lap and kissed my forehead before leaning back. "I know you're stressed, but I just want to go home and shower. I'll tell you everything when you're naked and dripping on my cock, okay?"

That sounded amazing. All I could think about was reclaiming him, but that wasn't in the cards yet. Greyson shut the door now that he'd made sure Laidan had everything under control, catching Dominic's comment. "Orgasms have to wait. We've got work to do."

Dominic groaned, dropping his head to the top of the seat. "I just got out of jail. What do we have to do now?"

"I called a family meeting," I said. "It's time to finish this once and for all."

Dominic's eyes widened, and he sat up with a wince. Fucking idiot was going to pull his stitches if he had them. Did they even do stitches in jail? If they superglued my boyfriend, I was going to burn that fucking place down.

His shock wore off at the likely feral look I was giving him, and he pulled my hand to his lips. "I'm fine, *mariposa*. Tell me more about the meeting. Are we going after Cash?"

"No. Joaquin."

Dominic didn't ask if I was sure about that, if I was okay, or if I wanted him to do it for me. He just gripped my hand tight in his. "Let's do this."

The boys were quiet on the drive to the Celestine, like I needed time to prepare. I didn't. Admittedly, I had a pit in my stomach every time I thought of ending my uncle's life, but then I remembered the flames on the walls, Dominic rushing away from me, a burned Nate carrying a worse-off Cameron in his arms.

My cousin nearly died because his father had told the Aces where to go. Joaquin betrayed not just the Marcosa family, but his own son. It was a decision he wouldn't survive.

As Greyson parked the car in underground parking, I shot a text to Rafael. I didn't know if it was necessary since I already had Tennessee and Moore's teams waiting to intervene, but I figured it wouldn't hurt.

Joaquin dies tonight.

Understood. On standby if you need me.

Stopping by the apartment so Dominic could change took precious minutes, then we were walking into the conference room as a unit, the boys at my back, guns loaded and ready to draw.

I was going to kill one uncle tonight, but we were ready to kill them all if necessary.

Joaquin sat close to the head of the table, smirking like there was nothing wrong with the world. I knew what he thought the meeting was about. He hoped I was coming to tell them I was engaged to Dominic. Greyson and I hadn't formally announced our engagement yet, but I knew word had spread through the family that there was a ring on my finger, and only an idiot could've been blind to Joaquin's choice of groom.

Gabriele, Leonardo, and Mathias nodded politely as I walked to the head of the table. Joaquin's greedy eyes followed me the whole way, laser-focused on the ring. His son was in the hospital fighting for his life, and all he cared about was fucking *jewelry*.

I was used to rage. My father had been prone to fits of it, and even my brother, as wonderful as he was, had the gene to lose his shit over nothing. Me? I controlled it. I wielded that anger like a blade and used it to cut down my enemies.

When the fuck had that become my own family?

As the boys took their places behind my chair, I didn't sit, instead dropping my palms onto the surface and taking deep, calming breaths.

That control I had was wearing really fucking thin.

Because he had no sense of self-preservation, Joaquin broke

the silence. "I see congratulations are in order. Well done, my boy."

I didn't need to see to know he was pinning Dominic with a proud father look. Now that I was here, all I could do was stare at my uncle's hands. They had guided me as a teen and thrown me into the air as a child. He was the man who'd made silly faces at boring dinners to make me laugh and snuck me candy behind my father's back. When had it all gone wrong? When had he turned into a power-hungry prick capable of throwing his own blood to the wolves?

A brush of fingers against my back sought to give me strength and support, but I wasn't balking. I was pissed.

We were criminals, but we had a code. Family first.

When had that stopped being enough for Joaquin?

My arms trembled with the need to punish, and I lifted my head to stare at him. "Did you know your son almost died last night?"

The words were whisper-quiet, yet in that room, they might as well have been a roar.

No one moved. No one spoke.

As I speared Joaquin with a glare, that stupid *I won* smirk finally dropped. "What?"

"Cameron almost died last night. He's in the burn unit right now. Did you know that?"

He mouthed the word *burned* like he'd never heard it before. His fists clenched on the table, and his neck reddened with anger. Even I would have believed the performance if I hadn't known better.

Were all Marcosas born good liars, or did we learn it at our fathers' knees?

"How?"

"His house burned down."

"His house," he repeated.

"Does this room have an echo?" I asked, turning to catch Dominic's eyes. He smirked but said nothing, too focused on my idiotic uncle to play. Too bad. I was just getting started.

Joaquin glared down at the table, much like I had. "I thought he was staying at the Celestine."

"No. Someone burned down his house with his wife inside."

That got me a scowl. "The O'Bannon girl. Is that what this is about? Your little bestie got hurt, and now you're coming after us?"

My other uncles shifted in their seats, knowing that his flippant attitude pissed me off on a good day. They were right to be nervous, but I forced myself not to do anything yet. I had to stay cool and level for a little bit longer.

I dragged in a deep, dejected breath, like this was the last thing I wanted to be doing. "No, this is about you, me, and something I should have ended a long time ago."

A spark popped up on his face like he'd won something, and I knew exactly what it was. He thought I was giving up. That this attack on Ash was the last straw for my fragile mind. He thought, as I suspected he always had deep down, that I was too emotional to run the Marcosa empire. That I was too weak to do what had to be done.

What a joy it was knowing he was going to be the example proving just the opposite.

"It's obvious that I've been too lenient with you. Too *sentimental*. I let things stand, hoping you would see the error of your ways and back me in earnest, as you should have from the beginning. That was my mistake. I hope this corrects that oversight."

The shot rang out before anyone recognized that not only did I have a gun, I'd pulled the trigger. Blood trickled down Joaquin's forehead as he slumped to the table with a hard *thump*.

There were no last words or second chances for someone like Joaquin. There was only death and the coldness of the grave.

For a moment, I didn't think any of my uncles even breathed.

"I assume you had a reason for that," Mathias drawled.

"You mean besides him giving out his son's address so the Aces could burn him alive and send us into war with O'Bannon as well as Cash? No."

It didn't take a genius to know he didn't appreciate my sarcasm. "Do you have proof of this?"

"Only three people knew the address: Cameron, Joaquin, and me. I doubt Cameron would willingly allow himself or his wife to burn, do you? Not to mention the *hours* that my cousin's been surveilling his father acting against the good of the Marcosa family and me as its head."

Emotions flitted across all three of my uncles' faces, from fear and anger to disbelief and, finally, begrudging acceptance. "We understand the reason he died, but did it have to be so public?"

Only they would consider a handful of men a public execution.

"Considering your recent *conversations*, it seemed like you'd forgotten my latest warning. It felt necessary to reiterate it in a way you couldn't misinterpret." They all shifted again, small tells giving away their discomfort, and I laid my gun on the table in plain sight. "I will not tolerate dissent, especially if that dissent involves our enemies. A betrayal that large only ends one way—death. This family is mine until the day I die. If you have a problem with that, tell me now, and I'll end all of our misery before it begins. Any takers?"

My men were motionless, but I could feel their restlessness as we all gauged what would happen with my remaining capos. Would they bend the knee and put any thoughts of usurping my throne to rest for good, or would we be hauling out more bodies than one?

There was nothing but silence, and I let out a slow, relieved breath. "Good. If I have even a moment of doubt about your loyalties, I will throw you out with tomorrow's trash. Understood?"

They all muttered agreements, while their eyes focused on anything but the spreading bloodstain on the table. "Get out."

Leonardo and Mathias walked out with uneasy, respectful nods, but Gabriele stayed in his seat. When it was just the four of us and the body, he sighed. "I worried you'd let him go too long."

"I already did." Maybe a small part of me had still been desperate for Joaquin's approval, one that had spent the last few years hoping he'd change his mind and agree that I was the right choice to lead. That part of me died when he did, thank god.

Gabriele hummed, leaning back in his chair. "He never was my favorite."

The feeling was mutual. Joaquin had never trusted Gabriele because he'd married into the life, while Joaquin had been born with a bloody spoon to his lips. But Gabriele had proven the only useful uncle I had so far. He had been the first to tell me about the capos' plans to usurp the throne and put a man on it, even before Dominic. He'd kept his distance, acting like an informant would to let me know Joaquin was getting more pronounced in his wishes to end my reign. Ally or not, Gabriele was a fair man with a firm grasp on loyalty. One I trusted as implicitly as I could right now.

"Who's going to replace him?"

Dominic cleared his throat. "Actually, I've got a good idea about that if Cameron isn't interested."

Since most positions were passed down among the family, my cousin would likely take his father's place as a capo, but I was curious to hear who'd won Dominic over in such a short time. "We'll discuss replacements in a few days. The men will need time to mourn."

"Of course." Gabriele looked at the body uncomfortably before turning back to me. "You know there are traditions..."

"I'm aware." The words were harsh, and I immediately fought to soften them. "I need to tell Cameron first."

"He's still sedated," Greyson said behind me. "We'll have to do it tomorrow."

Tomorrow evening would be the wake. Gabriele was right; traditions had to be upheld or I risked whatever power I'd snatched from my uncle's cooling hand. So tomorrow, I'd wrap my uncle as I'd done my father and brother, and then I'd burn his shell to ash.

"We'll tell him first thing in the morning."

Gabriele got out of his chair with a groan and rounded the table to clap me on the back. "Tomorrow, then. Don't forget to lay him down, or you'll have a bitch of a time with the shroud."

"I won't. Goodnight, Uncle."

"Goodnight."

I let Dominic and Greyson lay Joaquin's body on the floor and remove his clothes before we locked the door and went for the elevator. Tennessee and Moore would personally move the body to the freezer downstairs, but for now, Joaquin would lie there nude. It was petty and undignified as fuck, but it seemed like the least I could do.

We were all exhausted since I knew none of us had slept in days. Grey and I hadn't felt right resting with Dominic in jail, even if he was only in custody for a handful of hours. We clung to one another as we made our way into the penthouse, where I had to grab Dominic's arm to keep him from dropping onto the couch.

"What now? I just want to sleep." His groan was borderline whiny, and it made me smile for the first time in days.

"You're disgusting," I said frankly. "Go wash off the stench of jailbird, and then we'll go to bed."

"Only if you come with me."

I nodded, ready to get my hands on him so I could confirm he was really okay. Plus, I still needed to get a look at that wound.

Chapter Twenty-Six

Turning to Grey, I asked, "Are you joining us? The shower fits six."

His grin reminded me that he already knew that. "I'll take a shower in my room so you two have a minute."

"Are you sure?" Grey nodded, and I pressed up on my toes for a long kiss. "Thank you. I promise we'll have time alone soon."

Grey squeezed my hips with a smile. "I don't mind waiting. There's a lot going on."

That was true, but I didn't need him feeling neglected. "Meet us in bed in fifteen?"

"Sounds good."

I yawned as I stepped into the bathroom and turned on the water, knowing Dominic probably had gone for some clean clothes. My shirt was halfway over my head when Nate spoke.

"Mari."

I spun with a curse, only to see Dominic haul Nate to the wall by the throat. If I looked up rage in the dictionary, the way my boyfriend looked at the other man would be right there. "What the fuck are you doing here?"

"I came to check on Mari."

"Bullshit."

Nate sighed. "Look, I know—"

Dominic's fist interrupted whatever he was going to say. When his face twisted as he geared up for a second hit, I pulled him away. "That's enough. You're going to hurt yourself."

Nate's eyes drifted immediately to his injured side, and Dominic's narrowed suspiciously. "Maybe it's good that you're here after all. I've got questions for you."

With a carefully blank face, Nate nodded for him to continue.

"Why did your men save my life?"

"Wait, what?!" I might as well have been invisible for all the attention they paid me.

"I did it for Mari."

"Do you expect me to believe that?"

"No."

"How many Aces are under your control?"

Um, what?

"None. There are just some who don't like how far Cash is taking things."

"If Mari had been in jail, would your men have helped her?"

"If they could. We have a few women planted in that side of the jail who would've done most of the work. Some guards too." When he saw us staring, he shrugged. "I'd call in a lot of favors to get you out of jail alive, angel. Anything else?"

Apparently satisfied, Dominic stared at Nate for a long minute before turning to me. "Do you really trust him?"

"I'm going to try."

"Why?"

How could I explain it when I barely understood myself? "Because my gut is telling me to. Giving second chances is what I do for people I love, and while it may be a weakness, it's one I can't seem to forget. Nate's hurt me, but he's helped me too. I owe it to myself to see which side of the fence he falls on."

"He could kill you."

"I won't," Nate argued. We both ignored him.

"He could," I agreed. "I'm willing to take that risk."

Dominic still looked angry, so I slid close and wrapped my arms around him gently. "I'll be careful."

"She won't have to be. I won't hurt her."

"Shut up, fuckboy. No one's talking to you." With a sigh, he came back to me. "This is the last chance, Mari."

When I nodded, he hauled me closer and pressed a possessive kiss against my lips. I could feel his eyes burning into Nate's the whole time, but I kind of liked it. *Don't get toxic, Mari.*

Finally, he pulled away. "I don't like you. I don't want you here, but if Mari says you stay, you stay."

"I understand. I'll make it up to you, I promise," Nate said.

"Don't bother. I'm not interested in apologies. Just don't prove her wrong."

"I won't." Nate jolted, grimacing as the faintest sound of buzzing reached my ears. "But I have to go now. Cash is calling."

With a careful kiss to my forehead, one that focused all too hard on not touching Dominic, Nate slipped out of the room and the building again.

"I'm tempted to superglue the side of the building just to watch him get stuck there."

Laughing, I tipped my head back. "Thank you for not fighting me."

"Mmm-hmm. I'll take my payment in sexual favors." His grin was salacious, but a loud yawn cracked his jaw, and I laughed.

"You'll settle for help washing your back now and an IOU for later."

"Fine," he grumbled, letting me clean him off before helping me do the same.

By the time we were both dried and in bed, waiting for Grey to join us, we had no shortage of yawns, but I wasn't tired. Even when our third hauled himself into the room, curling around my back like he could protect it even in sleep, I couldn't rest.

Dominic lasted a few more minutes before laughing at my huffing and puffing. "What's wrong, *mariposa?*"

What wasn't wrong? "I'm worried we won't get him out in time."

I didn't need to say Nate's name; we all knew who I was talking about. Greyson, who never fell asleep before everyone else, squeezed me tight in agreement. When Dominic didn't immediately shoot down my fears, I let us lapse back into silence.

Eventually, he cuddled me closer, burying his face in my hair. "So am I."

Did that mean he was willing to forgive Nate? Even if it took years, just the idea of a steady, united group brought me unfathomable levels of comfort. Not willing to risk the fragile peace we'd created, I kissed his chest, refusing to poke at such a sore topic.

Instead, I turned to a much more important one. "When were you going to tell me you got stabbed in jail?"

Chapter 27
Nate

Where have you been?"

I hadn't even made it in the door of the compound before he was on my case. Normally, my first thought would've been to check what mood Cash was in, a habit I'd adopted long ago. But this time, the words grated.

My shoulder ached from the burns I'd gotten—despite already getting them taken care of—my lungs were on fire, and my brother thought he deserved to know my every move because he thought he owned me. Because he *did* own me.

Not to mention that I'd just walked away from the people I knew were my *real* family after getting what was as close to Dominic's acceptance as possible at the moment, just to come back into this hellhole of a life. I hated it here. I hated Cash.

All of this was for Mari—her safety and protection—but I couldn't force myself to pretend to be a good little soldier right now. Not when I could still see her splayed out on the floor of that house, the flames licking too fucking close to her skin for comfort. I wasn't sure I'd ever sleep again with that image burned into my brain.

"Out."

I made my way to one of the couches in the massive, mostly empty party room and groaned as I sank into the cushions. Ordinarily, I wouldn't dare sit on them since I knew what the others got into out here, but I needed a fucking break. Two seconds and I'd get up and disinfect myself.

Cash smirked, saying nothing about the unusual insolence. He didn't have to. The quiet cock of a gun was enough of a response.

Since I'd returned to the Aces, one thought had bounced around my head over and over until I thought I'd lose my mind from the sheer repetition.

Why didn't I go against Cash sooner?

The answer was staring at me from the other side of that gun. A faceless peon who watched my brother like he was the sun, moon, and stars combined. Cash himself was unstable, but it wasn't just him. He had an army of misinformed and misaligned humans at his back. Men who were too weak to walk away from what he offered.

Blow, money, women, and power—in that order.

Our father had taught Cash that weak minds were easier to control. Mario had taught him everyone had a price. Combining those schools of thought gave Cash his philosophy—find a man's weakness, and you find what it takes to control them, regardless of the strength of their mind.

"The hit in jail failed," I said, rubbing a hand over my jaw as if I was annoyed at the situation. I was, but not for the same reason as my brother, whose face shifted in agitation. "It was Dominic who went to jail, not Mari."

"The guard dog," Cash corrected. "I'm aware."

"We had to shift things last minute, and it obviously didn't work out. Apparently, she's got more protection on the inside than we expected."

Cash frowned, his fingers tapping an irregular rhythm on his chair. My eyes narrowed in on those fingers, watching the faintest twitch as they touched down, and I cursed myself for not doing it sooner. Cash was fearless when high and reckless when he was coming down, but his instability always grew to unparalleled levels when he was jonesing.

Once, I'd seen him gut a man with a dull kitchen knife because he'd mispronounced a word. When he was done, he apologized before snorting a line right in front of the guy, immediately going back to laughing and making plans.

"Dad didn't say anything about her having protection. Her dog should have been dead." Those fingers tapped quicker, and even Cash's gun-toting Ace leaned away.

"Maybe she got some after her friend was taken." I kept every part of me even: tone, facial expressions, body language. *This* Cash was likely to lash out at anything, and I didn't want him to find a reason to make me his target.

Shara had been the original target of the jail hit, but she'd gotten out of custody too fast. Mari's destruction of the Cardinal, the last real tether to our father, beyond seeing him in jail, had sent Cash into another stratosphere.

I had no doubt that if Mari had been arrested, they'd have never found her body. I didn't like how many fucking attempts on Mari he'd okayed, like she'd become his sole focus in his quest for power. He was getting obsessed, and an obsessed Cash was a dangerous one.

He cursed, and his face twitched too. A tic his habit had created. Right on cue, he impatiently beckoned to a woman in the corner. She was his usual type, just this side of too thin. Her hair was pulled back and clean, her face perfect with that no-makeup look that meant she was wearing a shit-ton of it. Her dress and shoes were clean and designer. She looked like she was ready for a night at a high-end club, not some drug-filled frat house.

The way she looked at Cash told me how out of it she was. It was exactly the way his gunman did. That was Cash's power. He was a maniac, but he had the charisma to enchant the masses into pretending he was a saint. It was fucking terrifying.

The woman licked her lips and carefully brought over the tray filled with white powder on steady hands. For a moment, I wondered if I could poison the coke. End the war before anyone else had to die. There were ways to lace it with something that would kill him in his sleep. I even knew a few contacts I could reach out to to get it. It would be a suicide mission, but at least Mari would be safe.

The woman dropped gracefully to her knees, not tipping the tray even an inch. Using a razor he'd gotten from somewhere, Cash scraped a small amount out of the middle and leaned forward to lick her bottom lip. Carefully, he smeared some of it across her mouth, letting her tongue taste the drugs before he lifted the rest, not to his nose, but hers.

I remembered why lacing the drugs wouldn't work.

Cash always had a tester for his food, his drinks—anything that went into his body, someone else tried first. He wouldn't even sip out of a sealed water bottle without a tester. I wouldn't be the first to attempt poisoning, and I certainly wouldn't be the last.

We all waited in tense silence until she sighed in relief as the drugs hit her. With a big grin, Cash leaned down and snorted the rest of the lines as quickly as he could. It was easily twice as much as anyone should've taken, but after years of addiction, his tolerance was higher than anyone I'd ever met.

When a slow, serene smile lit his face, I knew the drugs were working. A flick of his wrist sent the woman away, and as soon as she was out of sight, that serenity was gone. It was like the longer he'd used drugs, the faster his high wore off. What used to be hours was now minutes at most.

"Suit up, little brother. We've got places to go."

Unease filtered through my veins as I wondered what exactly he had planned. "Where are we going?"

"A wake." His grin was something beyond manic, if that was even possible. "Better wear black."

Chapter 28
Mari

Every underground family had traditions designed by the founders to create harmony and respect within the family. The Marcosas had plenty, but only one was the bane of my current existence.

When it came to the people born into the family, the leader prepared the body for burial. I'd watched my brother do it for our father, and when Antoni died, I'd done it for him too. It was a sign of respect, of honor.

Hence why I found myself huffing in annoyance just after dawn. Normally, I didn't have an issue with it, but no one had expected one of us to become a traitor. That changed things. I couldn't give the same reverence to Joaquin as I had my beloved brother.

Deciding on three major deviations from tradition, I didn't wash the body like I should have. I wanted Joaquin to be left with his sins in the afterlife. I went straight to wrapping him in the black shroud customary for our family. Tradition said it should have covered him from head to toe, leaving no ounce of skin open to view.

It was a protective thing, to guard the body from ill wishes or something. That didn't sound appropriate for Joaquin, so I left his face bare, showing the vibrant red streak down it and the hole the bullet left. Everyone would get to see what betrayal like his got you.

My final act of defiance was the most important. Tonight, when I set the pyre ablaze, Joaquin would burn without last rites or a priest to watch over his body. Just me guiding his descent to hell, where his spirit belonged.

The perfect penance for a dead traitor.

After putting the body back in the freezer and heading upstairs to the shower, I let myself wonder how I was going to tell my cousin Joaquin was dead. First his mother years ago, then Rey, and now his father. Sure, he hadn't liked Joaquin much, but he was still Cameron's father and I'd taken him away. The fact that I didn't regret it made things harder to swallow too.

Only practice kept me from jumping out of my skin as hands slipped over my hips and wrapped around my stomach. "Everything go okay?"

"Fine."

Greyson's stability behind me was a balm I needed, so I leaned into him, desperate to soak up some of it before I headed to the hospital. He let me, taking my weight and pressing warm, soothing kisses to every inch of skin he could reach. "How are you feeling?"

"Fine." He said nothing, but I could feel the disbelief radiating through him. "It had to be done."

"It did, but that doesn't make it easy," he agreed.

True enough. I thought about keeping my thoughts to myself,

but this was Greyson. He was safe. If I couldn't tell him, I couldn't tell anyone. "I'm worried Cameron will be angry."

He hummed in an almost agreement before pushing me off so he could grab the shampoo and lather up my hair. He worked diligently, making sure he massaged my head and neck until I was near boneless against him, then carefully worked his way down the strands. Tipping my head back, he carefully maneuvered me into the water to rinse it out so he could start all over again with conditioner. While he let that soak in, he went for my body and set his sights on the rest of me.

Every touch was sure, every muscle kneaded and relaxed beneath his hands. At one point, I had to lean against the wall because I was sure my knees would give out. Nothing about it was sexual, just intimate. The type of touch that two people who were each other's worlds could have. Grey touched me like I was his to protect and serve and worship, and it made everything so much better.

I loved that he could put his hands on me and, without words, give me everything I needed. Sex was wonderful, especially with him, but this was something else.

He had one of my feet balanced against his shoulder as he worked my calf and ankle into puddle-of-goo territory when he finally spoke again. "I think you're not giving Cameron enough credit. Yes, Joaquin was his father, but he was also blatantly anti-Mari. Cameron's loyalty has always been to you. He may be upset, but he'll understand why you did it. Trust him, Mari. Trust yourself."

"Maybe that's the problem. I'm not sure I *can* trust myself."

"Nate was—"

"Not the only problem." It was the truth. Nate was a catalyst to show me something much more glaring was happening. "I'm still as naïve as I was when I took this role."

"*Reina.*"

"No, I am. I trust people blindly, and then I get surprised when they stab me in the back. It's a habit."

He let go of my feet and twisted so he could rake careful fingers through my hair, getting the worst of the tangles before he took a brush through it. "It's not a bad thing to trust people, Mari."

"It is when they're the wrong people." He grunted behind me, so I kept going. "I knew Joaquin wasn't on my side from the beginning. The smart thing to do would've been to take him out at the start."

"That would've been suicide."

He was referring to the fact that my uncles would've taken me out for it, but I wasn't so sure. "I could've brought them to heel."

"Why is this such a problem for you?"

"How much suffering could we have avoided if I'd made the tough decision earlier?" I wasn't sure Grey would have an answer for me, I wasn't even sure I wanted one. Asking the question was enough.

"A lot," he admitted, knowing Joaquin had been a pain in my ass for years. "But that's not who you are."

"Maybe it should be."

"No." When I said nothing, Grey whipped me around and crowded me into the tile wall. "You are not your father. You are not Cash. You don't see opposition as a death sentence. It's what makes you human."

"I can't be human and run a criminal empire, Greyson."

"Says who?" he challenged. "You've been doing it for years and doing it well."

I had no answer for that, but I didn't feel better.

Grey huffed and leaned into me, shielding me from everything that wasn't him. His big hand snaked through the hair he'd just painstakingly cleaned, and he wrapped it around the base of my neck, thumb stroking my pulse. "Empathy is your burden, *reina*. It's part of what makes you great. Does it mean you give people too many chances? Maybe, but I wouldn't change you for anything. A queen can be ruthless and still have a conscience."

I wanted to believe that, but history was proving I constantly made the wrong choices. "Are you sure?"

"Yes, but if you need a reminder, just ask. If you're not sure you're making the right decision, lean on Dominic and me for counsel. We won't tell you what to do, but we can advise you." With a firm grip, he pulled my head to his chest. "We're here to help you. Let us do it."

We stayed there, wrapped in each other, until I felt the last of my resistance slip down the drain. Greyson was right. I'd hated how my father ruled because he had no compassion to temper the fear he wrought. No empathy to fuel the city's exploits, both underground and not. I didn't want to be like him or Cash. I wanted to be me.

The tough choices would always be there, but I'd take them every time if it meant I still had my soul.

We got out, dressing quietly next to each other so we didn't wake Dominic. He needed the rest and I wanted to do this without an entourage, yet I couldn't help but snatch Grey's hand as I passed. I held it the entire drive to Seattle General, only letting go when I stepped into my cousin's hospital room, which he'd apparently forced the staff to put Aislynn in too. It would take a while for him to be comfortable letting her out of his sight.

After she'd made a house call to check Dominic's and my lungs, Dr. Grant had told us most of Cameron's burns were second-degree, though some were third. Because of the number he had, and to avoid infection, they'd decided to treat them all as if they were third. He was hooked up to antibiotics and IV drips to help him heal and deal with the pain. The fewer people in the room, the better, but they'd made an exception for me this once, which I was grateful for.

My cousin lay grumpily in the bed, bandages covering the worst of his wounds, letting Ash fuss at him as he tossed barbed words her way. For her part, she seemed content to ignore him, happily plumping pillows or adjusting the blankets every two seconds. She had a somber gratitude hovering around her as she did the same to her husband, and if I hadn't known she loved him before, I did now.

"You're okay." Cameron's words were hushed with relief, and I forced my face to smile, though his flat lips said it wasn't a good one.

"I'm fine," I promised, staying back like I'd promised the nurses. "I need to tell you something, though."

Telling Cameron was awful, but he didn't seem upset. He didn't seem like...anything. Maybe he'd shut down, or maybe he was too high on the pain meds. I wasn't sure. When Ash gave me a shaky smile from where she perched on the bed at his side and asked me kindly to give him some time, I left, hoping he'd forgive me someday.

For now, I had a party to plan.

Chapter 29
Mari

Traditionally, wakes were somber as people settled in to wait over the soul of the dearly departed. For us, it was an excuse to party, and even the fact that Joaquin was a traitor didn't dampen our spirits.

Although, that was probably all the booze.

Everyone had made the drive back to the mansion for the funeral because even I couldn't burn a whole-ass body in the middle of the city. Cameron and Aislynn had to stay in the hospital, though she'd texted that they were having a private wake together, which I appreciated. My cousin needed someone with him, and his wife was the perfect option.

Meanwhile, I was strolling through the garden, pouring shots from the bottle in my hand for my buzzed men to use as they raised toasts, not to Joaquin, but to Rey and Antoni and even my father. Cameron's men also raised their glasses to stories of him as a child, though they were told less in honor of my uncle and more in appreciation of his legacy.

His shrouded body lay elevated in the center of the garden, the space between him and the stone slab below covered in ready-to-burn wood. There were small trinkets and photos from those brave enough to leave those memories with him, though I wasn't sure if, like the stories of his children, it was to honor what they thought were memories instead of the reality of his demise.

Either way, I hated seeing the pyre set up. The last time, it had been Rey lying there. The time before that, my brother. In moments like this, where grief crowded me like an unwanted shadow, it felt brand-new. Like I'd done no healing at all. It sucked.

Thankfully, my men stayed close by, keeping an eye on me. I'd let myself have a single glass of wine with Shara, who'd left almost immediately after she'd come, so I wasn't struggling through it all totally sober. Still, I couldn't wait for it to be over.

Unfortunately, duty called.

Because of my uncle's extensive history in the city, I'd had to issue invitations to all the leading factions, though I kept his traitorous nature to myself. Kosas and Ajilon had come and left almost as quickly, barely stopping to pay their respects. Haru had sent a text that he was unable to come at all. The only leaders who'd made themselves at home were O'Bannon and Two-Bit. The latter set himself up near the bar and merely raised a glass in toast when I spotted him, but O'Bannon was on the warpath.

"I hear my daughter's in the hospital *again*."

Honestly, I was surprised Ash had even told him. It was obviously her decision, but from what I knew, she'd barely spoken to her father since the wedding. He certainly didn't reach out to her often.

I nodded noncommittally. "She is. It's been taken care of."

"My little girl was almost burned alive, and you think burning a fucking building means it's *taken care of?*" The anger in his voice was real, but I didn't think it was actually about Ash being his precious daughter. Sean O'Bannon was a proprietary man.

Aislynn was his property, and someone had tried to take her away from him.

"Cameron was the only one truly hurt, and he got that way making sure his wife was safe. What matters is they're both okay."

He huffed, downing his whiskey like it was a shot and reaching for a bottle nearby. "If you think blowing up a building is enough to make up for someone nearly taking out one of my heirs, you're wrong."

"No, but since Ash is now a Marcosa, she's mine to avenge as I see fit. The building had sentimental meaning to Cash, so I took it from him like he tried to take Aislynn. When we get him on his back, I promise you can gut him for his part in Ash's pain if it makes you feel better."

When I thought he'd say something else, Kieran dropped a hand to his shoulder and whispered in his ear. Without looking away from me, Sean nodded, and the tension in the air dissipated. "I'm sorry for your loss. Your uncle was a good man."

My uncle was a betraying fuck, I wanted to scream. Instead, I gave O'Bannon a tight smile. "Thank you for coming."

"Keep my daughter safe, Mari," was what he said, but I could read between the lines.

Don't lose my investment, or I won't help anymore.

"Of course, Sean."

Dominic took his place almost immediately. "What did the Irish fuck want?"

"To tell me I was doing a shit job protecting his kid." Dominic huffed, and I laughed. "What did you need?"

"Greyson sent me to tell you it's time."

There was no announcement, but as I made my way toward the slab that held my uncle's husk, everyone stopped to watch. The unspoken command to follow my attention was too strong for even the drunkest of them to ignore. The sun had set, and torches had been placed everywhere to give us some form of light. We didn't use electricity in the wakes if we could avoid it.

As we got closer to the pyre, Dominic moved to be nearer to Greyson, giving me the floor. Just like before, I wasn't sure what I should say, but with Two-Bit in the crowd, I knew I couldn't say everything I wanted to.

Keep it short, it is.

"Death is the only sure part of life. Beautiful and humbling, it brings us together as much as it divides. Tonight, we gather like this to mourn a man who was instrumental in guiding this family for decades. I hope the afterlife is everything you dreamed of, Uncle."

Lifting the bottle I'd been carrying around all night, I poured a healthy dose onto my uncle's shrouded body. It wasn't unheard of, but it was definitely a sign of disrespect. My final one.

"Burn in hell," I whispered as I put the torch to the alcohol first and then the kindling below, making sure the fire was burning everywhere before I dropped the torch into it too.

There was no telling how long I stood there, watching the flames envelop my uncle's body, but I couldn't move. I needed to see, so I could tell myself he was really gone.

I heard the quietest *pop*, and then pain bloomed along my shoulder. I raised my hand automatically to check on what I expected was a burn from a falling ember.

It wasn't.

Red seeped through my fingers, running sticky down my skin as I realized what had happened.

Someone shot me.

I pulled my gun immediately, looking for who the fuck was ballsy enough to shoot at me in the middle of a Marcosa party. Dread twisted my gut as I caught a pair of eyes so familiar, they made my heart ache, but they weren't Nate's.

They were Cash's.

Greyson and Dominic didn't stop to ask questions, pulling their guns as one, even while their keen eyes went nearly feral at the sight of the hole in my jacket.

Grey's face was dark with retribution. "What the fuck."

Dominic spun around. "Who shot my girl?"

"That would be me." Cash's grin was as unstable as ever. "Sorry to interrupt, but we're the entertainment."

We were all too fucking shocked at the audacity of his interrupting what was culturally known as a *cease-fire* moment in time. You didn't shoot people at a funeral. Cash lifted his gun and fired, once again proving he didn't care about decorum one fucking bit.

"Take cover!" I yelled over the sound, knowing I was going to lose people tonight. We were all armed, but we'd been prepared for remembrance, not battle. Half my men were in the bag, and the other half weren't armed enough for this.

"Who the fuck fires into a funeral?" I grunted, leaning out from behind the viewing platform to shoot two of Cash's men before they could creep closer. My phone buzzed in my pocket, and I ignored it before realizing it was probably Nate. I was right.

I'm here.

I craned my neck, trying to look around the stone, but I pulled back as a chip was cut away with a bullet.

"What the fuck are you doing?" Dominic asked, hauling me farther into the safety of the middle.

"Nate's here." I yanked my earbuds from my pocket, connecting them as I dialed Nate's number, muttering as it rang, "Pick up, pick up, pick up."

"The kid's not our problem right now," Dominic growled. "Let's focus on getting out of here alive."

Fires backlit the windows, and I just knew Cash was going to burn the place down. *Fuck it, I don't like the damn house anyway.*

"Meet us by the lower garage," I said, tapping on Dominic's and Greyson's shoulders so they could hear too.

The doors weren't open, but the garage had an outside entrance we could use without electricity, one big enough for us to drive through. There was also a road nearby that would bypass the bullshit of the Aces' cars blocking us in.

No way was I letting my people die here.

The boys nodded, and Dominic lifted his head to yell. "Everyone out!"

Amazing how fast men could sober up when their lives were on the line. When I saw most of our men were fighting their way out, or occupying the Aces' time for us to get out, I refocused my efforts. I had three things to do.

Get Nate, get to the cars, get out.

But first, we needed a distraction. I peered around for something we could use to escape from our current hiding place and saw the bar cart not too far away. Pulling out my knife, I tugged on the hem of Dominic's shirt and sliced it off.

"Now's not really the time to get naked, *mariposa*."

"Oh, shut up and cover me," I said, rushing for the cart. A bullet whizzed by my ear, and one fired from the boys right after, the pained yell telling me they'd taken that Ace out as I ducked, wrapped my arms around the mass of bottles, and hauled the whole thing to our hiding place.

It took me less than a minute to prep the bottles, and then we were tossing them over the pyre, staggering the flames to get as much space clear as we could.

Grey peered out from behind the platform, and when no one immediately opened fire, he hauled me to my feet. "Let's go."

As one, the three of us stood, moving through the garden as quickly as possible. If we could make it to the side of the house without dying, we'd be okay. We spread out, trying to give them more targets to hit in hopes we could do it unscathed. "We're nearly out of the garden. Get there, Nate."

"I see you, baby. I'm coming." There was shuffling and more heavy breathing. "Just stay low and out of— Mari, look out!"

Nate's tinny voice blended into Dominic's and Greyson's roars as I twisted to find an Ace diving closer on the stone patio, ready for a potshot. One look at the gun and I knew he'd hit his target. There wasn't time to move, so I braced for impact as my men yelled, vowing to wear Kevlar when leaving the house until this fucking war was over.

But the bullet never came.

Instead, a hard body rammed itself into my side, stealing the breath from my lungs as we went down together. The aim was off, and I felt his head hit the ground at my side, wincing when he didn't get up. Two rapid shots were all it took to end the Ace, but I was too focused on the big man lying on me and the warm liquid that dripped onto my thighs.

"Where the fuck did he come from?" Dominic asked. Nate was still as the grave on top of me, and my heart was frantic at how true that could be.

"I don't know, but help me get him off!" I snapped. Dominic rolled him over, keeping his body between me and the melee as I leaped to Nate's aid. Grey stood over all three of us, our own god of war as he picked off anyone who came close.

Blood seeped from Nate's shirt, and I lifted it to see a small wound in his stomach. It wasn't anywhere immediately problematic, so I pulled off my jacket and stuffed it against the wound. It wouldn't pack shit for long. "We need to get him out of here."

"Will Cash let us steal his brother back?"

"I don't care." I knelt, trying and failing to haul Nate's arm over my shoulder more than once. Finally, Dominic huffed, handed me his gun, and grabbed Nate in a bridal carry that would've made me laugh any other time.

Nate groaned, coming to once Dominic started moving. "Mari?"

I stepped up close, keeping my eyes focused on the people around us. I didn't want another ambush. "We're getting you out of here."

"I didn't know."

"I know, baby. We'll talk about it later." I took my eyes off the surroundings for a single second. That was my mistake.

Two Aces popped up and fired. The shots pulled my attention, and they were both dead by my bullets in seconds, but the distraction cost me.

Dominic stumbled, his hold on Nate slipping before he righted himself, and I saw the splatter of blood through a hole in his jeans. Someone had grazed his leg just right, so it took a chunk of skin with it. "Fucking cocksuckers, that hurt."

"Can you walk?"

"I've got your fuckboy," he promised, and, hurt or not, I smacked him upside the head.

"I was asking about you, you asshole."

He turned, contrition all over his face, but it twisted as he looked behind me. I followed his eyes, and my gun wavered. "Greyson."

His name was a breath on my lips as I bolted for him. The bullet that had just grazed Dominic had driven Greyson to his knees by force. The other had nicked the side of his neck, and blood poured down his body. I grabbed him under the arms and hauled him to his feet, hissing under my breath as I did. "Up, get up. Get up."

"Mari."

"Don't even think about it." I yanked off my shirt and wrapped it around Grey's neck as tight as I could without cutting off circulation. "We're going to the car, all three of us. Now, run."

I didn't know how we made it to the garage. If we had a lucky break or Cash let us go to toy with us more later. I wasn't sure I cared.

All four of us were injured, and if I didn't get Greyson to a hospital soon, he was going to die. Not to mention Nate. As I hauled open the door and shoved a very pale Greyson inside, I hoped we'd make it in time.

Dominic snatched the keys from the hook on the wall with an, "I'll drive. You need to be with them."

"All four of you, get in the back." The moment we heard the voice, all of us had our guns up. It was instinctual, and even Dominic, who was farther away, had recognized the threat and hauled the driver's side door open. "What the fuck?"

I pulled open the passenger door and tried not to let my surprise show. I wasn't sure who I was expecting, but a smiling Two-Bit in my driver's seat wasn't it. "Whatever this is, I don't have time. Get out."

All I could think about was Greyson's drooping eyes and the clock that was ticking in my fucking ear.

They need help. My men are shot. Cash shot them.

Two-Bit crossed his hands over his stomach, settling in his seat. "Make time. We need to talk."

I peeked at my men, who were all shaking their heads, but it was the blood that made my decision. We didn't have time for squabbling. Greyson and Nate didn't have time.

If Two-Bit wanted to come for me now, he could get in

fucking line. Slamming the door, I crawled into the back seat and barked at Dominic to do the same. "Get us to the hospital, and I'll give you whatever the fuck you want."

•••

The GILDED EMPIRE series concludes in ***VICIOUS THRONE***

Also by Janie Crouch

All books: https://www.janiecrouch.com/books

HEROES OF OAK CREEK

Hero Unbound

Hero's Flight

Hero's Prize

GILDED EMPIRE (as MJ Crouch)

Broken Crown

Damaged Kingdom

Fierce Monarch

Vicious Throne

ZODIAC TACTICAL

Code Name: ARIES

Code Name: VIRGO

Code Name: LIBRA

Code Name: PISCES

Code Name: OUTLAW

Code Name: GEMINI

NEVER TOO LATE FOR LOVE (with Regan Black)

Heartbreak Key Collection

Ellington Cove Collection

Wyoming Cowboys Collection

Holiday Heroes Collection

RESTING WARRIOR RANCH (with Josie Jade)

Montana Sanctuary

Montana Danger

Montana Desire

Montana Mystery

Montana Storm

Montana Freedom

Montana Silence

Montana Rain

LINEAR TACTICAL (series complete)

Cyclone

Eagle

Shamrock

Angel

Ghost

Shadow

Echo

Phoenix

Baby

Storm

Redwood

Scout

Blaze

Hero Forever

INSTINCT SERIES (series complete)

Primal Instinct

Critical Instinct

Survival Instinct

THE RISK SERIES (series complete)

Calculated Risk

Security Risk

Constant Risk

Risk Everything

OMEGA SECTOR (series complete)

Stealth

Covert

Conceal

Secret

OMEGA SECTOR: CRITICAL RESPONSE & UNDER SIEGE
(series complete)

Special Forces Savior

Fully Committed

Armored Attraction

Man of Action

Overwhelming Force

Battle Tested

Daddy Defender

Protector's Instinct

Cease Fire

Major Crimes

Armed Response

In the Lawman's Protection

About the Author (Janie Crouch)

"Passion that leaps right off the page." - Romantic Times Book Reviews

MJ Crouch is the alter ego of USA Today and Publishers Weekly bestselling author Janie Crouch. Her books have won multiple awards, including the Romance Writers of America's coveted Vivian® Award, the National Readers Choice Award, and the Booksellers' Best.

After a lifetime on the East Coast, and a six-year stint in Germany due to her husband's job as support for the U.S. Military, Janie has settled into her dream home in Front Range of the Colorado Rockies.

When she's not listening to the voices in her head—and even when she is—she enjoys engaging in all sorts of crazy adventures (200-mile relay races; Ironman Triathlons, treks to Mt. Everest Base Camp...), traveling, and hanging out with her four kids.

Her favorite quote: "Life is a daring adventure or nothing." ~ Helen Keller.

facebook.com/janiecrouch

amazon.com/author/janiecrouch

instagram.com/janiecrouch

bookbub.com/authors/janie-crouch